To: Tab
Thank you so much
for the Posters!

Trashy Suspense Novel

JACQUELINE E. SMITH

♡ Jackie

Wind Trail Publishing

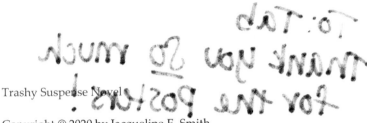

Trashy Suspense Novel

Wind Trail Publishing
PO Box 830851
Richardson, TX 75083-0851
www.WindTrailPublishing.com

First Paperback Edition, November 2020

ISBN-13: 979-8-5534284-8-8

Library of Congress Cataloguing-in-Publication Data
Smith, Jacqueline E.
Trashy Suspense Novel / Jacqueline E. Smith
Library of Congress Control Number: 2020921849

Cover Model: Hannah Alvarez
Cover Design: Wind Trail Publishing

Printed in the United States of America.

In loving memory of Emma Jean.

Excerpt from *Vivian's Crypt*
By D.H. Whittaker

Caroline Duval shivered as she trudged further and further, deeper and deeper into the dead woods surrounding the small town of Slaughter, Wyoming. She didn't believe in the ghost stories her fourth-grade students told, nor in the urban legends that the old folks whispered from their rocking chairs. There were no tall men made of shadows. There were no creatures lurking in the leaves.

Not anymore, anyway.

There had been a wolf, once. She was a majestic creature, with a thick gray-tan coat and striking amber eyes that seemed to reflect the glow of moonlight on freshly fallen snow. Caroline would never forget the first, the only night she saw her. She was driving home along a winding country road when, all of a sudden, there she was, standing at the edge of the forest.

The next morning, ten-year-old Vivian Drew's parents reported her missing.

Aloud, residents of Slaughter mourned for the child and prayed for her safe return. But in dark, shameful secrecy, each and every one of them sighed with wretched relief, because each and every one of them knew the real Vivian Drew. A mean-spirited and manipulative girl, Vivian was known for spinning lies, twisting words, and making false accusations. Occasionally, she would get violent, throwing rocks at her neighbor's dog or shoving her younger brother off of his tricycle. Once she'd even threatened two of her classmates with a knife.

As Vivian's fourth-grade teacher, Caroline had been among the first to volunteer for the search and rescue party. She, along with half the town, had trekked through miles of frost and mud and broken tree limbs, calling out Vivian's name and keeping a sharp eye out for a glimpse of her red hair or purple scarf. And with every step, with every fleeting moment, Caroline became more and more aware of a terrible, terrible truth: she didn't want Vivian to be found.

It was beyond shameful, utterly reprehensible. Even now, four years after what remained of Vivian's mutilated body had been unearthed deep in the heart of the forest, Caroline still lived with the guilt of knowing that a part of her had hoped for the deadly outcome.

The days following the discovery had been equally gruesome. Though few grieved for Vivian, many sought to avenge her brutal murder. So, the townsmen gathered up their rifles and set out in search of the only being in Slaughter capable of such a violent kill: the she-wolf.

Caroline's heart broke for the beautiful animal the same way it should have broken for the dead girl. After all, the wolf was simply acting on instincts. It wasn't evil. It was nature. But the hunters wouldn't hear of it, and after three days of heated bloodlust, they returned home with the wolf's pelt draped over their shoulders.

In the days following the animal's assassination, residents of Slaughter slept peacefully in the assurance that their enemy was dead. There would be no more children stolen from the playgrounds, no more bodies torn to pieces in the dead of night.

It wasn't until four weeks later, when Vivian's autopsy report was released, that an icy wave of dread swept back through the town, settling in the hearts and minds of every soul in Slaughter.

According to the coroner, there was no sign that Vivian had ever come into contact with a wolf, or any canine.

The bite marks on her body were human.

Chapter One

Welcome to Blue Ridge Books!
Our New Year's Resolution? Read More Books!
New Year's Sale: 20% Off All New Titles!
Check Out Our Auld Lang SIGNED Special Editions!

I'm thinking we may have gone overboard with the window signs. I mean, I guess they're cute in a sort of tacky-yet-charming way that suits our little store. And business is so slow after the holidays that they really couldn't hurt.

I just hope they're not too much.

Oh well. Even if they are, they'll be gone within a week or two. There's really only so long you can celebrate the new year with kitschy signs in your bookstore window.

I've just finished opening up shop, unlocking the cash register and organizing the table displays, when our antique shopkeeper's bell rings, alerting me to my first customer of the day.

"Good morning, Eloise," Hettie Brunsworth, one of my regulars, greets me with a warm smile.

"Hello, Hettie. How are you this morning?"

"I'm doing just fine. Thank you," she replies, adjusting her old mink stole. Hettie has always reminded me of a literary character from the 1920s. A quirky, classy woman in her mid-seventies, she's obsessed with faux fur coats and outlandish costume jewelry and you'll never, ever see her without bright red lipstick. She's the sort of person who's never met a stranger and never fails to remember the important details. The entire town loves her. And so do I. "Did you and Isaac have a good New Year's?" she asks me.

"We did. My cousins are in town so they brought their kids over."

"Oh, I bet Isaac enjoyed that."

"He did. He got to stay up late, eat junk food, and he finally had enough people to stage his backyard production of *Hamilton*."

Hettie stifles a laugh.

"That boy sure does love his Broadway, doesn't he?"

"That he does." One day, I'm going to be able to afford to take him to New York to see all of his favorite shows. I don't know how and I don't know when, but it's going to happen. "And how was your New Year's? Did you and Theresa go to any wild parties?"

"Oh Dearie, you know us. Every day is a party," she answers with a cheeky wink. "We've actually been doing a lot of work around the house these last few days. I don't remember if I told you, but my nephew, Danny, and his little girl, Adelaide, are moving here this weekend."

"No, you didn't tell me that."

"Well, he didn't want me to make a big deal out of it. He and his daughter have had a bit of a rough year. You see..." Hettie leans forward as if to share a secret, even though she and I are the only two

2

people in the store. "Her mother passed away very unexpectedly a few months ago. She and Danny were divorced, but of course, as the mother of his child, he still cared for her very deeply."

"I'm so sorry to hear that. How terrible for them," I murmur.

"Yes, it was very terrible. And it's been quite an adjustment for both of them. That's one of the many reasons I was so happy when he told me that they were coming to live here. To be around family and to live in such a wonderful community... I just think it will be very good for them."

"Oh, I agree."

We live in a small mountain town called Cedar Ridge, North Carolina. Although our residential population barely surpasses two thousand, during the winter months, we're something of a vacation destination. Most tourists come for the ski resort, but a fair few trickle downtown to the shops and art galleries. It's not perfect, and it may be more than a little old-fashioned, but Cedar Ridge is a safe and friendly community that always has and always will feel like home to me.

"You know, now that we've broached the subject, I was wondering if I might ask you a favor," Hettie said.

"Sure, anything."

"Danny happens to be a writer, and he's a very good one. He's even won an award or two, but don't tell him I told you that. Anyway, I know he's not going to want to be cooped up all alone once Addie starts school and I was thinking, well, you've got such a nice lounge here, and with the coffee shop right next door, it would just be the perfect place for him to get some work done during the day. Would you mind too terribly if I gave him your name?"

"No, not at all. He's more than welcome to work here." I technically set up the lounge to be a reading nook, but with its cozy couches and open fireplace, it could easily serve as an office for a long-suffering wordsmith.

"Oh, thank you. I so appreciate it. I think he'll really like it here. And I'm sure he'll enjoy getting to know you. Not like *that*, of course," she quickly adds, noting my look of alarm. "I promise, I'm not trying to set the two of you up. Although he is very handsome. And you, well, you're just as pretty as a winter rose..."

I can't help but blush.

"That's very sweet of you to say."

"I only speak the truth," Hettie smiles.

"But you know, I'm really not looking for anything..."

"Oh, I know, I know. And neither is he. I do think the two of you will end up being friends, though. You just have so much in common! You're both single parents. You're both fond of the written word. You're about the same age. Well, perhaps. How old are you, Dear?"

"Thirty-five."

"Ah, you see! He's just turned forty!"

I'm tempted to point out that I still have five years to go before I'm over *that* hill, but I hold my tongue. Age *is* just a number, after all. Besides, I'm thankful for my thirties. They've been the happiest years of my adult life. My twenties, on the other hand... they were a regular train wreck.

Ding.

4

The shopkeeper's bell rings again and a slender young man with curly black hair appears.

"Oh, good morning, Jason," Hettie greets him.

Speaking of train wrecks...

I'm kidding, I'm kidding. I've known Jason Harberger since the day he was born. Our families are old friends and he's always been like a little brother to me. I used to babysit him when he was six and I was thirteen. I was with him when he lost his first tooth, when he broke his first bone, and he came to me for advice when he developed his first crush. Now he's my employee, even though he hates that word and prefers that I call him my assistant.

"Well, well. Nice of you to show up," I tease.

"Sorry. I almost hit Floyd Whalen with my car this morning. Had to make sure he was okay. And that he didn't follow me into the store."

"Oh God, thank you," I tell him.

Floyd Whalen, bless his heart, is something of an odd duck. He's about seventy years old or so with flyaway gray hair and pale blue eyes that never quite seem to make contact with others'. He's frail and weathered and he wanders up and down the streets of downtown with a staggering limp. But it isn't his appearance that unnerves those who come into contact with him.

You see, we have an urban legend here in Cedar Ridge. A monster, if you will. It's called the Bogman. And Floyd Whalen is obsessed with it.

This thing, whatever it is, made its first appearance about five or six years back. A woman driving alone late at night reportedly saw a humanoid monster trudging along the side of the highway. Five more sightings followed within the week. However, it wasn't until a couple of tourists snapped a blurry photograph of a strange shadowy figure lurking down around Bog's Creek that the police, the press, and the people in general began to take the claims seriously.

The local media dubbed it the Beast of Bog's Creek, but by the time nationwide news stations picked up the story about two weeks after the first sighting, it had unofficially been rechristened the Bogman.

Most of us have accepted the Bogman in our own ways. Some fear it. Some, like Jason, are fascinated by it. And tourists absolutely love it. So much, in fact, that a few of the souvenir shops in Downtown Cedar Ridge began to sell Bogman merchandise.

Then there's Floyd Whalen. Floyd will tell anyone who will listen that he's seen it. That it attacked him, dragged him into the woods, and left him to die in the mud and snow.

And then he'll show you his scars.

"To tell you the truth, I feel sorry for the guy," Jason admits, adjusting his black-rimmed glasses.

"So does Theresa," Hettie sighs. "She thinks she can heal him, despite the fact that some people don't want to be healed."

"I wonder what really happened to him," I say.

"God only knows," Hettie mutters.

"Well, on that note, I'd better go get to work," Jason announces.

"Oh hey, before I forget, what days are you going to be gone next week?" I ask, pulling out my day-planner.

"Monday to Wednesday. I'll be back Thursday," Jason answers.

"Traveling?" Hettie asks. "Where are you going?"

"Philadelphia. A couple of my filmmaker buddies and I are going to spend a few days investigating the ghosts of the Eastern State Penitentiary."

"Oh, my. That sounds very... scary," Hettie supplies, fidgeting with her minks.

"*That* is putting it lightly," I remark.

"Eloise thinks I'm crazy," Jason says.

"Yes, I do."

I don't do creepy. Or haunted. Or anything that can get inside my head and keep me up at night. Frankly, I've dealt with enough demons in my waking hours to go looking for the kind that will terrorize me while I sleep. But if Jason wants to spend his hard-earned vacation time chasing ghosts around an abandoned prison, then more power to him. As long as he doesn't bring any ghouls or goblins back to my store, he can go wherever he wants.

"I must admit, I'm right there with you," Hettie tells me. "But you know, Jason, if you enjoy ghost stories, you should read my nephew's work. He's moving to town this weekend and I'm sure he would appreciate a young, fresh perspective."

"Yeah, absolutely," Jason grins. "I'd be happy to give him some feedback."

"That's wonderful. Thank you," Hettie smiles. "Now, I hate to say it, but I really must be off. I have to drive Theresa to her Reiki class. You kids take care, now."

"Have a good day, Hettie," I bid her.

The shopkeeper's bell rings once more as she opens the door and steps out into the frigid January air.

Like most of the stores in town, Blue Ridge Books closes at 5 P.M. It's then that I'm finally able to lock up, head home, and relieve my mom of babysitting duties. Not that she minds watching Isaac. She loves being a grandmother and Isaac absolutely adores her. Still, I wish I didn't have to depend on her so much.

Isaac and I live in a small, two-story house in a friendly, tight-knit neighborhood. It isn't extravagant by any means, but it does have a fireplace, three bedrooms, two bathrooms, and a spectacular view of the mountains. Although my mom and stepdad have offered many times to let us move in with them, I like having a place of my own. It might not be much, but it's warm and cozy and full of love. And that's really all we need.

Inside the entry hall, I kick off my shoes and hang my keys on their designated wall hook. Then, I make my way into the living room, where my mom and Isaac are watching *The Wizard of Oz*. Well, technically my mom is watching *The Wizard of Oz*. Isaac is sprawled out on the floor amidst a mess of crayons and scattered pieces of paper, sketching scenes from his favorite Broadway shows. It's a project he's been working on for a while now.

"What's going on in here?" I ask, smiling from ear-to-ear. It doesn't matter what I do or where I've been, coming home to Isaac is my favorite part of each and every day.

"Hi, Mom!" Isaac greets me with a sunny, gap-toothed smile. "We're watching Elphaba."

"Again?"

He's been going through a *Wicked* phase for about two weeks now, but since he can't watch it from home, he's content to settle for the next best thing.

"I told him that when you were his age, you were scared to death of this movie," my mom chuckles.

"Can you blame me?" I shudder. As far as I was concerned, there was nothing magical about being swept away by a *tornado* to a strange land of warty witches and terrifying tin men. Even as an adult, I don't particularly care for the premise. "So what did you two do while I was at work?" I ask, taking a seat on the couch next to my mom.

"We read a couple of books and made peanut butter sandwiches for lunch. Then we went for a walk in the snow. After that, we made some hot chocolate and now we're coloring and watching Elphaba," she answers.

"Sounds like a perfect day," I smile.

"And what about you? How was your day?"

"A bit slow, but after the holidays, that's to be expected," I answer, picking a few of Isaac's toys up off the floor and setting them next to me. "We did have a few customers, though. And Hettie stopped in to say hello."

In a town as small as Cedar Ridge, everybody knows everybody.

"That's nice. How is she doing?"

"Pretty well. She and Theresa had a good New Year's. And uh, her nephew is moving to town next week."

"Oh?"

"Yeah. He's a writer and she was wanting to know if it would be okay if he came and worked in the store."

"You sound like you don't want him to."

"No, no. It's fine. I really have no problem with it," I tell her honestly. "It's just... well..."

"What?"

"Even though she claimed she isn't trying to set us up, I think she maybe sort of... is."

"Would that be such a bad thing?" Mom asks lightly. Even though she's never come right out and said it, I know she's been hoping that I'll meet someone for a while now. And you know, I can't really blame her. After all, it's been four years since Isaac's dad and I split up. Maybe if that whole experience hadn't been so traumatic, I'd be hoping that I'd meet someone, too.

"I mean, I *guess* not..."

"But...?" Mom presses.

"I don't know. I don't think I'm ready. Besides, he's a *writer*. And I don't date writers."

"Why not?" Mom laughs.

"Because I have yet to meet one who isn't completely insufferable. Don't you remember that guy from last year? The one who wrote those weird cyborg assassin stories? He shows up for a book signing, complains that there isn't enough room in the store for his legions of fans, and pitches a fit because we dared to offer him filtered tap water instead of bottled water. And all the while, he's acting like he's doing *us* a favor."

"Well, maybe he was just having an off-day."

"Mom, he booked the signing himself! And the only people who showed up were a couple of tourists wanting to know if we had free WiFi. Then, he made me feel so guilty about his nonexistent sales that I bought *all seven* of his stupid books."

"Were they any good?"

Of course that's the question she asks. It's such a Mom question.

"I wouldn't know. I slapped a two-dollar price tag on them and stuffed them on the clearance shelf about thirty seconds after he left." If the reviews on GoodReads are to be believed, however, no, they are not good. Although, apparently, what his stories lack in substance, they more than make up for in scantily-clad women.

"You see? You didn't even give them a chance. What if that man turns out to be the next Ernest Hemingway?"

I don't know what world my mom thinks she's living in, but it must be nice there.

"I think I'm going to start dinner," I announce. "Isaac, Sweetheart, what do you want?"

"Spaghetti."

"We had spaghetti two nights ago. Try again."

"Okay, so you're just going to ignore me. I get it," my mom sighs. "But I still think you should give Hettie's nephew a chance. Who knows? He might just be the man of your dreams."

"The man of *my* dreams is Benedict Cumberbatch, but he had the nerve to go and marry someone else."

"Oh, I'm sure you'll learn to love again," my mom teases, rising up off the couch and kissing me on the cheek. "I'll see you tomorrow."

"Thank you." It doesn't matter how many times I say it, I know I'll never be able to thank her or my stepdad enough for everything they've done for me, and especially for Isaac. If not for them, his childhood would have been very, very different.

And that's something that I don't even like to think about.

Chapter Two

In my younger years, I was never really one for routine. Since becoming a single parent, however, I have found few things in life that keep me afloat quite like my morning ritual.

First, before I do anything else, I brew a pot of coffee and pour myself a cup. Then, I shower and change before pouring my second cup of coffee, which I enjoy while reading and watching the sun rise from our library on the second floor. The room is actually intended to be the third bedroom, but since it's only Isaac and me, we converted the extra space into a recreational room for books, music, and games. It's easily my favorite room in the house.

If I'm running according to schedule, I'll get about thirty minutes of blessed solitary reading before it's time to wake Isaac up and make breakfast. Then he gets dressed and, if it's a school day, we'll walk down to the bus stop together. If not, then he's allowed to watch television in my bedroom until my mom arrives to watch him.

Today just happens to be his first day back to school after winter break and he's about as thrilled as you'd expect any first-grader might be. Of course, he's excited to see his friends, but after almost three weeks of being free to sing and draw and study musical scripts to his little heart's content, he's returning to his classes with relatively low enthusiasm.

My morning ritual ends with me attempting to tame my wild auburn hair and applying a touch of mascara to my virtually invisible lashes. Although I don't necessarily consider myself a great beauty, I've never disliked the way I look. My nose is a little longer than it should be, and my lips are rather thin, but my eyes are pretty; wide and sky blue, the same color as Isaac's. Our eyes are actually the only feature we share. Otherwise, with his mop of blond curls and cute button nose, he's the spitting image of his father.

Glancing at the clock, I realize I have ten minutes to spare before I need to leave for work, but I head out the door anyway. With Jason gone, one of my Saturday employees, Blythe, will be helping me out around the store, and as much as I love Blythe, she's just a little... well... disorganized. Don't get me wrong, she's great with the customers. The problem is that sometimes she's *so* great that she lets them walk right out of the store without paying. Not intentionally, of course. She just enjoys talking with them so much that she forgets to ring them up.

Long story short, with Blythe as my coworker for the better part of the week, I need to make sure I'm caught up with everything before I open this morning.

I don't often say it aloud, but the truth is I love being at my store early in the morning. With golden sunlight streaming in through the windows and the smell of old pages and fresh coffee lingering in the air, it's like my own personal piece of Heaven.

I'm in the process of taking inventory of all of our new titles in the storage room when I hear the shopkeeper's bell ring. The sign out front still says **Closed**, but I left the door unlocked for Blythe.

"Hello? Eloise?" she calls out.

"In the back, Blythe!"

She appears moments later, wrapped in a thick gray shawl.

"How are you, Dear?" she asks, greeting me with a warm hug.

"Just fine," I smile. "How are you?"

"Wishing it was summer. I tell you, it just keeps getting colder and colder out there."

"I'll be sure to light a fire," I say. I made Jason go on a firewood run on Saturday before he left. "Thank you so much for helping me out around here this week. I really appreciate it."

"Oh, you're welcome. You know how much I enjoy being here. I just wish I could feel my toes!"

Winter in Cedar Ridge is beautiful, but it can be brutal. And since we're still in early January, we really haven't even seen the worst of it, yet.

"If you'd like, I can fetch you a blanket from the reading nook," I offer.

"Don't you worry, Dear. I brought my own!" she laughs.

"I should have known." Blythe always comes prepared. "Hey, what time is it?"

"We've got about seven minutes till we open. Would you like me to go unlock the cash register?"

"That would be perfect. Thanks, Blythe. I'll be out in just a second to get a fire going."

Once I've finished up with inventory and made a note of which titles I'll need to order before the week is up, I emerge from the storage room and head into the lounge, flipping the **Closed** sign on the front door to **Open** along the way.

I've only just knelt down to light the fire when the shopkeeper's bell rings.

"Why, hello there. Welcome to Blue Ridge Books." I hear Blythe greet the customer. I can tell by her tone that she doesn't recognize the person who's just walked in. Must be a tourist.

"Yeah, thanks." The voice that answers is brusque, baritone, and wildly ungracious. Like the speaker has neither the time nor the patience for small talk or warm welcomes. "Are you Eloise Bowman?"

Now, it's not all that unusual for customers to ask for me. My name is listed on the website, after all. What *is* a little strange, however, is that this guy knows me by my maiden name.

"Oh, dear me, no," Blythe answers. "I'm just the temporary cashier. But I can call her in here for you if you'd like."

"There's no need," I announce as I stride back into the store itself, fully prepared to give the person I'm about to meet a very passive-aggressive lecture on common courtesy. One look at him, however, and I'm strongly considering turning right back around and leaving Blythe to fend for herself.

The man in my store is intimidating, to say the least. He stands well over six feet tall, sturdy in stature and rugged in appearance. His eyes are actually a rather beautiful blue, but shadowed by a heavy, almost menacingly stern brow. Strands of his windswept brown hair fall inelegantly across his forehead and he has a scruffy beard. It strikes me suddenly that he would be rather handsome if not for the ugly scowl on his face.

Summoning up every ounce of bravado that I possess, I clear my throat and ask, "What can I do for you?"

"I'm Daniel Brunsworth. My aunt told me that I should come and talk to you."

Hold up. *This* guy is Hettie's nephew? That's impossible. The way she talked about him, she had me expecting a mild-mannered, middle-aged milquetoast. Not a tall, brawny mountain man who looks like he could survive for days roughing it in the Alaskan wilderness.

"Oh, right," I manage to choke out. "It's nice to meet you. I'm Eloise Keller."

"I thought Hettie said it was Bowman."

"It was. Bowman is my maiden name. I'm divorced now, but I still go by Keller because it's my son's last name."

"How old is your son?"

I hate to admit it, but I'm a little surprised he's asking. He doesn't seem at all the type to be interested in other people's kids. Or other people in general.

"Six."

"That's a great age."

"He's a pretty great kid." Not that I'm biased or anything. "Hettie mentioned that you have a daughter. How old is she?"

"She'll be eleven next month."

"I guess she started school today."

"Yeah. I'm trying not to think about it," he admits, shoving his hands into his pockets.

"Was she nervous?"

"No, but I am."

Oh, my goodness. Is the ice beginning to thaw?

"Don't be. Cedar Heights is a wonderful elementary school. Who's her teacher?"

"Actually, she's at the North Hill Academy."

"Oh, okay." And by that, I mean *oh, wow*. North Hill Academy is the only private elementary school in Cedar Ridge and it is definitely not cheap. I know it's absolutely none of my business, but I can't help but wonder how he's able to afford it. Maybe Hettie's helping him. With all her fake furs and costume jewelry, I can totally see her being an eccentric millionaire. "Well, she'll get an excellent education there. I've heard nothing but good things."

"I'm really just hoping that she's able to make some friends. She's had a rough year."

"Yeah, Hettie told me. I mean, she didn't go into detail or anything. She just mentioned that she'd lost her mom and I'm... I'm so sorry. For both of you."

"Thank you," he tells me, glancing down at the floor.

Okay, it is definitely time to change the subject.

"So uh... Hettie also told me that you're a writer."

"Are you?" Blythe chimes in. "How wonderful! What do you write?"

"Oh, you know. This and that," Daniel answers. I guess he's not one to talk about his work. And I can't really say I blame him. Writing is rather a personal profession.

"Well, just so you know, you're more than welcome to work here," I tell him. "We sometimes get a little busy around lunchtime when all the tourists are in town, but overall, it's a pretty peaceful atmosphere."

"I'll keep that in mind. Thanks."

"Would you like me to give you a tour?"

"Sure. If you're not busy."

Oh. I did not expect him to take me up on that. Okay, then.

"Not at all," I tell him. Then, I turn to Blythe, who happens to be watching us with an inordinate amount of interest. "We won't be long, Blythe."

"Take your time," she grins. I can only hope and pray that Daniel doesn't read anything into her overtly suggestive tone.

Thankfully, if he does, he doesn't acknowledge it.

"So, the store is divided into three sections: fiction, non-fiction, and collectibles," I explain, guiding him back through the aisles. "Collectibles can refer to just about anything from rare, first-edition books worth a small fortune to plastic action figures worth about fifty cents. Most of our books are used, but we do have a few shelves dedicated to new releases."

Daniel adopts a pensive air as he casts his eye over the Mystery/Thriller selections.

"What's your favorite genre?" he asks.

"Oh, goodness... I'm not sure I have a favorite," I answer. "I enjoy the classics, of course: *Pride and Prejudice*, *To Kill a Mockingbird*... pretty much anything you'd read in a high school English class." That gets a chuckle out of him. "I also read a lot of light-hearted contemporary fiction, a little bit of romance, and of course, nowadays, I'm reading a lot of middle-grade books with Isaac."

"Your son?"

"Yes."

"What is he reading now?"

"We just started the *Magic Tree House* books."

"My daughter loved those," he says.

"Oh yeah? What's she reading?"

"Hettie bought her about a dozen Judy Blume books for Christmas and she's been devouring them."

"You know, we actually had someone sell us a few signed Judy Blume books last year."

"I bet those didn't sit on the shelf very long."

"Oh, they never even made it to the shelf. I kept them for me," I grin. "One of the many advantages of working for myself."

"So, you own this store?"

"I do."

"Was it a dream of yours or...?"

"It was actually something I sort of grew into. I began working here part-time in high school, just sweeping the floors and organizing the shelves. I eventually got promoted to running the cash register and working inventory. I finally became a full-time employee after my divorce. Then, when the previous owner, Mrs. Snyder, decided to retire, she asked if I'd be interested in taking it over for her."

"Sounds like you've done well for yourself."

"Well, I've had a lot of help. But I do my best," I say. "And what about you? How did you get into writing?"

"By accident," he remarks. "It was never something I wanted to do, or even considered. But my senior year of college, I was a few elective hours short, so I enrolled in a creative writing class, thinking it would be easy."

"Was it?"

"It was awful. It was so much work that for a few weeks, I thought about dropping out. But then my professor called me in to discuss my first assignment. I thought for sure he was going to tell me I had no business writing and that I needed to find myself a new elective. Instead, he asked me if I'd mind if he submitted my short story to a state-wide fiction contest."

"That's incredible," I tell him. "So I'm guessing you sort of fell in love with it after that?"

"I don't know if I'd call it love, but it did keep me motivated. I never imagined I'd still be doing it almost twenty years later, though."

"Well, it's never too late to try something new," I remind him. "If you grew your beard a little longer and threw on a plaid shirt, you'd make a pretty convincing lumberjack."

At that, he actually throws his head back and laughs. It's a miracle.

"That's not something you hear every day," he says.

"Welcome to Cedar Ridge."

"Ah, that's right. Almost forgot where I was for a second."

"Have you spent much time here?"

"Yeah, actually. When I was a kid, my family and I would visit Hettie here every summer. I grew up in Chicago and I loved the city, but when I look back, I was always happiest here. Then, after Addie's mom died, bringing her here just made the most sense."

"Oh, of course. You have history here. You have Hettie and Theresa. And, you know, I might be a little biased, but Cedar Ridge really is a wonderful place to grow up."

"I'm guessing you speak from experience?"

"I do."

"Have you lived here your entire life?"

"No, actually. I spent four years at college in Raleigh, which is where I met my ex. After we got married, we moved to Winston-Salem. It wasn't until we split up four years ago that Isaac and I moved back here. And I don't hesitate to tell you it was the best decision I've ever made."

"I'm glad everything worked out for you."

"Well, like you said, bringing him here just made the most sense."

Daniel smiles down at me and suddenly, I find myself totally reevaluating my first impression of him. He isn't rude or angry. He's an artist who doesn't open up until he feels comfortable in his surroundings. He's a father trying to make the best decisions for his daughter in a new town. He's a man adapting to a new role in a new life, and although I doubt he'll come out and say it, I get the impression that that new life scares him to death.

And I, for one, know exactly how he feels.

"So uh... would you like to see the lounge?" I finally ask.

"Lead the way."

My mom is waiting for me at the window when I arrive home later that evening.

Let the record state that this is not a regular occurrence.

"What's going on?" I ask her, shedding my coat. "Is everything okay?"

"Yes, everything's fine," she answers with an uncharacteristically cutesy smile. "I'm just eager to hear about your day."

"... Why?"

"Oh, I don't know. School started back up again, so you were probably busy with students and teachers looking for books for their English classes. You might have also had some parents come in, looking for a new book now that they have a little extra time to sit and read. Or you may have spent the morning with a certain *writer* who just moved to town and is probably very lonely - "

"Okay, so, you talked to Blythe today." I don't know why I'm surprised. My mom and her friends are top-notch busybodies.

"Tell me about him!"

"I can't imagine there's anything I can tell you that you don't already know."

"You can tell me what you think of him."

"I thought he was nice," I answer, making my way into the living room where, once again, Isaac is laying on the floor, coloring. Tonight, he's watching *The Music Man*.

"Who's nice?" he asks without looking up from his drawing.

"Hettie's nephew," I answer. "He's very nice."

"Hettie has a nephew?" Isaac asks in his adorable little kid voice. He's at that age where everything seems wondrous, even the simple idea of one of his favorite friends having a nephew.

"Yes, she does."

"What's his name?"

"Daniel."

"How old is he?"

"He's forty."

"Oh. He's old."

"Hey now," I laugh. "I'll be forty in just a few years. Does that make me old?"

"Well... a *little*."

"Oh, really?" I demand, dropping to my knees and snatching him right up off the ground. He shrieks with laughter as I tickle his sides and kiss his cheeks. Finally, I show him mercy, but I don't release him. Not just yet. "So how was your day at school?"

"It was okay," he answers.

"Just okay?"

"Yeah."

Even though he's only in the first grade, I worry desperately about Isaac and how he's treated when I'm not with him. I know his teachers love him and I know he has friends... but I also know that he's different. Let's face it, there aren't many six-year-olds out there who can recite Arthur's monologue from *Camelot* word for word.

"Did you learn anything new or exciting?"

"No. But Shayla let me share her cookies at lunch."

So the highlight of his day was cookies. Maybe he *is* just like other kids after all.

"Well, I hope you still have enough room in your tummy for Mona's."

Isaac gasps. Mona's is a local pizza parlor and his absolute favorite restaurant.

"Yes!" he exclaims. I can't help but laugh.

"Why don't you go upstairs and change and then we'll head out?" In the blink of an eye, he's on his feet and dashing up the stairs with the speed and precision of... well, of a hungry first-grader anxious for garlic bread. Once I hear his door slam, I turn to my mom and ask, "Would you and Lenny like to join us?"

"Thank you, but I think we'll stay in tonight. Lenny's still watching his cholesterol. What I *would* like, however, is to hear more about Hettie's handsome nephew."

My poor mom. She holds out so much hope for me. Even in spite of my astonishingly bad track-record when it comes to romance.

It all began in seventh grade when I fell for the boy who only asked me out so he could cheat off of my history tests. I was so hurt at the time, I couldn't imagine that any of my future boyfriends could possibly be worse. Then I got to high school and dated, in chronological order, the guy who cut class so he could smoke and sell marijuana behind the gymnasium, the bad boy who dressed like a rock star and ended up getting suspended for bringing a knife to school, and the "nice" guy who called me an uppity bitch after I told him I wasn't ready to sleep with him.

By the time I met Lance Keller during my sophomore year of college, I was old enough to know that he wasn't good for me but still young and naïve enough to believe that I could fix him. In my mind, we were a modern-day Beauty and the Beast. I was the bookish girl from a small town. He was the shy, reclusive son of one of the richest men in Forsyth County. But all the wealth, privilege, and love in the world weren't enough to rid him of the demons that had plagued him for years.

"I already told you, he seems like a really decent guy," I finally answer, banishing the ghosts of all my failed relationships from my mind.

"Blythe said he seemed to like you."

"Well, I certainly hope he didn't *dislike* me."

"Do you think you'll see him again?"

"Mom. It's Cedar Ridge. I'm bound to see him again."

"You know what I mean."

"If he decides to come back and work in the store, then yes, I'll see him again."

"And would you like that?"

I never get the chance to answer, however, as Isaac chooses that moment to come bounding down the stairs, dressed in his best dinner jacket and blue bow tie.

"I'm ready!" he announces.

"Oh, my! Don't you look handsome!" I smile.

Mona's is a far cry from the fanciest restaurant in town, but Isaac loves dressing up whenever we go out. It doesn't matter where we go, he is always the most debonair little fellow in the room. And my God, I love him for it.

Then again, I love him for everything.

Chapter Three

"Hey, Blythe? Can you keep an eye on things up here? I have to run to the back just real quick." It's only the second day of the new semester and I've already had four phone calls from frantic parents asking if I have any copies of *Mythology* by Edith Hamilton. I was able to track down books for the first three, but number four is proving to be something of a challenge. Though there's always a chance that I have a few extra copies stashed back in inventory.

"Sure thing, Honey."

So far this morning, we've had five customers. Three of them were tourists, one was a young lady who often comes in on Tuesdays hoping to get her hands on new releases, and one man just came in to wander. Alas, there's been no hide nor hair of Daniel Brunsworth.

I can't say I'm all that surprised. It was all Hettie's idea that he should set up shop here, anyway. He probably only stopped by yesterday as a favor to her. Like I told my mom, I'm sure I'll still see him around town. And I really would like to. I'd like to keep up with how he and his daughter are faring here.

Right now, however, I have more pressing matters at hand, namely finding a fourth copy of Edith Hamilton's *Mythology*. And finally, after searching every shelf and rummaging through every box, I do. It's tattered and water-stained, but it's intact and readable.

Emerging from the storage room, I hold the book high over my head and march triumphantly back to the front of the store.

"Ha! Victory!" I exclaim.

My world comes to a screeching halt, however, when I find myself face-to-face, not with Blythe, but with a towering and rugged wordsmith. Daniel Brunsworth has returned, armed with a black backpack and a to-go cup from the coffee shop next door, and he's watching me with mild surprise and - dare I say it - amusement.

"Oh! Hello," I greet him, desperately trying to salvage what little remains of my dignity.

"Having a good morning?" he asks lightly.

"Yes. Thank you." I clear my throat and set the worn and weathered copy of *Mythology* down behind the cash register. "How are you?"

"Doing okay. I thought I might take you up on your offer to get some writing done here."

"Well, that's great!" And unexpected. Though not unwelcome. "Come with me and I'll help you settle in."

He follows me into the reading lounge and selects the armchair closest to the fireplace, which is still dark.

"Sorry it's a little cold in here," I apologize. "We've been busy this morning."

"That's not a bad thing," he says, unzipping his backpack and pulling out a laptop computer.

"True," I acknowledge. "So how did your daughter - I'm sorry, what did you say her name was?"

"Addie. Short for Adelaide."

"That's beautiful."

"Thanks."

"So, how did Addie enjoy her first day of school?"

"I think she liked it okay. She said her teacher was nice and she's excited about her art class. I can tell she still misses her friends back home, though."

"Oh, of course," I say, kneeling down to collect a couple of logs for the fire. "If you don't mind me asking, where did you move from?"

"I was actually up in New York, but Addie lived with her mom in California, out in Irvine. After the accident, I moved out there to... well... to settle a few things. And to let Addie finish out the first half of the school year in an environment she knew."

"She's lucky to have you."

"No. I'm the lucky one."

I should have known he'd feel that way. It's the same way I feel about Isaac.

Once I've got the fire lit, I slip out of the lounge, leaving Daniel to work in peace. I need to get to work myself. I have a sneaking suspicion I'll be scrounging the back-alley bookstores of Cedar Ridge for a few more copies of *Mythology* before the day is done. Might as well get a head start.

About thirty minutes into my crusade, the shopkeeper's bell rings and Hettie's wife, Theresa Haddock steps inside. She's accompanied by an older man, dressed in an oversized brown coat, who peers around my bookstore with wild, unfocused eyes.

Floyd Whalen.

I try to suppress a grimace.

Theresa doesn't seem to notice.

"Hello, Elsie!" For reasons I've yet to figure out, Theresa only ever calls me Elsie. I've corrected her. Several times, in fact. But to no avail. To Theresa, I am - and apparently will forever be - Elsie.

"Good morning, Theresa," I greet her. "Hi there, Mr. Whalen. How are you doing today?"

"S'well as you can expect, all things considerin'," he grumbles without meeting my eye.

I'm not about to ask him what he means by that. Asking Floyd to elaborate is a mistake you only make once.

"Floyd is thinking of writing a book," Theresa informs me.

"Is that right?" I ask.

Theresa is a sweet woman, wild and Bohemian. She's the kind of person who wears scarves even when it isn't cold outside and always smells of incense and eucalyptus oil. She wears about twelve earrings in each ear, has an elephant tattoo, and I've never once known her to leave her house without at least three decks of Tarot cards.

She also happens to have a soft spot for the downtrodden and the doomsayers.

"That's why we're here. I want him to meet Danny," Theresa explains.

"Oh." It's all I can say as I very seriously consider how tricky it would be to help Daniel escape out the store's back exit without anyone noticing.

Alas, Daniel must have heard Theresa's voice because he emerges from the lounge mere moments later.

"Hey, Theresa," he smiles.

"Hello, Danny." Although I get the impression that Daniel is very much not a hugger, Theresa throws her arms around his neck and holds him fast, just like an aunt seeking to comfort a frightened child. "How are you today?"

"I'm great."

"Hmm. Your aura suggests otherwise."

Daniel narrows his eyes and casts me a stealthy sidelong glance.

"Yeah, I'll have to work on that," he remarks. "So, what brings you by?"

"I want to introduce you to someone," Theresa beams, taking Floyd gently by the elbow and presenting him to her nephew. "This is Floyd Whalen. He lives down at the far end of Hermitage Lane. He's retired now, but he worked in the lumber industry for over forty years. And he has an extraordinary story."

"Oh yeah?" Daniel asks lightly. He knows where this is going.

Cocking his head slightly to the side, Floyd looks Daniel up and down with those pale eyes. Then he takes a tentative step forward.

"Have you heard of the Beast, young man?"

"The Beast?" Daniel asks.

"The Beast of Bog's Creek. Tall as two grizzlies. Russet fur, matted with mud and blood. Long, glistening fangs. And a pig's snout as ugly as anything you'll ever see. Oh, but his eyes... you never forget the sight of them golden yellow eyes."

"Is... that right?" Daniel asks, visibly caught off guard. And understandably so. "And this monster... lives here?"

"That's right. Right here in Cedar Ridge. Dwells deep down in the darkest neck of the woods. But every once in a while, it makes its way into town or finds itself wanderin' along the highway."

"There are quite a few in town who've seen him," Theresa adds. "Hettie, of course, thinks it's all nonsense, but since you love a good horror story Danny, I thought that Floyd's testimony might interest you."

"Yeah, it sure does," Daniel finally musters, forcing his face into something that remotely passes for a look of sincerity.

"I've seen it, you know," Floyd mutters gruffly, almost as though he's sharing a secret. "It came after me one night. Swiped me right up off the ground. Dragged me to the edge of the woods and left me for dead. Woke up in the hospital a few hours later. Couple o' hunters found me 'bout to bleed to death and called an ambulance. I wasn't supposed to make it, but seven years later, here I am."

"Wow," Daniel remarks. "That is... quite a story."

"Isn't it? I was meditating on his testimony earlier this week and I got to thinking about how wonderful it would be to take that experience and turn it into something that he can share with the world. Like a book." Theresa smiles brightly at her nephew.

"Yeah. Yeah, that *would* be great," Daniel says, running a hand through his hair. "I could probably give you the names of a couple of people who might be able to help get you started."

"Well, what about you?" Theresa asks.

Daniel grimaces.

"Gee Theresa, you know I would love to, but now just really isn't a good time" he claims. "I mean, I've got two deadlines of my own I've got to meet, Addie's still getting settled in at her new school, and with all the boxes we still haven't unpacked? I'm sorry, I just can't."

"Oh, that's all right, Dear. Of course, I understand. As a matter of fact, I have something that just might help you. And Addie." As she speaks, Theresa reaches into her pouch and pulls out three stones; one blue and marbled, one green and earthy, and one pale pink and shiny, a quartz of some kind. "This is a Blue Apatite," she explains, holding up the first stone. "It's a stone of manifestation. It helps to clear confusion and negativity while nurturing your ability to achieve your goals. Then this green one is called Chrysoprase. It's a healing stone, and it's also known for restoring hope in a hopeless heart. And this," she picks up the pink stone, "is actually my very favorite. Rose Quartz. It's the stone of love and compassion."

Daniel must be used to receiving healing stones from his aunt because he accepts her gift with a gracious smile.

"Thanks, Theresa. This means a lot."

"You're welcome. I know that you're not really into all of this, which is funny to me since you're an artist *and* an Aquarius - " At that, Daniel raises a skeptical eyebrow. " - but I think, in times of change, even the smallest act of kindness goes a long way."

"And you're right. Thank you. I really do appreciate it. And I know Addie will, too."

"Well, I guess we'd better be on our way. I have a Reiki class beginning in about thirty minutes," Theresa says, glancing around for Floyd, who's wandered off and is poking around the new releases. "And Danny remember, if you ever need someone to watch Addie or if you're interested in a Healing session or even if you just want a nice home-cooked meal, you call us right up. We're here for you."

"I know. And thank you."

Theresa engulfs Daniel in one last nurturing hug before she turns back to me. "Thank you so much for giving our Danny a place to write, Elsie."

"Oh, it's my pleasure," I assure her.

"You take good care of him. And take care of yourself. There are some very big changes headed your way. You need to be ready." I blink, not entirely sure what she means by that. She must not foresee anything too concerning, however, because instead of elaborating, she flashes a bright, sunny smile and says, "Love and light! Let's go, Floyd."

Floyd turns to obey, but before he leaves, he takes one last look at Daniel.

"That Beast is out there. You mark my words," he grumbles.

Then he follows Theresa out the door.

Daniel is the first to break the silence.

"Well, that was... unusual."

"That was Floyd."

"Is there any, uh... substance? To everything he was talking about?"

"That depends on who you ask," I reply. "There are others who claim to have seen it...

34

whatever it is. But he's the only one who's ever supposedly come in contact with it."

"So what is it?"

"A lot of people think it's a monster of some sort, you know, like Bigfoot or the Mothman. But there are a few skeptics out there who are convinced that it's just an ordinary animal, maybe a bear or a large deer. There's also the theory that it might be human, even though all the eyewitnesses swear that it isn't."

"What do you think?"

"I think I'd rather we were just known for the ski resort," I answer.

"You don't like the idea of monsters in the woods?"

"I don't like the idea of monsters anywhere," I reply.

"Why not?"

I take a moment to formulate my answer.

"Because there's enough uncertainty in the world without having to wonder whether there's something supernatural crawling around my backyard."

"I'm going to go out on a limb here and guess you're not much of a horror fan?"

"Not even a little bit."

Daniel smirks then and suddenly, I remember what Theresa said earlier. Why she brought Floyd to meet him in the first place.

Daniel loves a good horror story.

"Oh no," I groan. "You write horror, don't you?"

"Yeah, kinda," he admits with a laugh.

"I am so sorry."

"Why are you apologizing?"

"Because I feel like I just insulted your passion."

"Horror is hardly my passion," Daniel says. "It just happens to pay the bills."

"Still, I'm sorry I don't... appreciate it."

"I won't hold it against you," Daniel assures me.

"Thank you," I smile sheepishly.

He observes me for one more brief moment. Then, with the slightest hint of a smile, he turns and retreats back into the lounge.

Chapter Four

At the beginning of the school year, I exchanged phone numbers with a few of the other Cedar Heights moms and we created a group chat. Originally, it was intended to keep up with homework assignments, class announcements, and to discuss any questions or concerns we may have had. Of course, it only took about two weeks for it to evolve into a social hotline. Sure, we'll talk about something school-related every once in a while, but we mostly discuss movies we don't have time to see, manicures we can't afford to get, and all the ways our own parents still manage to drive us crazy.

This morning, I wake up to a series of text messages as I often do, but they're not about the first grade bake sale, the upcoming winter carnival, or the latest true crime documentary to drop on Netflix.

There was a sighting.

The Bogman is back.

And the local news outlets are already celebrating.

The Legend Lives On: Bogman Returns!
Hello Bogman, Our Old Friend!

Welcome Back, Boggy: Infamous 'Beast' Reemerges After Four Years

Linda McAllen was on her way to her early-morning shift at Preston Park Medical Center when she saw it: a tall, hairy creature making a mad dash into the forest.

"It was the movement that caught my eye," Nurse McAllen claims. "I was driving; the same route that I drive every morning. It was still dark so naturally, I had my lights on. All of a sudden, there it was. It moved so quickly, I didn't get a good look at it. But I do know that whatever it was... it wasn't human."

Although Nurse McAllen couldn't positively identify the creature, she knew immediately what it had to be...

"Oh, you've got to be kidding," I groan.

I don't bother reading the rest of the article. It can't possibly tell me anything I don't already know. Besides, I need to get up and make breakfast for Isaac. I can't waste my morning poring over this nonsense.

Of course, word spreads like wildfire in a town as small as Cedar Ridge, and by the time I make it to work, the streets of downtown are bustling with locals and tourists alike, all asking the same question. It's sort of like being in the opening sequence of a Disney movie, but instead of singing about the funny girl who likes to read or the street rat who stole a loaf of bread, all of the colorful townspeople are wondering whether or not their neighbors have heard about the Bogman. And of course, everybody's answer is "Yes."

Even Daniel's heard the news.

"So, I guess old Floyd was right," he remarks, once again setting up shop in the lounge. "Is this how it always is?"

"I couldn't tell you," I reply. "I wasn't living here the last time Bogman hysteria swept through Cedar Ridge."

"Ah. So, we're both in for a new experience."

"Lucky us," I quip.

"You know, you never told me what you think it is."

"Didn't I?"

"No. You diverted the question. So, I'll ask again. Do you believe in the Bogman?"

I pause for a moment, trying to figure out exactly how to answer him.

"The truth is... I'm not entirely sure what I believe," I admit. "On a conscious level, no. I don't think that monsters actually exist. But at the same time - "

Ding!
CRASH!

Before I can finish, the door to the bookshop slams open, nearly knocking my shopkeeper's bell right off of its hook, and a stocky young man with bristly blond hair and wide hazel eyes bursts inside.

"Hey yo, Jason!" he calls out.

"Logan!" I snap before I can help myself.

"Oh hey, Ms. Keller!" Logan grins, strutting into the lounge. "Where's J-Man?"

For the most part, Jason has always had pretty decent taste in friends. Logan Taylor is the exception. He's loud, he's obnoxious, and he's got an ego on him the size of an ocean-liner. I truly don't know how Jason puts up with him.

"He's still out of town with the crew. I thought you went with them."

"I wish. Couldn't get the time off work," Logan whines. "So, will J and the guys be back soon?"

"Yeah, tomorrow."

"That's not soon enough. I need them here *now*. We've got a Bogman to catch!"

"Of course you do," I mutter.

"You scoff but mark my words, little lady. The Bogman is out there. And I'm going to be the one to prove it."

"Little *lady*?" And here I was thinking he couldn't possibly get more irritating.

"In the meantime," he continues, "I'm going to need some books on roughing it in the wilderness. Whatever you've got. I know your selection is kinda limited."

"Are you seriously thinking of going out there?" Daniel asks.

"Hell yeah, I am! How else am I supposed to document the greatest cryptozoological discovery of the twenty-first century?" Logan asks, all but basking in his own eminence. His spell of self-admiration is temporarily broken, however, when he takes a closer look at Daniel. "You look familiar."

"Yeah, I've got one of those faces."

"This is Hettie's nephew, Daniel. He's just moved here," I tell Logan.

"Oh. Well, welcome. I hope you enjoy snowstorms and monotony," Logan says. Then, he turns back to me. "So, Ms. Keller, about those survivalist books?"

And we're back to this.

"Whatever we have in our *limited* supply is going to be in nonfiction under 'Guides and Manuals,'" I answer. "You might also check out the nature section."

"Thanks," he winks. I'm dead serious. He actually winks at me. I don't know whether to laugh or vomit.

"He seems like a piece of work," Daniel mutters once Logan is out of earshot.

"You have no idea," I grumble. "But hey, if he wants to spend his money here, I'm not about to stop him. Even though I'm fairly certain those books will end up as coasters for his specialty set of collectible beer mugs."

"Actually, they're called steins."

"That is *not* the point," I reply, casting him a sidelong glance. To my delight, he laughs.

"So, you don't think he's actually going to catch a monster?"

"No, I don't think he's actually going to *read*."

That's when Daniel laughs again, so loudly this time that Blythe hears it all the way from the cash register.

"Sounds like you kids are having a good time in there!" she calls.

Hastily, I busy myself sweeping the floor around the fireplace so that Daniel won't see me blushing. Thankfully, he doesn't seem to notice.

"Boy, it's nice to be called a kid again," he says. "Back in New York, I was always surrounded by twenty-somethings, fresh out of college. I was beginning to feel like the only old guy in Manhattan."

"Sounds like a title for your autobiography, if you ask me," I tease.

"Ha. You're funny."

"Why thanks."

Just then, Logan reappears with an armful of used books.

"Thanks again, Ms. Keller. And hey, before I go... don't you have like, a loft or something here?"

I do, actually. All of the old buildings downtown have two or three stories. Every once in a while, I think about converting my second story into a cafe or perhaps moving the lounge up there and expanding my floor space down here. But then I remember that that costs money and I have a six-year-old and so the second floor remains an extra storage space for stuff that's probably been up there longer than I've been alive.

All that considered, I'm sure I'm happier with the cobwebs and dust-bunnies than whatever harebrained scheme Logan is about to suggest.

"Where are you going with this, Logan?" I ask.

"Well, I'm just thinking that if you're not using it, maybe Jason and I could turn it into our headquarters. You know, we could move in all our film stuff, hang some maps up on the - "

"No."

"You didn't even let me finish."

"I heard enough."

"Come on, are you worried that we'll trash it? Because you know Jason will keep it tidy... maybe."

"It isn't that." Though, now that he mentions it, it is a valid concern.

"Then what? Are you worried it will distract him from his work?"

"I just don't want any of that... *stuff* in my store."

"What stuff?"

"The Bogman stuff."

"But it's science!" Logan argues.

"It's not science. It's creepy and weird and I don't want anything to do with it."

Of course, that isn't good enough for Logan.

"Why don't you take some time to think about it and then you can get back to me?" he asks. Then, before I have time to argue, or even speak, he turns and dashes out the door as boisterously as he entered.

"I'm not going to change my mind!" I call after him, but he's already gone. Heaving an aggravated sigh, I turn back to Daniel, who doesn't even try to hide the smirk behind his beard. "Sorry about that."

"No, no. Don't apologize," he tells me. "So, does this mean you're a believer after all?"

"I'm not going to go so far as to say I'm a believer. I'm just not about to take any chances," I reply. "That's what I was going to say earlier. Even though I don't think I believe, I can't say that I know for sure that there isn't something out there. Because I don't. No one does. And that's what scares me the most."

"And you don't like being scared," Daniel concludes.

"No. Do you?"

"Sure, I do. It's fun."

"You and Jason." I shake my head.

"Is he your boyfriend?"

"My assistant. He's obsessed with ghosts and monsters and spooky urban myths."

"Does he read a lot of horror?"

"He reads it, he writes it... He lives for it. His dream is actually to become a filmmaker specializing in horror, and that's why he's not here right now. He and a few of his friends went off to investigate an old haunted prison. I'm sure he'll be thrilled to know the Bogman has returned."

"Hmm." Daniel nods and stares down at his computer screen. His brow furrows and he appears lost in thought. Suddenly, I find myself feeling rather self-conscious.

"I'm sorry. That was probably a lot more than you wanted to know," I tell him.

"No, no. It's fine," he says, meeting my eye once again. "It wasn't you, I promise."

"Still, I really should let you get on with your work." Just as I really should be getting on with mine. "As always, let me know if you need anything."

"Thanks."

With a polite smile and a nod, I turn to leave and go about my business, but then he calls out to me again.

"Eloise." I look back at him. "I enjoy talking with you."

This time, I can feel the blush all the way from the roots of my hair to the tips of my toes.

"Likewise."

Excerpt from *Mausoleum*
By D.H. Whittaker

It was a clear night in Springlake, Michigan as three figures slipped silently into St. Matthew's Cemetery.

Paul Ortiz was there for the hell of it. It was something to do on a Friday night. Besides, he was an adventurer at heart, and God knew adventures were hard to come by in their nice, respectable suburbs.

Morgan Hirsch was in it for the clicks and the content. She was already a social media celebrity by Springlake's standards. But a series of snaps from the resting place of a recently-deceased delinquent? That would be enough to catapult her into nationwide super-stardom.

Blake Solomon couldn't have cared less about the call of adventure or the number of likes on his Facebook page. He was there for Cole Bailey, that sick, twisted son of a bitch.

Cole Bailey, who'd carved a pentagram into his baby brother's stomach.

Cole Bailey, who'd hunted his neighbor's beloved pitbull for sport.

Cole Bailey, who'd driven sweet Briar Jamison to madness with his perverse obsession.

As far as Blake was concerned, death was too good for that sociopath. Especially an accidental death. According to police reports, Bailey had been kicking around the abandoned railroad tracks, probably in the hopes of finding another animal to torture, when he'd fallen and hit his head on the metal rails. He'd died instantly. No pain. No suffering.

No justice.

To add insult to injury, his grieving mother had requested they lay him to rest, not in the ground, six feet closer to hell, but inside the polished walls of the mausoleum. Old Mrs. Bailey must have known her son's burial site was bound to be desecrated, so she'd done her best to make sure he was out of reach.

But that wasn't about to stop Blake. Where there was a will, there was a way. If he couldn't dance on Cole Bailey's grave, he could damn well take a sledgehammer to the walls that held him.

The mausoleum itself was a peaceful building with cool, filtered air, tranquility fountains, and a small garden of potted plants. It seemed more like a temple than a resting place for the dead.

"Okay, guys. This is it," Morgan whispered, holding her phone up so her multitude of live-stream viewers could get a better look. "We are actually inside the mausoleum where Cole Bailey was buried just last week."

"I wonder if he's started decomposing yet," Paul mused gleefully.

"We're about to find out," Blake muttered under his breath.

Clutching his weapon, he marched ahead of his companions and down a darkened hallway. He skidded to a stop, however, when he saw the flicker of candlelight and a shadowy silhouette kneeling beneath Cole Bailey's tomb.

"Jesus - " he hissed.

Not at all startled by his sudden appearance, the figure turned to face him.

"Hello, Blake."

Chapter Five

"Mom, is the Bogman real?"

I'm in the process of zipping up Isaac's puffy winter coat when he asks the question.

"Who told you about the Bogman?" I ask in return.

"Shayla and Jenny. And Jeremy. And Mia." So basically, his entire class. Which begs an answer to a whole new question: why do all these six-year-olds know about the Bogman? Did their parents tell them? Did they overhear the older kids discussing it at lunchtime?

"What did they tell you?"

"That it's a monster that lives in the trees and it comes out at night. And it likes to look in windows to see if you're still awake. And if you are, it eats you."

"And what did you say?"

"That there are no such things as monsters. Except in *Monsters, Inc.*"

"And you're right," I assure him.

"But Shayla says her grandma *saw* it!" Isaac exclaims, his lower lip quivering.

"Well Sweetheart, sometimes grown-ups' eyes play tricks on them, especially when it's nighttime.

Do you remember in *Snow White* when she's running through the forest and all the trees have spooky faces? But then the sun comes up and she realizes that they were never spooky at all?"

"Yeah."

"That happens in real life, too. Sometimes a grown-up will see something and, because it's dark outside, or maybe even because they're scared, their brain will trick them into thinking it's something else."

"Why would their brain do that?"

"Because brains are silly," I tease, ruffling his adorable golden curls. "Now go get your boots on. You don't want to miss the bus."

Once Isaac is safely on his way to school, I grab my purse and my sack lunch, brush the thin layer of fresh snow off of my car, and make the ten-minute commute from my house to my business. As much as I've enjoyed having Blythe at the store with me this week, I'll be glad to have Jason back. Granted, he'll probably spend the entire day talking my ear off about ghosts and the Bogman, but he's much better at lifting heavy boxes of books than I am. And he doesn't mind when I send him on arbitrary errand runs.

All joking aside, I'll really just be happy to see him. He's been one of my best friends for so long and a real source of strength and comfort these last few years. And I miss him when he's not around.

I've just finished unlocking the cash register and organizing the checkout counter when the front door opens and he walks in, looking for all the world like a kid at Christmas.

"Hey!" he greets me with a brief hug. "Did you hear the Bogman's back?"

"Has anyone *not* heard the Bogman's back?"

"Okay, I'm sorry. I know how you feel about him, but this is going to be huge. It already *is* huge. Get this. I met up with Logan last night. He's already started compiling every article, every police report, and every witness statement from each sighting back when all of this began. He even found this detailed analysis of the picture that those tourists snapped, so we reached out to the guy who did that to see if he'd be interested in going over his process with us and maybe even recording a segment for the documentary."

"Wow." That is a *lot* of information. "So... a new documentary, huh?"

"It's going to be amazing, El. We're going to start interviewing witnesses this weekend. Logan's actually picking up some new recording equipment as we speak," Jason tells me. "This is it. This is going to be the film that changes our lives. I can *feel* it."

"That's great. I'm happy for you. In the meantime, how do you feel about taking inventory on all of the new titles?"

"You didn't even try to lift those boxes, did you?"

"Nope."

"Wimp. You're such a wimp!" Jason declares, but he heads back to the storage room anyway.

"Not a wimp. A single mother who can't afford a chiropractor!" I call after him as the front door opens again.

"Why would you need a chiropractor?" Daniel asks.

"Because I threw out my back. Hypothetically."

"Oh. Okay." I appreciate how he just accepts my strange explanation without any sort of hesitation, and I expect him to carry on with his business as usual. But he doesn't. Instead, he lingers for a moment at the front counter and asks, "So uh, how's your day been so far?"

I blink, unsure of how to answer. Is he flirting with me? Or is he just making polite conversation?

"Well, it's only nine, so you know... pretty short."

Oh, my God, that was so awkward. Thankfully, Daniel laughs, though it may just be out of courtesy. Or pity.

"Although," I continue, hoping to redeem myself with actual social skills, "Isaac did ask me about the Bogman this morning. So I guess it got off to a bit of a rocky start."

"Addie asked me about it, too."

"What did you tell her?"

"That there's nothing to be scared of. That I wouldn't have brought her anywhere that wasn't safe. And that there are no such things as monsters."

"Do you have a picture of her? If you don't mind me asking."

"No, not at all."

He pulls his phone out of his pocket and opens his photo album. He selects a picture of a preteen girl in a blue and green plaid private school uniform. Her brown hair is tied up in a high ponytail and she smiles with her mouth closed, like she's shy or maybe embarrassed.

"She's adorable," I tell him.

"Thanks. I think so, too," Daniel grins, swiping backward. "Here she is at Christmas." He shows me a picture of the same darling girl, sitting beneath a gorgeous tree, surrounded by discarded wrapping paper. This time, she's dressed in candy-cane pajamas and holding a brand-new arts-and-crafts kit.

"How sweet. Is she an artist?" I ask.

"Sort of. She's really into those cartoon books. What are they called...? Manga?"

"Oh, yeah. We have some here in the young adult section."

"Well, after... everything that happened, I noticed her drawing more and more. And when I asked her what she was working on, she told me they were characters for her manga. So, Santa went shopping and found her the arts-and-crafts set."

"That's wonderful," I smile. "You're a good dad."

"I'm trying," he sighs, scrolling back through his photo album. As the pictures pass, I notice there are very few of him, until one particular image catches my eye.

"Hey, wait a minute." I reach out to stop him and, without realizing what I'm doing, grab his hand. His fingers are still cool, but his touch is like a spark against my skin, and I'm suddenly very aware of my heart beating. Especially when he glances down at me with those blue eyes. Hastily, I retract my hand and direct his attention back to the pictures on his phone, specifically the one of him sitting at a table, surrounded by stacks of books. "Do you do book signings?"

"Every once in a while," he answers.

"Wow, I feel silly. I didn't realize you had a book out," I admit.

"You mean you didn't go home and Google me?" he teases.

"I mean, obviously I knew you were a writer. And Hettie mentioned that you'd won a few awards. But you can win awards for a lot of things. Like Lin-Manuel Miranda. He won the Pulitzer Prize for *Hamilton*." My six-year-old son taught me that. I didn't even know he knew what the Pulitzer Prize was.

"I can assure you I've never won anything that prestigious or written anything that significant."

"Nevertheless, if you're ever interested in signing books here, I'd be more than happy to set that up for you." Even as I make the offer, I can hear myself complaining about the last book signing I agreed to host here at the store. I guess that makes me a hypocrite. And a shallow one at that.

Oh well.

"I appreciate that," Daniel grins. "Thanks, Eloise."

The way he says my name sends a shiver straight down my spine, all the way to my very core.

"Don't mention it," I breathe.

"Eloise!" Jason calls from the storage room after nearly two hours of organizing the inventory.

"Up front!"

We only have two customers right now, both of whom just sort of wandered in. I'm usually pretty good at figuring out who's here to buy and who's here to browse and these two are definitely browsers.

"Hey." Jason appears, carrying a fresh stack of hardbacks. "These were supposed to be out Tuesday, but they just came in today. Do you want me to clear a space with the new releases?"

"If you don't mind, that'd be great. Oh! And when you're finished, come with me into the lounge. I have someone I'd like you to meet."

"10-4." Apparently, that means "understood" in radio lingo.

While Jason tackles the new release display, I log into my business email to make sure we aren't missing any other shipments. Thankfully, we're not, but with the weather the way that it is in January, it never hurts to check.

Thud-Thud-Thud-THUNK!

Even though I'm pretty used to it by now, the sound of half a dozen hardback books tumbling to the floor still startles me. I whirl around, expecting to see Jason scrambling over his own feet to clean up the mess he's made of my merchandise. Instead, he stands frozen, eyes fixed and mouth agape, completely oblivious to the scattered books surrounding him.

If I didn't know better, I'd say it was like he'd seen a ghost.

"Jason?" I ask, hurrying over to him. "Hey, what's going on? Are you okay?"

"It's him," he mutters, sounding dazed.

"What?"

"It's really him."

"Who?"

"D.H. Whittaker." He breathes the name with a strange sort of reverence. I follow his eyes to the lounge, where Daniel sits, staring intently at his computer screen.

"*Who*?" I ask again.

"Eloise, you own a bookstore!" Jason scolds. "D.H. Whittaker! You know, the author of *Vivian's Crypt? Morphling?* He's the master of modern horror! Do you remember that movie that came out last year? *Knick Knack?* The one about the demon?"

"Does that sound like something I would see?" I ask him. Although, now that he mentions it, I might remember seeing a trailer for it. It looked terrifying.

"*He* wrote that! The book anyway," Jason explains.

"Well, Jason, I hate to break it to you but the guy in there isn't famous. He's Hettie's nephew."

"Hettie can't have a famous nephew?"

"She can, but I'm thinking if she did, she would have told me."

"I'm telling you, Eloise, it's him. Look him up!"

"I'm going back to work now."

"Fine. If you won't look him up, I'll just go in and ask him if - "

"Don't you dare!" I hiss, grabbing his arm.

"Why not?"

"Because he's new in town, he doesn't know a lot of people, and I don't want you going in there and making him feel uncomfortable."

That's when Jason's eyes go wide behind his thick black frames.

"Oh, my God, you like him."

And now I'm blushing.

"No, I don't," I lie.

"You do!"

"Jason - "

"You have a crush on D.H. Whittaker!"

"For the last time, it's *not* him!

"It *is*! Look, we have a whole shelf of his books in Horror. Come on, I'll prove it to you."

Knowing that he isn't going to give this nonsense a rest until he's at least attempted to prove his point, I follow him back to the Mystery/Thriller section, which includes our admittedly modest horror selection. Even so, I catch a glimpse of D.H. Whittaker's name almost immediately.

"Here. This is one of his newer works," Jason says, grabbing a book off the shelf and handing it to me.

"*Mausoleum.* Creepy," I remark.

"Look at the back of the dust-jacket. I'm sure there's a picture of him."

I flip to the back of the book and sure enough, Jason's right. There is a picture. And when I see it, all the blood drains from my face. His hair is a little shorter and he doesn't have a beard, but those piercing eyes are unmistakable.

The man staring back at me is the spitting image of Daniel Brunsworth.

"*Now* are you convinced?" Jason asks.

"This... doesn't mean it's *him*," I try to argue, but a tremor in my voice gives me away. "A lot of people look like other people. Maybe D.H. Whittaker has a doppelgänger."

"You know, he has a book *about* a doppelgänger. You should go ask him about it. Right now, because he's in our reading nook. Oh, my God, D.H. Whittaker is in our reading nook. Do you think he's working on a new book? Did he tell you?"

"No, he hasn't said a thing."

"Did you ask him?"

"No."

"Why not?" Jason presses.

"Because it's none of my business."

"Can I ask him?"

"No!"

"What am I supposed to say when you introduce us, then?"

"Oh, you can forget about me introducing you. At least until you calm down."

"Ugh, Eloise, come *on*. D.H. Whittaker is one of my heroes. You can't expect me to be calm!"

"I can and I do. Especially when we're not even certain that it really *is* him."

"You're kidding. You saw the picture! You *know* it's him!" Jason insists.

"No, I don't. And neither do you. And I don't want you interrogating him, talking to him, or even looking at him until you remember how to act like a normal human being."

"Wow, you've really got it bad for this guy, don't you?"

I don't dignify that with a response.

Chapter Six

Saying goodbye to Daniel this evening wasn't nearly as awkward as I was afraid it would be.

Saying hello to him tomorrow morning, however, might be a different story.

Because Daniel Brunsworth is D.H. Whittaker. I may have been reluctant to accept it earlier this afternoon, but I'm all too certain of it now.

I've been doing my research for the past ninety minutes, ever since I put Isaac to bed. Any other night, I'd be asleep by now as well, but I couldn't stop thinking about Jason and his crazy fanboy ramblings. Which, as it so happens, turned out to not be quite so crazy after all.

It all began with a simple Google search.

"D.H. Whittaker is an American author of horror, suspense, and supernatural thrillers. He is best known for titles such as Morphling *and* Knick Knack, *the latter of which was adapted into a major motion picture by Boundless Studios. His books have sold over 25 million copies worldwide."*

Twenty. Five. Million.

The number alone was enough to leave my head spinning. Then I saw the pictures. Specifically, I saw the pictures of D.H. Whittaker signing books at a literary festival.

And one of those images is the same one that Daniel has saved to his phone.

So that's it, then. The new guy in town, the father seeking a better life for his daughter, the witty, rugged, down-to-earth man I'm trying very hard not to fall for... is an internationally acclaimed literary superstar.

And I had no idea.

And I own a bookstore.

Of course, instead of simply accepting all of this and calling it a night, I decided to investigate further. That's why I'm still sitting here, nearly two hours past my bedtime, staring at a computer screen in the middle of my darkened bedroom. Because one article leads to another, which leads to another, which leads to another.

I guess this is what Jason means when he talks about falling into the internet's black hole. Earlier this evening, I couldn't have told you the first thing about D.H. Whittaker, other than what I already learned from Daniel himself. Now, thanks to Google, I could write a dissertation on his early life; his education, his first few years in the limelight, the time he crashed his new Mercedes in Reno, and every other bit of frivolous trivia the world wide web has to offer.

Then there are the stories that aren't so frivolous, like the evolution of his relationship with his ex-wife. Those are the stories that are keeping me awake into the odd hours of the night.

I don't want to read about her. I *shouldn't* read about her. Not only is it disrespectful, it's also a huge invasion of privacy, especially considering her tragic fate and my friendship with Daniel. But I can't help myself.

Her name was Lisa Bell, and her romance with Daniel was a roller coaster, to say the least. According to two different articles, she was a model and an aspiring actress when she met Daniel at a party in Beverly Hills. From then on out, their relationship moved at breakneck speed. Two weeks after they met, they were living together, and three months after that, Lisa was pregnant. They eloped in Vegas on Christmas Eve and then Addie was born in February, almost a year to the day after her parents first met.

One of the articles has a picture of Daniel and Lisa cradling their newborn in the hospital. When I see that image of a young Daniel and his baby daughter, a fresh wave of guilt washes over me, and I remember that I'm reading about real people and not characters in a book. This is a man I know, a man I've befriended. And I'm sitting here absorbing the most personal and precious moments in his life as though they existed solely to satisfy my own selfish curiosity.

Feeling a dreadful headache coming on, I shut down my laptop and nestle myself beneath my comforter. Although I don't know who I'm kidding if I think I'm going to get a single wink of sleep tonight.

Sure enough, the sun rises far earlier than I'd like, and I, unfortunately, must rise with it.

I did manage to sleep a little, but I tossed and turned and had bizarre dreams. And my appearance reflects my weariness.

Thank God for concealer. And coffee. Oh, I need so much coffee. And not the off-brand instant coffee I buy at the grocery store. No, I need real coffee. Fancy coffee. That's why, on my way into work, I make the executive decision to stop in at the coffee shop next door to my store.

It probably goes without saying that The Mountain Cafe is one of the busiest spots in Downtown Cedar Ridge, especially on a Friday morning. The line of customers, an even mix of residents and tourists, extends almost to the front door and every table is occupied. While I wait, I glance over this morning's specials and try to decide what I want to order. I know I could get by with just a regular coffee but I'm craving a sweet, sugary vanilla latte and -

Oh.

Oh, no.

He's here. Daniel. D.H. Whittaker.

I don't know how I missed him. He's sitting alone at one of the tables by the front window, sipping at a steaming cup of coffee and reading one of the local newspapers. He looks for all the world just an ordinary guy, but I can feel myself fidgeting as I remember everything I read about him last night.

Maybe it's not too late to get out of here. He didn't notice me when I walked in. Surely, I can sneak out just as easily.

Oh, but then I won't get my coffee. Though, I could send Jason to fetch it for me. Of course, I'd have to wait until Daniel is back at my store. I can't let Jason be alone with him unsupervised. But then I'd be alone with him, which is exactly what I'm hoping to avoid right now.

I should have just stuck with my instant-coffee. Instant-coffee never gets me in trouble.

"Eloise?"

Damn. I waited too long.

Forcing a neutral expression, I turn and try to act surprised to see Daniel looking at me.

"Hey!" I greet him with a nervous squeak that is about ten pitches higher than my regular speaking voice.

Mercifully, he doesn't seem to notice. He just smiles.

Then, he rises right up out of his chair and makes his way through the masses to join me in line. And just like that, I am frozen on the spot.

"Haven't seen you in here before," he says, making casual conversation like he isn't the literary equivalent of a rock star.

"Usually, I make my coffee at home," I explain. "Just needed something a little stronger today." *Because I was up half the night internet-stalking you.*

"Ah. Understand," he says. "I've actually been meaning to stop by the store and grab some coffee for the new house, but this place is so good, I keep putting it off."

"Their lattes are addictive," I agree. "When I first moved back and took over the bookstore, I had to make a conscious effort not to stop here every morning. Otherwise, I'd be spending every last dime on coffee." It's a comment that I don't mean to make, but the words are out of my mouth before I can stop them. Money is the absolute last thing I want to discuss with anyone, but especially with Daniel.

"I'm afraid I'm already there," he jokes as we approach the counter.

"Hi. What can I get you?" the young barista asks.

"A vanilla latte, please," I reply, pulling out my wallet.

"No, no. I've got it," Daniel says, producing a ten-dollar bill before I've even had the chance to remove my credit card.

"Are you sure? You really don't have to," I tell him.

"Consider it rent for all the space I'm taking up in your reading lounge," he grins.

"Well, thank you. I appreciate it."

"My pleasure," he answers. "So, are you heading over to the store now? Or do you have time to sit for a moment?"

That's when, for a multitude of reasons, my heart skips a beat. I really shouldn't stay. I have emails to check, budgets to balance, secrets to keep... But one look into his intelligent eyes and I know I can't refuse him.

"I think I could spare a moment."

Taking my latte, I thank the barista and follow Daniel back to his table. Like a gentleman, he pulls a chair out for me before taking his own seat.

"You know, I used to write in a coffee shop like this back in New York," he tells me. "If Hettie hadn't told me to stop in and meet you, I'd probably be spending all my time here."

"What was it like there?"

"Where? The coffee shop?" he teases. I sneer playfully across the table. "New York is loud. It's always busy. It can be hard to breathe at times. But at night, there are about a thousand different colors lighting up the sky. There's music on every street corner. It's a constant celebration of life for people of every orientation, every nationality, every race."

"It sounds amazing."

"You've never been?"

"I always meant to visit. I still plan to someday, once Isaac's a little older." Or once I can afford it.

"It's a great place."

"You miss it, don't you?"

"I did at first. But then I went back for a meeting the first week of December, and I was surprised by how agitated I felt, and how eager I was to get back to Addie." Daniel smiles fondly at the thought of his daughter. "You know, a year ago, I couldn't have imagined life outside of New York. Now, I can't imagine life without her."

"You should bring her by the store sometime. I'd love to meet her."

"I will," Daniel promises. "And what about your son? Will I get to meet him?"

"If I can talk him into coming to work with me. His grandma usually lets him eat extra cookies and watch old movies with audio commentary though, so she's kind of the favorite."

"Audio commentary?" Daniel laughs.

"Don't ask."

Any insecurities or reservations I may have had concerning Daniel melt away as we regale each other with tales of our kids. Our conversation carries us all the way to 8:50, a mere ten minutes before my store opens.

"Oh, my goodness, I didn't realize how late it was," I gasp, leaping up out of my seat. "I need to get going."

With fumbling fingers, I reach for my empty coffee cup and all the napkins I've left strewn about the table, but Daniel stops me.

"I'll take care of all this. You just go."

"Really?"

"Yes, really. Go. I'll be over in just a few."

"Thank you, Daniel." I almost hug him then, but decide it is definitely too soon. Especially when I'm going to be seeing him again in about five minutes.

"Don't mention it."

Gathering my purse and my coat, I scamper out the door and sprint the short distance to my beloved Blue Ridge Books. Much to my relief, Jason is already there, dusting off the counter.

"There you are!" he exclaims. "What the hell is going on? You're never late!"

"I know. I'm sorry. I lost track of time."

"What were you doing?"

"I ran into Daniel at the coffee shop and we got to talking and - "

"Oh, my God. Were you on a date?"

"No," I answer firmly, brushing past him to get to the cash register.

"You were, weren't you? You were on a date with D.H. Whittaker!"

"I don't know how to tell you this, but you're beginning to sound like my mother. It wasn't a date."

"Did he buy your coffee?"

"Irrelevant."

"It was a date."

"It wasn't a date, and you need to wipe that word from your vocabulary because he'll be here any minute."

And suddenly, Jason is as fidgety a fanboy as I've ever seen him.

"Oh, my God, really? Did you tell him about me? Does he know that we know? Can I ask him about his new book? Because I Googled it last night and it sounds *really* cool. It's called *Renfield*. You know, like R.M. Renfield from *Dracula*? It's a modern-day prequel told from his perspective and that's got to require a lot of research - "

"Jason." Now I'm using the same warning voice I use whenever Isaac gives me grief about not wanting to brush his teeth.

"Okay, I'm sorry. Normal, right?"

"At this point, I'd settle for quirky," I remark.

"Deal," Jason grins.

I'm a mere moment away from rolling my eyes when the shopkeeper's bell rings and Daniel appears.

"Ohh-h-h!" Jason gasps. Loudly. I shoot him a scathing look and he quickly turns his high-pitched trill into a cough.

"Hello, again," I greet Daniel.

"Are you open for business?" he asks.

"We are, indeed. And, speaking of business..." I lead in, with a considerable amount of reluctance. "This is my associate, Jason."

"Nice to meet you, Jason," Daniel says, reaching out his hand.

"It is an honor and a privilege, Sir," Jason answers, all in a rush.

I throw him a look that hopefully says, "*Too much.*" Jason backtracks and tries again.

"I - uh... I've heard a lot of good things about you," he smiles. A very eager smile.

And I know Daniel notices.

"Thank you," he replies.

"You know, uh, I happen to be a writer, too," Jason says. "A screenwriter, that is. I mean, sure, I've dabbled in books here and there, but film is my preferred medium."

"That's great," Daniel tells him. "I'd love to read your work sometime."

"Oh, my God, really? Because you know, I just happen to have a few pages in my backpack and - "

"Maybe some other time, Jason," I intervene before Jason can pitch him his entire portfolio.

"But he said - "

"I know, but he has work to do right now. And so do you," I remind him.

I can tell Jason wants to argue, but thankfully he seems to get the message that, for the moment, less is more. The truth is I would love to see Daniel take Jason under his wing and make all of his dreams come true, but that isn't going to happen if Jason completely overwhelms him with his unabashed albeit endearing enthusiasm.

"Fine," Jason finally agrees. "I uh... guess I'll go do inventory or something. Again, it was great to meet you, Mr. Wh - er..."

"Brunsworth," I supply. "Hettie's nephew, remember?"

"Right, right. Hettie's nephew. Great to meet you, Hettie's nephew!" Jason exclaims before darting off to the back.

"Yeah, so, that's Jason," I tell Daniel.

"He seems... passionate," Daniel observes.

"That's a good word for him." I may have gone with crazy or obsessive, but passionate works, too. "I'll do my best to keep him out of your hair."

"Don't worry about it. Believe it or not, he's not the weirdest I've encountered."

Oh, I definitely believe it.

Chapter Seven

Severe Weather Alert.
The National Weather Service is tracking a severe storm system, moving northeast through the southern states. This system is expected to bring high winds and heavy snow to the southern Appalachian Mountains. Please check your local weather forecast for more information.

Snowstorms in Cedar Ridge are nothing out of the ordinary and come the winter months, residents know to be prepared for them. I have an entire section of my hall closet dedicated to my emergency-preparedness stash; an idea inspired by a picture I saw on Pinterest. My emergency supplies include toilet paper, water bottles, extra blankets, a first-aid kit, two flashlights, a portable phone charger, and lots and lots and *lots* of batteries. I also always make sure to keep the pantry stocked with foods with a long shelf-life.

Thankfully, meteorologists are predicting this particular storm will be relatively mild. At least, compared to a few we've seen in the past. We'll probably start seeing snowfall later on this evening before the storm itself moves into the area at around 1 o'clock in the morning. It will make for a quiet weekend inside, but I can't pretend that that isn't my favorite kind of weekend.

Nor can I say that snowstorms aren't great for the book business. Half the town, it seems, has stopped in today in search of something to read while they ride out the inclement weather.

"So, should I be worried about this snowstorm?" Daniel asks me while I tend the fire in the lounge.

"Not as long as you don't lose power," I reply.

"Oh, don't even joke about that," he warns me.

"I'm not joking. Last year, we had a storm come through that knocked out power in the entire town for almost a week. I had to drive almost an hour out to Boone just to charge my phone."

"Well, I'm going to tell Theresa to offer up some sacrificial sage or whatnot to the weather gods, because I truly don't think my preteen daughter could survive thirty minutes without her phone," Daniel remarks dryly.

I can't help but smile.

That smile vanishes, however, when the shopkeeper's bell rings and Logan rushes into my store, a lot like a blustery blizzard. He scans the room with a wild, almost feral look in his eyes, and for half a moment, I worry he's come to warn us that our fearsome friend the Bogman has made another unwelcome appearance. Then I notice the stack of Whittaker books in his arms and I realize his true intentions here are far less noble.

What happens next is a blur. I drop my fire iron and leap to my feet at the exact moment that Logan finally zeroes in on Daniel.

"I *knew* I recognized you!" he hollers loud enough for half of Main Street to hear.

"No!" I gasp, tripping over my own feet in an attempt to cut him off before he reaches Daniel.

"Mr. Whittaker, Sir, you have no idea what an honor this is for me. I'm your biggest fan and I was wondering if - "

"Nope, sorry! Wrong guy!" I exclaim.

And that's when I do the unthinkable and grab Logan by his brutish shoulders.

"What? Eloise, no! You don't get it! This man is a freaking *genius* - "

"No, he's not."

Now I'm physically pushing him out of the lounge, which, considering how much larger he is than I am, is no easy feat.

"Please, can't I just get *one* autograph?"

"I told you, you've got the wrong guy!"

"But I - "

"Nope! Get out!"

And with one final shove, I send Logan stumbling out of my store and onto the frosty sidewalk.

Shutting the door firmly behind me, I take a few moments to catch my breath before I realize that every soul inside the bookshop has fallen completely and utterly silent. I turn slowly to see customers of all ages staring at me with wide and curious eyes.

"Sorry about that," I apologize hastily. "That's just Logan. He... ate glue as a kid." I have no idea if that's true or not, but it seems as good an explanation as any.

"Why was he asking for an autograph? Do you have someone famous back there?" one of my regulars, a middle-aged gentleman who often comes in to peruse our selection of rare vintage books, wants to know.

"No, no," I answer far more emphatically than necessary. "You see, Logan is friends with my employee, Jason and... they're both really big nerds. Huge horror geeks. And I think, somehow, Jason may have convinced Logan that my friend Daniel is actually... that hot police chief from *Stranger Things*."

I'd be surprised if any of the folks in my store have actually seen *Stranger Things*, but it's too late to backtrack now. I'm committed.

The good news is that the only woman who seems suspicious steps around me and into the lounge, I assume to take a closer look at Daniel.

"You know, he *does* bear a resemblance!" the lady exclaims.

And with that, everyone goes back to their own business. Everyone, of course, except Daniel, whom I don't at all have the courage to face, but whom I also know I can't ignore.

"You watch *Stranger Things*?" he asks as I slink back into the lounge, avoiding eye contact at all costs.

"I tried. It was too scary. But all my friends are just obsessed with it," I answer as I kneel down to retrieve the fire iron I left lying on the floor. At the same time, Daniel closes his laptop and even though I'm still not looking at him, I can feel him watching me.

"So, how long have you known?" he asks.

My heart begins to pound as I try to figure out just how I want to answer that. I'd hate for him to think I've been lying to him... or worse, trying to take advantage of him. But I don't want to make him feel uncomfortable, either.

"Unofficially... almost a day," I tell him. "Jason recognized you yesterday, but I didn't fully believe him until I..."

"Until you what?"

Oh, my goodness, I can't believe I'm about to admit this to him.

"Until I went home and Googled you."

To my sincere and utter relief, he chuckles under his breath.

"You know, I didn't believe Hettie when she told me you didn't know. I thought surely you were just hoping to get me into your store for..." he trails off, but I get the gist. I appreciate him trying to spare my feelings, though.

"For personal and financial gain?" I supply.

"More or less."

"Is that why you were so surly the day we met?"

"Glad to know I made a good first impression," he jokes. "But to tell you the truth, yeah. I came in fully prepared to lay down the line but you..."

"I...?"

"Turned out to be just as kind and lovely as Hettie said."

"Oh." I smile as a warm blush floods my cheeks. "Well, thank you - "

"Eloise!" Jason appears suddenly, calling out my name and looking frantic.

And just like that, a moment that might have been is ruined, gone forever.

"What is it, Jason?" I ask. I can't deny I'm rather cross with him at the moment. You see, Logan isn't a smart person. There's no way he figured out who Daniel is on his own. Someone had to have told him. And that someone wasn't me.

"Logan just texted me. He said that you threw him out?"

"Yeah, because he came in here demanding *autographs*," I hiss, rising up to my full height to properly scold him.

Jason's face falls.

"Oh."

"You told him about Daniel, didn't you?" I cross my arms and shoot him my best Disapproving Mom Glare.

"Maybe. But in my defense, I *also* told him that it was classified information!"

"Jason, do you really think that Logan Taylor knows what classified means?"

"I know, I know." Jason buries his face in his hands. "I'm sorry, all right? I know I shouldn't have told him... but he's my best friend! And you, Mr. Whittaker... I don't think you need me to tell you that you're one of the greatest minds in horror alive today - "

"Jason..." I warn.

"Sorry." Jason clears his throat. "And sorry to you, Mr. Whittaker."

"Just call me Daniel. And it's all right."

Jason smiles and heaves a sigh of relief.

"So uh, now that the cat's out of the bag, so to speak, do you think it would still be possible for me to show you a few pages of my screenplay - "

"Jason!" I cut him off yet again.

"Right. Too soon. My bad." Jason holds his hands up in surrender and begins backing away. "You know, I think I'm just going to run and give Logan another call and maybe drop a few hints. Or threats. Or maybe I'll just outright beg him not to say anything."

"You could always remind him that I know his mom and that if he even thinks about spreading this around, I have access to all of his embarrassing childhood stories that I will happily share with his favorite author," I say.

"Maybe I could even publish a few," Daniel muses.

"That sounds a lot like blackmail," Jason observes.

"Does it?" Daniel quips.

"I'll talk to him," Jason reiterates.

And with that, he's gone.

Now it's my turn to apologize.

"Daniel, I am so sorry about all of this."

"Why? It wasn't your fault," he tells me.

"I know, but it happened in my store. I feel responsible."

"Please don't. If anything, I should be thanking you for jumping in to save me. Left to my own devices, I probably would have just sat there and let it happen. So, thank you."

Even though I don't think I've done anything to deserve his praise or his gratitude, I smile and say, "You're welcome." Then, unsure of what else to do, I shove my hands into my pockets and say, "I should be getting back to work."

"One more thing," Daniel stops me. "I uh... know this has probably been a lot for you to take in, and I'm sorry."

"Daniel, you don't need to apologize. I saw the way those boys reacted when they realized who you were. I completely understand why you didn't want to say anything."

"It isn't even that," he says. "After everything that Addie's been through this year, losing her mom, uprooting her entire life to move in with a father who wasn't around nearly as much as he should have been... I just want her to have some sense of stability. The last thing she needs is for her new classmates to find out that her dad is the guy who wrote *Knick Knack* and *Vivian's Crypt*."

As a mother, I'm ashamed to admit I hadn't even considered that. Of course his first instinct as a parent is to protect his child at all costs.

"I'm going to have another talk with Jason. Logan, too," I promise him. "I don't think either of them knows about Addie. If they did... I like to think that they'd both behave a little better in the future."

"Tell them I'll sign anything they want if they keep their mouths shut."

"I know you're joking, but believe me, you do *not* want me to tell them that."

"Why not?" Daniel asks, his blue eyes dancing with firelight.

"Because they would absolutely take you up on it."

Chapter Eight

As predicted, the snowstorm rolls over the mountains and into Cedar Ridge at 1 o'clock in the morning, startling me from an uncharacteristically contented slumber. Nestled beneath my heavy comforter, the last thing I want to do is climb out of bed, but I need to check on Isaac and make sure he's okay. My poor, sweet, sensitive boy. He's so scared of storms. I tried my best to prepare him for this one, but he still went to bed clutching his teddy bear that's dressed like Glinda the Good Witch.

Shivering, I make my way out of my bedroom and across our upstairs landing to Isaac's room. As I feared, he's wide awake and staring out his window with frightened blue eyes.

"Isaac?" I gently call his name.

"Mom?"

"Yeah, Sweetheart. It's me," I whisper. "Are you doing okay?"

"Uh-huh," he whimpers. "Is the storm almost over?"

"I'm afraid not."

Isaac sniffles and hugs his bear tight.

"Can I come sleep in your room?" he asks. My heart melts.

"Of course, Sweetheart."

"Glinda, too?"

"Glinda, too."

Still holding his bear as close as he can, Isaac jumps out of bed and runs into my open arms. His little body is warm and his curls still smell like his green-apple-scented shampoo. It's my favorite smell in the world. Even better than coffee and old books.

I give him a quick kiss on the cheek before taking his hand and walking with him back into my room.

"Can we watch TV?" Isaac asks once he's tucked in beneath my comforter.

It does not escape me that my son, at the tender age of six, might have a mild TV addiction. I am also well aware that, as his mother, I may be partly to blame for this. It's true that some nights, like when he's sick, I'll let him watch TV in here with me until he falls asleep. Most of the time, however, I'm pretty good at sticking to my No-TV-After-8 rule.

"I don't think so."

"But I'm scared."

"Tell you what," I whisper, nestling in beside him. "If you can close your eyes and fall asleep right now, without the TV, then tomorrow, we'll light a fire, we'll drink hot chocolate, and we'll build the best and biggest blanket fort that has ever existed."

Even in the darkness, I can see Isaac's eyes light up.

"Can we have a campout?"

"Well, duh," I tease him. "What's the point of building a blanket fort if we don't camp out?"

"And we can make s'mores and listen to music?"

"We can do anything you want." Except watch TV after 8.

"Okay," Isaac agrees quickly.

To my great relief, he manages to fall asleep within minutes. I, on the other hand, am suddenly wide awake. It might be the storm. More likely, it's adrenaline. Whenever I worry about Isaac, all of my senses kick into hyperdrive.

For a split second, I'm tempted to turn on the TV myself, but if Isaac wakes up again and sees it on, he'll never get back to sleep. So instead, I grab my phone off of my nightstand and begin to browse.

First, I hop over to Facebook to see if any of my friends are sharing their storm experiences. The only new posts I see, however, concern either politics, school fundraisers, or a neighbor's dog who's gone missing.

Then, I check my email. Not that I'm expecting any groundbreaking messages at one in the morning, but every once in a while, I find something interesting in my inbox. Tonight, I just happen to stumble across an email from my own bookstore. It's a newsletter that Jason sends out once every three months announcing community events, upcoming sales, and a recommended reading list. This month's list includes titles such as *Dating an Alien Pop Star* by Kendra Saunders, *Winter's Curse* by April Wood... and *Broken Mirror* by D.H. Whittaker.

Out of sheer curiosity, I click on the link to Daniel's book, which leads me to a synopsis and review. It's probably the last thing I should be reading in the dead of night, in the middle of a storm, with no one but my six-year-old son to protect me. But after everything that Daniel shared with me earlier, I realize I want to know everything. I want to know him. And knowing him means knowing his work.

"Deep in the woods of an isolated summer camp, evil lies in wait in the form of a simple broken mirror."

Evil in the woods? Strike one.

As someone who's lived most of her life in a small town surrounded by woods, I've never appreciated how so many horror enthusiasts flock to the forest for inspiration. Besides, we already have our own monster roaming the wilderness behind our backyards.

An isolated summer camp? That's strike two.

A story about a summer camp is a story that involves children. And if I fear one thing above all other mortal fears, it's losing Isaac. As a mother, I see him in every child, male or female, real or imaginary. The last thing I want is to read a story about kids being attacked by a mirror demon.

And strike three? Well, there is no strike three. But the first two are more than enough to convince me that *Broken Mirror* isn't a book that I'd enjoy.

I wonder if he's written anything a little milder, a little nicer. Somehow, I doubt it, but I suppose I could always ask him. That is if I ever see him again.

Okay, that's a little melodramatic of me. I'm sure I'll see him again around town. But after our misadventures this afternoon, I wouldn't be surprised if he chose to work elsewhere from now on.

Sighing, I shut my phone off and set it back down on my nightstand. I know myself well enough to know that if I'm not careful, I'll slip right back into that vast black hole of internet intelligence. And that just can't be healthy for me.

The weekend passes in an icy blur and before I know it, dawn is breaking on Monday morning. Although our little town took a beating, schools and stores alike are still open for business. Unfortunately for me, because two nights of sleeping in a tent on my living room floor have left me an agitated, achy shell of my former self.

But the fort made Isaac happy, and his happiness is what gets me through.

"So, the old store is still standing," Jason declares, carrying out a box of books to restock the shelves.

"Until the next one, anyway," I mutter. Daniel may have forgiven Jason for the whole Logan debacle, but I'm still a little miffed. And Jason knows it. Otherwise, he wouldn't be making small talk.

"You know, the storm may have actually ended up being a good thing. I uh... got a lot of work done on my screenplay this weekend," he says.

He'd better not be going where I think he's going with this.

"Good," I tell him.

"Do you think it might be all right... you know, if I maybe... showed it to Daniel?"

He went there.

"Absolutely not."

"Okay, I get it. You're still pissed. And you have every right to be! But I genuinely did not know about his daughter. If I had, you know I wouldn't have said anything."

"Yeah, okay, that's great, but I still don't want you pestering him if he comes back."

"If?" Jason asks. "What do you mean, *if?* Did he say something to you? Does he hate me?"

"No, he didn't say anything. And no, of course he doesn't hate you."

"Then, why wouldn't he come back?"

"Would *you* want to - "

Ding!

That's when the shopkeeper's bell rings, interrupting me and sparing Jason from what would have undoubtedly escalated into yet another lecture.

I glance around and my heart leaps into my throat when I see Daniel, decked out in his usual winter attire, looking as stern and handsome as ever.

"Mr. Whittaker! I mean - Daniel," Jason gasps. "How nice to see you again, Sir."

Daniel blinks. I can almost guarantee that it is far too early for fawning fanboys.

"... Thanks, kid," he finally says.

"Is there anything I can get you? A bite to eat or a hot beverage, perhaps?"

"I think I'm good."

"Right. Well... I'm just going to finish... what I'm doing here. And then I'll just... you know, be in the back. But if you need *anything* at all - "

"I'll send Eloise to fetch you, straight away," Daniel promises.

"Great," Jason grins from ear-to-ear. Then, as if this weren't already the most embarrassing moment of my entire life, he gives Daniel two thumbs up.

Thankfully, Daniel seems to have a gift for remaining calm and cool in the face of pure humiliation.

"So, how did you and Isaac fare this weekend?" he asks me once we're alone. Or rather, as alone as we can be with Jason just a few aisles over.

"We actually had a lot of fun," I answer. "He doesn't like storms, so we built a blanket fort in our living room and watched his favorite movies."

"Sounds like a great weekend to me."

"And what about you? What did you and Addie do?"

"We roughed it out over at Hettie and Theresa's. A lot of our stuff is still in boxes so they were gracious enough to let us crash there."

"Oh my goodness, I bet you had a blast," I grin. I've been to several parties hosted by Hettie and Theresa. Their house is amazing. It's full of light and color and a multitude of plants and cool knick-knacks from around the world.

"We did, Addie especially," Daniel says. "Hettie made the mistake of letting her into her closet. She was in there for hours working on her cosplay."

"Her what?"

"She likes to dress up as characters from her favorite manga books," Daniel explains. "She's already planning for the day she's allowed to have her own cosplay website."

"Something tells me that she and Isaac are cut from the same cloth," I muse.

"Maybe they'll meet one of these days," Daniel remarks casually. "Hettie actually wanted me to let you know that you and Isaac are welcome anytime."

"Oh." I'm pleasantly surprised by the invitation. "That's so sweet of her."

"Yeah, well, she thinks the world of you. Theresa, too. Although, I've got to ask..."

"Yes...?"

"Why does she call you Elsie?"

"As soon as I figure that out, I will let you know."

"So you have no idea?"

"None whatsoever."

Daniel laughs.

"That's so Theresa, isn't it?" he asks. "She actually tried to teach Addie how to read Tarot cards this weekend."

"How did that go?"

"Let's just say that she is definitely my daughter."

Now it's my turn to laugh. That laugh, however, aggravates the ache in my back and my shoulder and I wind up wincing in pain.

"Ow..." I moan.

"You okay?"

"Oh, yeah. Just suffering from aches and pains that I never would have felt ten years ago."

"Where does it hurt?" he asks.

"Mostly here," I answer, reaching for the tender spot below my right shoulder.

"May I?" he asks.

In that moment, my mind goes completely blank, and I can only follow his lead as he gently guides me around until my back is practically pressed against his stomach. I'm so close to him, I can feel his breath on the back of my neck. Then, gripping my shoulder with one large, strong hand, he moves his thumb in firm circles, kneading out the pain with masterful efficiency.

His touch is magic, and I realize just how easy it would be for me to lose myself to him. I wonder if he knows, or even suspects, the effect he has on me.

"How's that?" he asks once he releases me.

"You know," I begin, turning back to face him. "If this whole writing thing doesn't work out, I'd be more than happy to hire you as my own personal masseuse."

At that, Daniel throws his head back and laughs.

"Well, you do learn a few things when your aunt's a professional healer... energy therapist," he answers awkwardly. "Now that I think about it, I'm not exactly sure what Theresa calls herself."

"She's a woman of many talents," I supply.

"Yeah, let's go with that," Daniel grins. "Man, I'd forgotten how much I love that about this town."

"Love what?"

"How everyone here knows one another. How you all treat each other like family."

"We try. I'm not sure we always succeed," I tell him. "To be honest, ever since I moved back, I've felt like a little hermit."

"Why is that?"

"Probably because whenever I'm not here, I'm at home with Isaac. Yeah, I'll stop by the grocery store a few times a week, but I don't really go out. All of my friends in town are also moms, so we really only 'hang out' over text. We never meet up for brunch or go to the movies because none of us have the time," I explain. "I guess that's why I love being here at the store so much. It's how I stay connected with everyone."

"I get that," Daniel admits. "Back when I was still in New York, I wasn't exactly the life of every party, but my priorities definitely weren't what they are now."

"Being a single parent changes things."

"It sure does."

Ding!

The shopkeeper's bell rings again, announcing our first real customer of the day.

"I guess I should let you get to work," Daniel tells me.

"I guess I should let you do the same," I reply.

He smiles at me then, his blue eyes lingering on my face before he turns away, leaving me feeling light, dizzy, and utterly breathless.

Chapter Nine

"Jason, I've got a question."

It's 5 o'clock, the store is empty, and Jason and I are in the process of closing up shop for the day.

"Shoot," he says, mopping up the last bit of melted snow that customers have tracked in on my nice hardwood floors.

"If I were going to read one of Daniel's books, which one would you recommend?"

"Why don't you ask him?"

"It seems... rude, somehow," I answer, punching our final numbers into the calculator for the third time. Somehow, I keep coming up short.

Of course, I may be just the tiniest bit distracted.

"How does showing an interest in his work seem rude?" Jason asks.

"Because he already knows I don't like horror and if I ask him which of his books he thinks I should read, it would seem like I'm asking which of his books he thinks I'll hate the least."

"That... is insane," Jason remarks.

"No, it's not. It's perfectly logical."

"Maybe to you," he mutters. "I guess if I were going to recommend one of his books to a non-horror fan, I'd go with *Morphling* or *Underworld*. *Morphling* is terrifying, but it's psychological and not supernatural, so you might be okay. You'd probably be better off with *Underworld*, though, which is about a group of tourists who get lost in a cave."

Okay. I might be able to handle that.

"*Underworld*... I wonder if we have a copy."

"We don't," Jason tells me. "It's one of his earlier, lesser-known titles. But I can lend you my copy."

"Really? You wouldn't mind?"

"Not at all. As a matter of fact, it's in my backpack."

Oh my. Isn't *that* convenient?

"Is it, now?" I ask, raising an eyebrow.

"Okay, I know what you're thinking, but I *promise* I wasn't going to pester him for an autograph! I was just... you know... keeping a few books on hand just in case an opportunity presented itself."

"I'm choosing to believe you."

"Thanks. I appreciate it," Jason says. "So... you guys are getting pretty close, huh?"

"Pretty close? Jason, I hardly know him."

"Uh-huh. Right. Let's review the facts. You've known him for what, a week now? And he's already taking you out on coffee dates, you're going out of your way to read his books, and he's giving you sensual back-rubs in broad daylight in the middle of your store."

"Wha - !?" My jaw drops. I had no idea he saw that. "Okay, first of all, that was not a *sensual back-rub*. I had a knot in my shoulder from sleeping on the floor all weekend and he graciously offered to help work it out."

"'Work it out.'" Jason smirks.

"Second, as you so astutely pointed out last week, I own a bookstore. It's my job to familiarize myself with the authors of the day - "

"And just how intimately are you planning to 'familiarize' yourself with - "

"And *finally*," I cut him off before he can say something I'll have to fire him for. "If I claimed to be dating every person who'd ever bought me a coffee, I'd be dating half the town."

"What's that old saying? 'Methinks the lady doth protest too much?'"

"That old saying is Shakespeare, genius."

"Hey, he knew all about matters of the heart," Jason argues.

Let the record show that Jason's only exposure to the Bard is a single viewing of *Romeo + Juliet* starring Leonardo DiCaprio, and I'm the one who made him watch it. It was back in the days I used to babysit him. I was sixteen and hopelessly in love with Leo and Jason was nine and couldn't have cared less about anything happening in Verona Beach. Now, looking back, I'll admit he was probably a *little* young for that movie, but the fact remains that Jason Harberger just isn't very cultured.

"So, are you going to let me borrow that book or not?" I ask him, changing the subject once and hopefully for all.

"Oh, I am. *If* you admit that you like him."

"Why?" I sigh. "Why is this so important to you?"

"Because you're my friend and I care about you," he answers. "And because it's fun to think there's a very real possibility that I could be a groomsman in D.H. Whittaker's next wedding."

"That's it. You're done."

"Okay, okay, I'm sorry," Jason laughs. "See? I'm going to get the book right now."

He disappears into the back and returns moments later with a well-loved hardback novel. The image on the cover is a hauntingly beautiful depiction of an underground cave, illuminated by red candles.

"Here you go," he says.

"Thank you."

"Look, I know it's you and old books are kind of your thing, but please take good care of it. It's a first edition."

"I will guard it with my life," I promise him.

That evening, after I tuck Isaac into bed and kiss him goodnight, I pour a cup of lavender tea, wrap myself up in an oversized fleece blanket, and curl up on the couch with *Underworld*.

As Jason said, it starts with a group of friends exploring a cave in the heart of Colorado. I'm happy and more than a little surprised to find I actually enjoy the first couple of chapters. Daniel's descriptions paint such a vivid picture of the Rocky Mountain wilderness, I almost feel like I'm experiencing it firsthand.

Then the setting shifts and I begin to enjoy the experience less and less. The deeper the characters delve into the cave, the darker and more sinister the story gets. Friends begin to turn on one another. Shadows come to life. Slowly, they begin to realize that the walls are changing around them. The way back is no longer the way back. It's the same dizzying distress of *The Blair Witch Project* but with the added bonus of cave-induced claustrophobia.

I don't think I'll be finishing this book.

Grimacing, I set *Underworld* aside on my coffee table, lift myself up off the couch, and go about turning off the lights and getting ready to turn in for the night. I'm just preparing to take my empty tea mug into the kitchen when I see it. Or rather, sense it.

Something's... off.

Glancing around, I take note of every fixture, every surface. Nothing seems amiss. And yet I find myself frozen to the spot, wondering why my house suddenly feels unfamiliar.

It's the book, I try to convince myself. *You're letting it get inside your head. You're at home. You're safe.*

Although I'd never in a million years go back to my life with Lance, I will admit that in moments like this, it would be nice to have someone else around. Someone who will take care of me; who will promise to protect me and reassure me that everything is going to be all right.

Someone like Daniel.

Unwittingly, my mind drifts back to our encounter this morning. The way he looked at me. The way he touched me. If only he were here...

Then again, if it weren't for him and his disorienting fiction, I wouldn't be standing here, paralyzed with fear in my own living room. Having him around would probably just make it worse.

Of course, I don't believe that for a moment. Daniel may have made a living scaring the daylights out of readers around the world, but I know he would be the first to tell me he didn't want me to be afraid. He would take my hand and pull me gently against his body, just like he did earlier this morning. This time, however, I'd be facing him, gazing up into those piercing blue eyes. I imagine reaching up to wrap my arms around his broad shoulders while he slips his hands around the small of my back -

Just then, the grandfather clock in the corner of the living room chimes once, alerting me to the late hour. It's way past my bedtime, yet somehow, I'm still wide awake.

Taking one last look around to ensure nothing is out of place, I finally set my tea mug in the kitchen sink. Then, I turn off every light and head upstairs as a soft and silent snow begins to fall outside.

"Mom? What does the Bogman look like?" Isaac asks. He's sitting at the kitchen table, halfheartedly stirring his Lucky Charms while I rinse out my own cereal bowl in the sink.

"The Bogman?" With everything that's been going on recently, Daniel and D.H. Whittaker and the snowstorm, I'd almost forgotten about our resident monster. Of course, as soon as Isaac asks the question, I remember Floyd Whalen's vivid description of a beast with matted fur and golden yellow eyes. And that is the absolute last image I want my sweet boy carrying around in his head. "I don't know what it's supposed to look like."

"Is he big?"

"Sweetheart, we talked about this, remember? The Bogman isn't real. He's just make-believe."

"But what if he *is* real?"

The question is innocent enough, but it's the tremor in his voice that turns my stomach and makes my blood run cold.

Something's happened, I realize. He must have heard something at school. Or maybe he caught a glimpse of one of the pictures online.

"Hey, what's going on?" I ask, kneeling down to face him. "Why are you asking all these questions?"

My baby draws in a shaky breath.

"I saw him outside last night."

"What?"

"The Bogman. He was walking outside in the front yard."

Now my heart is pounding with the same terrible sense of dread that I felt standing in the living room just a few hours ago.

"I don't - I don't understand," I tell him, my voice trembling. "Why do you think it was the Bogman?"

"Because it looked like a monster," he answers.

We live in the middle of our street. Our front yard is not well-lit. Whatever he saw, or whatever he thinks he saw, he couldn't have gotten a very good look at it from his second-story window.

"Are you sure you were awake? Maybe it was just a scary dream."

"I *saw* it, Mom," he insists.

"Why didn't you come and get me?"

"I thought he might hear me. Monsters hear *really* good."

I have no idea where he picked up that idea, but it was probably from something I let him watch.

"Well, listen. If you see him or anything else outside your window again, I want you to come and get me, okay?"

"But what if he hears me?"

"He won't," I promise him. "And even if he does, you're safe here. You're always safe in your home."

But even as I speak the words, I find myself once again flashing back to the night before, to that eerie uncertainty. I had been fully prepared to sweep those feelings of fear under the rug, but now...

Now I'm wondering if perhaps I should have listened to my intuition a little more carefully.

That's why, after I send Isaac upstairs to brush his teeth and grab his backpack, I wrap my coat around my shoulders and slip outside. The morning clouds are gray and heavy and the world around me is blanketed by a fresh layer of snow. If someone - or some*thing* - was running around outside my house last night, all of the evidence is buried beneath four inches of icy powder.

Taking a few steps further, I turn my attention to the woods just beyond the edge of our small neighborhood. They've always been so beautiful to me. The gorgeous trees at the base of the surrounding mountains were part of what drew me to this street in the first place. At the time, the towering pines and sturdy Carolina hemlock seemed like a protective barrier, the walls of a living sanctuary. But now, draped with morning mist and heaped with snow, my beloved woods appear a menacing maze of secrets and shadows.

The perfect hiding place for monsters.

Excerpt from *Underworld*
By D.H. Whittaker

"I can't do this," Joan whimpered, staring wide-eyed into the tight, narrow passage.

"You have to," Stella urged.

"I can't go underground." Joan began to panic, her breath coming in short, shallow gasps.

"We're already underground!" Richie reminded her.

"Don't yell at her!" Theo snapped.

"I'm not yelling!" Richie hollered.

"Stop it! Please, just stop it!" Tonja begged. "We'll never get out of here alive if we start fighting!"

"We can turn around. If - if we can just retrace our steps -" Joan rambled.

"We already tried that. It didn't work," Richie muttered through gritted teeth.

"But that makes no sense!" Joan cried.

"Nothing here makes sense!" Richie exploded. "We're five miles under, upside down, trapped in some godforsaken hellscape! I've heard voices screaming at me in the walls and seen dead bodies crawling on the damn ceiling! We're not going to get out of here by retracing our frickin' steps!"

What happened next was a blur.

Theo didn't realize he had struck Richie until he saw his lifelong friend lying on the ground, a steady stream of blood trickling down and around his eyes like crimson tears.

"Richie!" Stella screamed, dropping to her knees to cradle his head.

"What the... hell - " Richie sputtered.

"Rich, I - I'm sorry..." Theo stammered, his hands trembling.

"Did you just... you just tried to kill me..."

"No! I didn't - "

"Get the hell away from me, man!" Richie growled.

"Okay, okay, that's enough!" Tonja stepped in. "Both of you need to get yourselves together. Joan, do you still have that first aid kit?"

"I - I think so," Joan muttered.

"Right. Then here's what we're gonna do. We're gonna get Richie cleaned up. You two boys are going to shake hands and apologize. And then, we're going to get the hell out of this cave."

They all agreed.

While Tonja knelt down to tend to Richie's wounds, Theo slunk back against the wall, closed his eyes, and took several deep breaths. But it wasn't until he felt Joan lace her fingers through his that he was finally able to calm his racing heart.

"Are you okay?" she whispered.

"No," he answered honestly. "Are you?"

"No."

Theo wished he had the words to reassure her that they were going to be all right, that soon they would see the sunlight and that, within a matter of hours, maybe even minutes, their time in the underworld would be merely a memory. But all such sentiments evaded him, and he realized, with a sickening sense of dread, it was because he didn't believe they were true.

They were never going to find their way out.

The cave was going to bury them alive.

And it was never going to let them go.

Chapter Ten

Ever since I inherited Blue Ridge Books from Mrs. Snyder two years ago, I have missed a grand total of three days of work. Two of those absences, I was taking care of a very sick little boy. In one instance, I was as sick as he was and my poor mom was taking care of both of us. Other than that, I have always shown up to work.

That being said, I come very close to calling in sick this morning. Not because I'm feeling ill, but because I'm afraid that whatever Isaac saw last night, whatever I felt last night, is still out there. And if it's going to come back, I want to see it with my own eyes. I want to know what it is... and be sure of what it isn't.

In the end, however, I decide against it and make my way into work. Chances are that whatever it is won't come back and I'll waste the day sitting by my window, waiting for something that may not even exist.

Besides, with all the recent activity in town, business has been busier than ever. In fact, I've no sooner unlocked the cash register than the shopkeeper's bell rings and three of the moms from Isaac's school appear.

"Good morning, Eloise," Nora Beauchamp greets me with a broad, sparkling smile.

"Well, this is a nice surprise," I say. I know all three from school functions of course, and Nora is even a member of our first grade group chat. "How are you ladies doing this morning?"

"We're doing just fine, thank you," Mary Beth Holdridge replies.

"Are you looking for anything in particular?" I ask. "You know, we just got the new Ellen Gardner book in."

"Actually, we came to see if we could leave a few flyers for the Winter Carnival here with you," Lauren Greene answers.

Every third weekend in January, Cedar Ridge puts on a Winter Carnival. It's not a grand spectacle by any means, but it's always fun and just festive enough to help ward off the post-holiday blues. There are games, lights, snow sculpting, and every night ends with a fireworks display. Isaac and I go every year.

"Oh, absolutely," I reply.

"Thanks, Eloise. You're a gem," Nora tells me.

"I tell you, this Carnival has really snuck up on us," Lauren sighs. "The committee has been working night and day just to pull it off. But we all truly believe that this year will be our best year ever. We've got rides, we've got guest speakers. We even have a theme."

"A theme?" I ask. That's new. As far back as I can remember, the Winter Carnival has never had a theme.

"Take a look," Mary Beth grins and hands me a flyer printed on light blue paper.

The City of Cedar Ridge Presents Its Annual Winter Carnival: Come Out And Celebrate The Year of the Bogman!

Immediately, I feel the blood drain from my face.

"What's that?" Jason asks, appearing on the scene. "Oh. Good morning, ladies."

"Hi there, Jason," Mary Beth smiles.

"We're just dropping off a few flyers for the Carnival this weekend," Nora informs him.

"Sweet," Jason grins, reading over my shoulder. Then, he gasps. Loudly. Right in my ear. "No way! Year of the Bogman?!"

"You like it?" Lauren grins.

"I *love* it!" he exclaims. "I'm sure *she* doesn't..." he adds, throwing me completely under the bus.

I feel my jaw drop as my friends turn to look at me with concerned, curious eyes. Of course, before I can defend myself, the shopkeeper's bell rings again and Daniel appears in a flurry of fresh snow.

"Damn, I think it's getting colder out there," he grumbles, taking two steps inside the store. He takes an automatic step back, however, when he notices the small crowd amassed around the checkout counter. "Oh, hey. Sorry. Didn't mean to interrupt."

"Well, hello," Lauren says, eyeing him up and down with keen interest. In fact, all three of my friends have stopped to stare at him. And I can't say I blame them. Let's face it, in a town as tiny as Cedar Ridge, it isn't every day a handsome stranger comes strolling into the local bookstore. "And who might you be?"

"Uh, Daniel. Brunsworth." It's funny. For a man used to meeting millions of fans around the world, he sounds remarkably unsure of himself in front of these three women.

"Oh, of course! You're Hettie's nephew. The writer!" Nora exclaims.

"You're a writer?" Lauren asks, her eyes lighting up.

"Uh, yeah. Sort of."

"Oh, how fascinating," Mary Beth sighs. It's only then that I remember that Mary Beth is a single parent, too. She and her husband split up about a year and a half ago. He left her for a woman who works at the Cedar Ridge Ski Resort. It was the talk of every preschool playdate. "I'm Mary Beth. It's a pleasure to meet you."

"Likewise," Daniel replies, shaking her hand.

"You know, I've dabbled a bit in fiction myself," Lauren cuts in. "I mean, I haven't published anything yet. With three kids and a husband, I don't have a whole lot of extra time on my hands. But we do have a Cedar Ridge writers' group that meets up every other Wednesday night down at the library. If you're interested, I can leave a card - "

"Or," Mary Beth interrupts. "If you'd like someone to show you around town, I'd be happy to be your guide. Or if you want to go out for dinner or even just meet up for a cup of coffee, you should give me a call."

"That's very sweet of you," Daniel says. Finally, he seems to have found his footing. "But you know, unfortunately, I don't really have a lot of spare time, what with work during the day and taking care of my daughter in the evening."

"Of course," Mary Beth nods. "Well, if you ever feel like a night out, just know the offer stands."

"Thanks, I appreciate it," Daniel grins.

"Well, it's been wonderful meeting you, and Eloise, always delightful catching up, but we still have half a dozen stacks of flyers to distribute," Nora announces, leading her friends out the door. "Let's go, ladies."

"Bye, Daniel," Mary Beth waves.

"Don't forget about the writers' group!" Lauren calls.

As soon as they're gone, Daniel takes a deep breath.

"You okay?" I ask him.

"Oh, yeah. It's just... not what I was expecting first thing in the morning."

Meanwhile, Jason is still poring over the flyers for the Carnival.

"Oh, man. This is going to be *awesome*!" he exclaims. "ToBOGganing, Build Your Own Bogman, not to mention all the rides and the games and... you're still not sold on this at all, are you?" he asks me.

"The Bogman Carnival? No."

"Why not? Plenty of places celebrate their local legends. There's a Mothman Festival in West Virginia. The Loch Ness Monster has her own gift shop in Scotland. Why shouldn't Cedar Ridge embrace the Bogman?"

"It just feels like we're asking for trouble. We don't even know what this thing is and until we do... maybe we shouldn't be antagonizing it."

"Antagonizing it? We're throwing it its own carnival! It should be flattered!" Jason argues. "I mean *look* at this! They've even arranged for Santiago Edwards to make an appearance!"

"Who?" I ask.

"Santiago Edwards?" Daniel says. "I know him."

Jason gasps.

"Get. Out. Are you *serious*?"

"Yeah. I was a guest on his podcast last year. Pretty cool guy."

Jason stares at Daniel, eyes wide and mouth agape. I, on the other hand, am completely lost.

"Who is Santiago Edwards?" I ask.

"He's a famous cryptozoologist," Jason answers.

"I'm not even sure I know what that is."

"He studies cryptids; creatures of mythology and folklore. You know, like Bigfoot, the Loch Ness Monster - "

"The Bogman?"

"Exactly," Jason says. "And the coolest thing is he's completely self-made. He started out like ten years ago sharing videos on Facebook and now he's an internet sensation. His YouTube channel has over 250,000 subscribers. God, it would be such a dream come true if we could - " I can actually see the little lightbulb inside of Jason's mind flicker to life as he turns back to Daniel. "Mr. Whittaker... You don't think that you could ... Would it be possible ... That is, if you don't mind..."

"Jason, breathe," I advise him. "And please take a moment to think before you continue."

"Do you think you could maybe ask Santiago if Logan and I could interview him for our Bogman documentary?" Jason asks all in a rush.

You know, I really don't believe Jason did a whole lot of thinking, but thankfully, Daniel doesn't seem to mind.

"If he's not busy, I could probably introduce you," Daniel tells him. "Can't promise more than that, though."

"I'll take it!" Jason jumps. Literally. He jumps right up off the floor. "Thank you, Sir! And you know, I would ask you if you'd like to be featured in the documentary, but I understand that you're trying to keep a low profile here and I respect that. Although if you change your mind and decide you'd like to be a part of it - "

"Hey, Jason?" I interrupt. "Quit while you're ahead."

"Right. I'm just gonna go, you know, organize some books or something. Have a pleasant morning," Jason grins before scampering off to the back of the store.

"I really don't know what I'm going to do with him," I sigh. Truly, I've experienced more second-hand embarrassment in this last week than in my entire thirty-five years.

"He isn't afraid to go after what he wants. You've got to give him that," Daniel points out. "So, is this Winter Carnival something you think a ten-almost-eleven-year-old would enjoy?"

"Yeah, I think so. I mean, it isn't huge or anything, but there are activities for every age. And most of the town comes out, so she might even see a few friends there."

"Between us, I think she's still working on the friends thing," Daniel confides.

"Oh." I haven't even met Addie and yet my heart is breaking for her. And not for the first time. "Well, it... it can't be easy. In a new school. And at her age. Fifth grade can be... tough."

"Yeah," he agrees. "You know, I think I will bring her out to the carnival. It may be a good way to really introduce her to the town."

"I bet she'd like that."

"Will you be there?" Daniel asks.

I don't know why, but the question catches me completely off-guard.

"Um... I'm not sure. Still debating."

"How come?"

"Because... of the weather."

"The weather?"

"Yeah. I checked and there is a *lot* of snow in the forecast." Even though he's already well aware that I'm a wimp, I don't want Daniel to know that I'm seriously considering skipping one of my favorite events of the year because of my irrational fear of what may or may not be the Bogman.

"You know, it is a *Winter* Carnival," Daniel points out.

Well, he's got me there.

"True. I just... I'm not sure it's a good idea this year."

"Is there any way I could persuade you to change your mind?"

Suddenly, my heart is beating so wildly against my chest that I'm afraid I might actually faint.

"I... I don't know."

"I'll buy you a vanilla latte."

Oh my God, he remembers my coffee order.

Oh, I am in so much trouble.

"Extra foam?" I ask.

"I think I can make that happen," he grins.

I swear this man will be the end of me.

"Okay."

By the time I make it home, reports of a new Bogman sighting are circulating online and I'm beginning to seriously reconsider the promise I made to Daniel. I *want* to spend more time with him. More than anything, in fact. I want to meet Addie and I want to introduce them to Isaac. I want to spend these cold winter nights reading books in Daniel's arms. I want *him*.

But Heaven knows I am not about to venture anywhere that might provoke another Bogman emergence. Or worse, an attack. I mean, it's only a matter of time, isn't it? If this thing is out there, and if it's the sort of monster that everyone seems to think it is, then sooner or later, it's going to attack someone. And what then?

I take a moment to compose myself before I head inside. I don't want to worry my mom or Isaac. Especially Isaac.

Finally, I let myself in.

"Hello!" I call, stepping into my cozy, comforting home.

"Hi, Honey!" My mom's voice calls back from somewhere beyond the living room. "I've got to run, Hettie. Eloise is home... Yes, I'll see you Friday! Bye!" Moments later, she appears, grinning from ear-to-ear. "Hello, my beautiful daughter."

"Hey," I reply, kicking off my boots. "What did Hettie have to say?"

"Oh, you know, just shootin' the breeze. We were thinking we might meet up at the Carnival on

Friday. And..." Mom smiles at me with a knowing look in her eye.

"And... what?"

"And I heard that you might be meeting someone out there, too."

I've lived in Cedar Ridge long enough to know how quickly gossip travels here, especially between the town's old biddies. So it really shouldn't surprise me at all that Hettie and my mom already know about my plan to meet up with Daniel at the Carnival.

And yet...

"How did you find out so soon?" I ask.

"Hettie!" My mom answers as though that should be obvious. Granted, I suppose it should be.

"How did *she* find out?"

"Well, Daniel texted her and asked her if she and Theresa would be going to the Carnival, and of course, she said they were. Then she asked him if he was thinking about going and he said yes, and that he was going to be there Friday because that's when *you* were going to be there. So of course, Hettie had to call me straight away to tell me the news."

"Of course," I echo.

With that, I breeze past my mom and make my way into the living room where Isaac is sprawled out in his usual spot in front of the TV.

"Hey, Sweetheart," I sing, kneeling down to plant a big kiss on his cheek.

"Hi," he answers.

"Did you have a good day?"

"Uh-huh."

"I'm glad." Hopefully, he's forgotten all about last night's visit from the Bogman, although I somewhat doubt it. In so many ways, Isaac is much braver than I've ever been. When it comes to monsters, however, I'm afraid he's just as big of a scaredy-cat as I am.

Which, of course, brings me back full circle to my earlier internal debate concerning the Winter Carnival. What kind of mother would I be, forcing her son to attend a carnival that will be full of Bogman snow statues and Bogman costumes? My poor boy will be having nightmares for months!

I just can't do that to him.

"What's wrong?" my mother asks me. "Are you feeling all right? You look like you're about to be sick."

"I'm fine. I'm just... I'm not sure about this weekend," I admit.

"What? Why not?"

But of course, the last thing I want to do is mention the Bogman or the Carnival in front of Isaac.

"Hey, Sweetie, why don't you run upstairs and wash up?" I suggest to him. "I'll go to the kitchen and get dinner started."

"Okay!" Isaac agrees and takes off running.

Meanwhile, my mom follows me to the kitchen.

"Now, Eloise, I know it's been a little while since you've been on a date, but you know there's really - "

"It isn't that." Although, the idea of dating does sometimes make my stomach turn. Even though this, technically, isn't a date. "It's the Bogman theme."

"Oh, Honey. Come on, you know the town is just having a little bit of fun."

"But there was another sighting! And Isaac is already so afraid of it. Did you know he thought he saw it outside his window last night?"

"He gets that from you. You've always had an overactive imagination."

"That's not the point," I argue. "It doesn't matter if he imagined it or not. It scared him half to death. It scared me too, for that matter."

"Maybe if he sees people having fun with the idea, he'll be less afraid of it," my mom reasons. "And that might go for you, too."

"You know, Mom, I don't think you've ever told me what you think about all this Bogman stuff," I realize.

"I think the people of this town enjoy having something to believe in. I don't have to tell you that it isn't every day something exciting happens around here. The Bogman gives them something to talk about... something to sort of spice things up. But do I believe that he actually exists? No."

"Really?"

"Eloise, you're so smart. Do you really believe in monsters?"

"I... don't know," I admit. "But after everything I went through with Lance, can you blame me for being a little overly cautious?"

"No. I guess I can't," my mother sighs. "But I also don't want to see you missing out on something great because of him. He's already taken far too much from you."

"I know."

With a smile, Mom takes me into her arms.

"I love you, Eloise."

"I love you too, Mom."

Chapter Eleven

Friday arrives with surprise blue skies and a brilliant sun sparkling on the snow. It's a breathtakingly beautiful day here in Cedar Ridge, the kind of day that we soak up and savor in the wintertime. The streets are bustling with preparations for tonight's Carnival and everyone is in a good mood.

Especially the two aspiring filmmakers who are, at this very moment, hatching evil schemes right here in my respectable bookstore.

"Okay, so like, what if we wait for him backstage?" Logan asks. "Spence says that he knows a guy who might be able to sneak us in - "

"Sneak us in? Dude, it's a makeshift stage that they built like, two hours ago. There's nowhere *to* sneak us in!" Jason argues. "I say we stick with our original plan and have Daniel introduce us."

"But you said that wasn't a guarantee."

"It's *not*," I remind them from my place at the checkout counter.

"You know, I still can't believe you lied to me, Ms. Keller," Logan remarks.

"Oh, I'm so sorry," I deadpan.

"That's all right. I'm sure you'll find a way to make it up to me."

"Fat chance," I mutter, abandoning my post and retreating into the lounge where Daniel is hard at work.

"How's it going out there?" he asks.

"You might want to let your friend know there's a very real chance that he'll be ambushed tonight."

Daniel chuckles.

"He hunts monsters for a living. He can handle it," he assures me.

"Has he ever actually seen one?" I ask.

"He says he has. And he's collected some pretty compelling evidence over the years. He'll probably talk about it tonight," he says.

"Oh."

"You're not going to listen, are you?"

"No, it sounds terrifying. Besides, I'll have Isaac there with me and I'm sure he wouldn't be interested." That is one of the many wonderful things about having a six-year-old son. I have a built-in excuse for getting out of everything.

"No, probably not," Daniel agrees. "You know, I'm really looking forward to getting to meet him."

"Yeah, I am too," I sigh without quite realizing what I'm saying. "I - I mean, I'm looking forward to seeing you... getting to meet him..." I clear my throat. "And I can't wait to meet Addie."

"Well remember, she's a little shy. But I think tonight will be good for her," he says. "I think it will be good for both of us."

"I think so, too," I smile.

"Hey, I just realized something."

"What's that?"

"I don't have your phone number. And I'm thinking I'm going to need it if I hope to find you tonight."

"Oh." And now I'm blushing. He's not even flirting with me and I'm blushing. At least, I don't think he's flirting. Is he flirting? "Well, uh... here."

I take his phone and type in my number.

"Great. I'll let you know when we get there tonight," he tells me.

"Great," I echo. "Well... as usual, I'll be up at the front if you need anything."

"Thanks, Eloise," he smiles.

Although the Winter Carnival doesn't officially begin until 7 o'clock, the fairgrounds are already bustling with citizens and tourists alike by the time Isaac and I arrive at ten till. And when I say bustling, I mean this place is completely *packed*. I don't know if it's the clear weather, the promise of Santiago Edwards, or simply the lure of the Bogman lore, but I've never seen crowds like this. Not here. Not in Cedar Ridge.

Our Chamber of Commerce must be thrilled.

"Mom, why are there so many people?" Isaac asks.

"I guess it's just a nice evening, Sweetheart," I answer.

Isaac knows all about the Bogman theme. I wasn't about to bring him here under false pretenses. But I'm sort of hoping that if we don't acknowledge it, we won't notice things like the Bake Your Own Bogman Cookies or the guy running around in the seven-foot-tall Bogman costume. Granted, these particular Bogmen are designed to be family-friendly monsters rather than an actual depiction of the supposed beast roaming our woods. In fact, with their big eyes and brown and green fur, they almost look like characters out of a Pixar movie.

As we venture further into the fairgrounds, I keep my eyes open for a booth or an activity that doesn't look too busy. To my surprise and utter relief, it doesn't take us very long to find one.

"Hey, do you want to go get your face painted?" I ask Isaac.

"Yeah!" he exclaims.

Grasping his hand, we approach the booth, manned and operated by the local high school art club.

"Hi, there!" one of the boys greets Isaac as he hops up onto the stool. "What would you like? We have a special going on our brand new Bogman design."

Of course they do.

"No, I don't think I would like that," Isaac tells him.

"That's no problem. We can also do superheroes, animals, and emojis," the boy says, offering Isaac a laminated sheet with a selection of designs.

"I like the snowman," he announces.

"One snowman coming right up!"

"What about you, Ms. Keller?" one of my regular customers, a young lady named Samantha, asks me. "Would you like to get your face painted?"

"Oh no, that's all - " I begin to decline, but something stops me. I barely even remember the last time I had my face painted. And why is that? It's fun. A little touch of magic. And the proceeds benefit the high school. "You know what? Sure. I'd love to get my face painted."

Isaac grins at me as I take a seat next to him. The snowman on his cheek is already beginning to take form.

"And what would you like?" Samantha asks me.

"Let's see..." I take a moment to browse the selection. "Why not a few wintery swirls?"

"Ooh, those are my favorite," Samantha declares. "Would you like some sparkles to go along with them?"

"Sure." Daniel will hopefully be here soon. I might as well look my glittery best.

Once Samantha finishes with me, I step off to the side to keep an eye on Isaac... and snap a picture or two of him looking adorable. I can tell by the look on his face he's trying very hard not to giggle while the boy paints the snowman's details onto his sweet, rosy cheek.

"Eloise Keller?"

I turn automatically to the sound of my name and find myself face-to-face with an unfamiliar yet reasonably handsome stranger. He's tall, though not quite as tall as Daniel, and he has an athlete's build. His dark brown hair is clean-cut and tidy and his eyes are the color of warm caramel.

"Yes?" I ask

"I'm sorry, I don't mean to alarm you," he apologizes. "I'm told that you run the local bookstore."

"Yes, that's right." One of them, anyway.

"I was wondering if I might talk to you about setting up a book signing. You see, I'm in town for a little while working on some research for a new book, and I figured while I'm here, it might be nice to get involved with the community."

"So... you're an author." Cedar Ridge seems to be running rampant with those recently.

"Yes, ma'am. Name's Cortland Hill. It's a pleasure to meet you."

"Yeah, likewise," I reply. "And um, sure. If you'd like to set up a book signing, I'm sure we can make room on our calendar. Why don't you call the store sometime next week and we can discuss it?"

"Better yet, why don't I stop by and bring a few signed copies with me? That way, you can put them out on display, maybe generate a little extra business for you."

"Oh.. Well, thank you. That's very... considerate." I have an exceptionally difficult time spitting out the word, but I don't want to be rude.

Just then, my phone dings in my purse.

One New Message: 718-352-9997

hey it's daniel. just got here. parking took forever.

Thank God. I very nearly heave a sigh of relief.

"Expecting someone?" Mr. Hill asks.

"Yes, actually. I need to go find him. But it was wonderful to meet you."

"You too, Eloise," he reciprocates with a rather unnerving sense of familiarity. "I'll see you soon."

Great, I think, watching him disappear into the crowd.

Before I have time to dwell, however, the boy painting Isaac's face announces, "All done!"

"How does it look, Mom?" Isaac asks.

"It looks great, Sweetheart," I tell him, shaking off my nerves and jitters. "Hey listen, do you remember when I told you about my friend, Daniel? Hettie's nephew?"

"Uh-huh."

"Well, he's here somewhere. Is it okay with you if we go say hi?"

"Yeah," he answers.

"Yeah?" I smile. "Okay, let me text him back to see where they are."

Hi! Just got our faces painted. Where are you? I write.

just passed a guy making balloon animals.

You're heading in the right direction. We'll try to meet you halfway.

So, I take Isaac's hand and we begin walking back toward the fairgrounds' entrance. Maneuvering our way through the multitude of Carnival-goers, I marvel once again at just *how* many people are here. It seems as though the crowds have nearly doubled in the short time since we arrived and for a moment, I'm worried that we might not actually be able to find Daniel and Addie.

Thankfully, Daniel is much taller than most and quite literally towers over the crowd.

"Eloise!" he calls out when he sees me.

My heart stops on the spot.

"Hey," I smile as we finally reach each other. "You made it."

"I did," he grins.

It's only then that I realize that he's alone.

"Where's Addie?"

"Oh, we came with Hettie and Theresa and they stopped to look at some jewelry," he explains.

"You do know that's asking for trouble, right?" I tease.

"No, asking for trouble was inviting the crazy aunts along in the first place" he jokes. Then, he leans forward to take a closer look at my face. "Hey, I like that."

"What?" I breathe.

"Your paint and glitter... thing."

Oh, my God. My face paint. It's been less than ten minutes and it's already managed to slip my mind.

"Oh, right," I laugh. "Thank you."

"Mom." Isaac taps my hand. "Tell him I have a snowman."

"Why don't you tell him?" I ask.

But Isaac shakes his head.

Thankfully, Daniel seems to know exactly what to do.

"Let's see that snowman, kid," he grins, kneeling down to my son's level. Isaac hesitates. Then, ever so slowly, he turns his head to show Daniel his design. "Wow. That's really cool."

"Thank you," Isaac replies shyly.

"Isaac, this is my friend, Daniel," I introduce them.

"It's nice to meet you, Isaac," Daniel says.

"Are you *really* Hettie's nephew?" Isaac asks, eyeing Daniel with the utmost suspicion.

This isn't at all the question Daniel had been expecting.

"I am," he answers with a laugh.

"I thought nephews were kids," Isaac remarks.

"Well, I was a kid once upon a time."

Isaac glances up at me, as though he needs me to confirm this. He's still not quite sold on the idea that every grown-up he knows was once as young as he is.

"You know, Sweetheart, Daniel has a daughter," I tell him, changing the subject. "She's actually only a few years older than you are."

"That's right. Her name is Adelaide," Daniel says.

"Like from *Guys and Dolls*?" Isaac asks.

Now *that* catches Daniel completely off-guard.

"Actually, she's named after her grandma... You've seen *Guys and Dolls*?"

"No, but he's studied it," I answer, running a hand through my little boy's golden curls. "Isaac loves everything Broadway."

"Well, that's cool. Do you want to be an actor?"

"No. A director," Isaac tells him.

Looking equal parts surprised and impressed, Daniel turns back to me.

"This kid's somethin' else, huh?" he asks, rising back up to his full height.

"You have no idea," I smile.

"Well, I have no idea how long Addie and the aunts will be looking at jewelry, but while we wait, maybe I could treat the two of you to some hot chocolate? Or a vanilla latte?"

"I like hot chocolate," Isaac announces.

"Yeah?" Daniel asks. "Well then, let's go find some."

Sadly, there are no vanilla lattes to be found at the Winter Carnival, but I'm more than content to settle for hot chocolate.

Once we each have a cup of steaming cocoa (plus an extra cup for Addie, of course), we begin making our way toward the handmade jewelry booth. While we walk, I can't help but notice a few people stopping to not-so-subtly stare. And I guess I can't say I'm all that surprised. After all, Daniel is a new face in a town where everybody knows everybody. I'm sure they're all wondering exactly who he is.

They're probably also wondering if we're on a date.

Which, of course, we're not.

But I can understand why someone might think we were.

Especially considering how Hettie reacts when she spots us together.

"Oh! Oh! You found her!" she exclaims, wrapping me up in a tight embrace. "Oh, Eloise, look at you! You are positively radiant."

"Thank you, Hettie. You look as festive as ever." As always, she's decked out in her faux fur and gaudy jewelry, some of which she's probably just purchased.

"And Isaac, look at you! Are you getting taller?" Hettie asks.

"Yes," he answers.

"I thought so. You are growing up so quickly."

"Too quickly," I comment.

"They all do," Hettie warns, casting a fond glance at the young girl standing between her and Theresa.

Addie.

She's taller than I expected, but just as sweet and pretty as she was in the pictures I've seen of her. Her soft brown eyes are gentle yet reserved. An effect, I'm sure, of all she's endured in the last six months. Still, she attempts a smile as Daniel introduces her.

"Eloise, this is my Addie," he announces proudly. "Addie, I want you to meet my good friend, Eloise."

"Hi, Addie," I smile.

"Hi," she replies shyly.

"And her son, Isaac," Daniel adds.

"Do you like *Guys and Dolls?*" Isaac asks. Of course that's the question he asks.

Addie looks politely confused.

"What?" she asks.

"It's an old musical," Daniel explains.

"Your name's in it," Isaac tells Addie.

"You know what, Sweetheart? Why don't you ask Addie about something else?" I suggest, patting him on the shoulder. I know my son well enough to know that if I don't cut him off now, he'll be talking about *Guys and Dolls* all night.

"Okay. Do you like *Wicked?*" Isaac asks.

Well, I guess I should have seen that coming.

Chapter Twelve

Over the course of an hour, we actually get to enjoy quite a bit of everything the Winter Carnival has to offer. We play games, we pose for silly photo ops, and Daniel and I even take Addie and Isaac tobogganing.

"I have a feeling I'm going to regret that in the morning," Daniel mutters to me, wincing as he stretches out his lower back.

"I have a feeling I will, too," I agree. "But it was worth it."

"Totally," Daniel grins. "This whole night has been worth it."

My heart absolutely skips a beat.

"I hope Addie's had fun," I say.

"I think she still is," Daniel assures me.

Right now, we're watching on as Hettie and Theresa take the kids through the Winter Lights Maze. I can hear Isaac laughing as he attempts to outrun and escape the grown-ups, only to be foiled by every twist and turn.

"You know..." Daniel continues. "I can't even remember the last time I did something like this."

"Really?"

"Addie was barely two when her mom and I split up. After that, I moved across the country and really couldn't be bothered to go back except for holidays and a few special occasions. And even then, I wasn't always... present," he admits. "I guess being here, seeing all this, makes me realize just how much I've missed out on."

His confession catches me off guard and for a moment, I can only stand in silence, trying to figure out the right thing to say.

"Well, you know, it's never too late," I finally tell him. "I know that sounds so cliché. But you're here for her now. And after everything she's been through this year, now is what matters."

"You think?" he asks, staring down at me with those intense, intelligent eyes.

"Yeah, I do."

The longer his gaze lingers on my face, the slower time seems to pass until finally, it stops altogether. The sights and sounds of the Carnival fade away, and all that remains is Daniel, illuminated by the soft glow of twinkle lights on the snow. Feeling bright and airy and without a care in the world, I take the slightest step towards him and -

"There he is!"

And just like that, the spell is broken as Jason and Logan trample onto the scene, film gear in tow.

"Mr. Whittaker! I mean... Mr. Brunsworth," Logan gasps as he fights to catch his breath. "We've been looking everywhere for you."

"It's almost 8:30, which means Santiago Edwards should be going on any minute," Jason explains. "And we were just wondering, or at least, you know, we were hoping - "

"Sir, did you ever get the chance to ask him about us?" Logan cuts right to the chase.

"Not officially," Daniel answers. "All I did was email him letting him know I'd be here tonight and if he had time after his talk, I'd stop by and say hello."

"And?" Logan presses.

"Did he respond?" Jason wants to know.

"He said he'd see me tonight."

"Yes!" Logan exclaims. "We're in!"

"I didn't say that," Daniel points out. "But I think I can at least introduce you."

"That's good enough for us!" Jason exclaims.

"What's good enough for you?" My mom asks, appearing like a gust of winter wind with my stepdad shuffling along behind her.

"Well hey there, Mrs. North! Mr. North." Logan greets my parents with an obnoxious grin.

"Hello, boys," my mom replies. "And just what exactly are all of you up to?"

"Not all of us. Just them," I tell her, motioning to Jason and Logan.

"Daniel's going to introduce us to Santiago Edwards," Jason explains.

"I see." My mother sounds very impressed even though I know for a fact she doesn't have a clue who Santiago Edwards is. I also know for a fact that she isn't about to ask, because that was exactly the lead-in she was waiting for. "And *you* must be Daniel," she beams.

"Yeah," Daniel replies, looking rather sheepish for a guy who hangs out with monster hunters and movie stars.

"It's so wonderful to finally meet you. I'm Eileen North. I'm Eloise's mom. And this is my husband, Lenny."

"Nice to meet you," my stepdad, a man of few words, nods.

"It's a pleasure," Daniel replies.

"Oh, the pleasure is ours. We've just heard so much about you from Eloise," my mom gushes. "You know, you're very handsome. And so *tall*. My goodness..."

"Mom." I cast her a warning glance.

"I'm sorry," she sighs.

"Not to disrupt the lovefest or anything, but we really need to get going if we're going to make it to the presentation," Logan informs us, clearly itching to get to Santiago Edwards before it's too late.

"What presentation?" Hettie asks as she and Theresa return with the kids. "Oh, hello, Eileen! Lenny."

"Hettie!" My mother embraces her friend. "And Theresa! Don't you both look lovely!"

"Hi, Grandma and Pop-Pop," Isaac waves.

"Hello, my darling boy." My mother scoops him up and embraces him as though she hadn't seen him less than two hours ago. "Are you having fun?"

"Yes. This is my new friend, Adelaide," Isaac says, pointing to Addie.

"Okay, yeah, this is cute and everything, but we've *really* got to go, man," Logan insists.

"Where are you going?" Hettie asks.

"Santiago Edwards is giving a talk here tonight and Mr. Whi - Daniel said that he would introduce us," Jason explains.

"And his presentation begins like, *now*," Logan adds.

"Oh. Well then, you need to get going," Theresa says.

"That's what I'm trying to tell them!" Logan exclaims.

"Go. We'll catch up," Daniel tells him.

"Are you sure you don't want to go and listen to your friend's lecture?" Hettie asks.

"Nah, it's all right. Besides, I don't think it's anything the kids would be interested in."

"Well, that's not a problem. We can watch them!" Hettie volunteers.

"Absolutely!" my mom agrees. "In fact, if you and Eloise wanted to go out for a drink or a bite to eat after the presentation, we'd be more than happy to take the kids home and get them to bed. Wouldn't we, ladies?"

"Yes, of course!" Hettie answers while Theresa nods emphatically by her side. "Of course, since we'll have Danny's car, you'll have to drop him off at our place afterward. Is that all right with you, Eloise?"

Oh, my God. They planned this.

"You know, I'm actually feeling a little tired..." I say.

"Oh, nonsense. You're too young to be feeling tired," my mom argues. "Besides, you work so hard. You deserve a night out. Doesn't she Daniel?"

"I think so. But only if you're feeling up to it," he tells me.

"I..."

Yes, of course I'm up for it. I'm up for anything that involves you.

Oh, but why do Jason and Logan have to be here? And why do we have to go and listen to your friend talk about monsters? I don't like monsters.

Oh, but I like you. I really, really like you.

"Sure," I finally answer. "Let's go."

Santiago Edwards is not what I'm expecting.

For starters, he's much younger than I imagined a hardened and intrepid cryptozoologist might be. It's hard to tell from my seat in the audience, but he may even be younger than I am.

For another thing, he has green hair and is dressed in ratty jeans that he probably bought in the late nineties, a black blazer, and a white t-shirt that says **Sasquatch is my Homeboy**. He's very boisterous and surprisingly comical as he bounds around the stage, answering questions and presenting what he claims is undeniable proof that cryptids do indeed exist. Watching him, I can't help but think that he seems more like a comic book character than a monster-hunter.

And you know what? I kind of like him.

"Okay, so let's talk about the E-word. You all know which word I mean. That pesky E-word that skeptics like my cousin Theodore just love to throw around to make the family cryptid enthusiast look like a total loser. That's right; I'm talking about *evidence*.

"Now, any of you who have ever had the pleasure of debating a skeptic have probably been beaten over the head with arguments about evidence, or should I say lack thereof. And you know, I guess I can understand where they're coming from. After all, they've never seen a tall, hairy monster traipsing through the woods or a sleek and shiny plesiosaur diving down into the depths. Why should they believe in something that they haven't seen?

"Here's the thing, though. They may not have seen these creatures, these cryptids, these *monsters*... but there are plenty of credible witnesses out there who have. And *that* is what I find so compelling, not just about cryptozoology as a science, but about what's happening to you right here in Cedar Ridge. Just out of curiosity, how many of you have seen or personally know someone who has seen the Bogman?"

An unnerving number of people raise their hands.

"Look at that. Magic. Pure magic," Santiago smiles. "Now let me ask you another question. How many of you think he's really out there?"

This time, nearly three-quarters of those in attendance raise their hands, including Jason and Logan. Out of the corner of my eye, I notice Daniel glance my way, but we both keep our hands in our laps.

"And you see, that, to me, is even more beautiful than any eyewitness testimony," Santiago continues. "All my life, people have asked me why I believe in monsters and myths. They tell me that I have no reason to believe. But see, that's where they're wrong. I have every reason to believe. Because what is life without fascination? Without curiosity? I for one would hate to think that we as humans know everything that there is to know, that we've discovered all that there is to be discovered. Otherwise, what's the point?"

He goes on like this for about fifteen minutes before opening up the floor for questions from the audience.

Once it's all over, Jason, Logan, and I follow Daniel back around the stage where Santiago is signing autographs for a few of the city council members.

" - and could you please make it out to Abby and Nicole?" one of the women is asking.

"Absolutely," Santiago grins as he scribbles his signature across what looks to be an ordinary scrap piece of paper. "There you go."

"Thank you. And thank you so much for being here tonight. It was a real treat."

"Oh, it was my pleasure," Santiago grins. Then, setting his Sharpie aside, he turns his attention to Daniel. "Well, if it isn't the man after my own nightmares. How are you doing, good Sir?"

"Doin' okay. How about yourself?"

"Can't complain. Though I've got to admit, you are the last person I expected to see in Cedar Ridge, North Carolina. What, are you here for a book signing?"

"I actually live here now," Daniel tells him.

"Oh, right. I heard about everything that happened. I'm really sorry about all that."

"Thanks, I appreciate it."

"How's your little girl? Is she doing okay?"

"She's adjusting."

"Well, this seems like a nice place to adjust. Real neat town from what I've seen of it. But you know, I've got to ask... What do you think of the Bogman?"

"You know, I really couldn't tell you. These guys, however, are setting out to make a documentary about him," Daniel says, indicating Jason and Logan.

"No shit," Santiago declares. "What do you have so far?"

"Uh... well... not much," Jason admits rather breathlessly. "But we've been collecting every picture, article, and interview we can get our hands on. And we've been reaching out to a few people to see if they'd be interested in appearing. And I've just got to tell you that we are huge fans of your work and meeting you tonight is just about the coolest thing ever."

"And we also wanted to ask if you'd be in our documentary," Logan says, point blank.

"Please," Jason adds.

"Are you kidding? Hell yeah, I'll be in your documentary!" Santiago exclaims.

"Really?" Jason gasps.

"Sure thing," Santiago says. "I'd been thinking about conducting a little research of my own here, and you guys just gave me a reason to stay. So, when are you shooting?"

"Whenever you're available," Logan answers with as much tact as he can muster. "We were actually thinking as long as the weather isn't too bad, we might actually venture down to Bog's Creek tomorrow."

"Oh yeah? What's the forecast look like?" Santiago asks.

"Iffy," Jason answers reluctantly.

"Do you guys have night-vision on your camera?"

"Yeah..." Logan replies, his eyes wide with anticipation.

"Well, the night is still young," Santiago observes. "Why don't we head down there and get some footage now? In fact, we could all go. Make a real adventure out of it. What do you say?"

Chapter Thirteen

I should have said no.

I wanted to say no, but I know I would have been the only one.

So I said yes. And now I regret it.

Bog's Creek trickles through what used to be summer campgrounds but has since been converted into the Thurman National Wildlife Refuge. Consisting of over eight thousand acres of hiking trails, mountain streams, and dense forests, Thurman is a popular destination for tourists and a recreational escape for residents.

And now, a humble home for our local monster.

In the light of day, Thurman is beautiful, peaceful. A winter wonderland of trees glittering with snow and a blanket of soft frost on the ground.

But in the dead of night?

It's like stepping into another world; a dark vacuum of shadows and ice. The chill in the air is menacing and it's only too easy to imagine that there's something out there, watching us from the depths of the forest.

"So, Santiago - it is all right that I call you Santiago, right?" Logan asks.

"For sure, bro," Santiago answers.

"Sweet," Logan declares. "So, anyway, I just wanted to ask you... how did you get into all this?"

"Is this for the documentary?"

"No. Strictly off the record."

"When I was ten, my sister and I went to visit our grandparents in Dover, Massachusetts. There was this park about half a mile from their house where we'd go to play almost every day. One afternoon, we were walking home with our grandfather when, out of the corner of my eye, I saw this... this *thing* scampering into one of the neighbors' backyards. I stopped walking to try and catch a better look at it and... it was like my mind couldn't make sense of what my eyes were seeing.

"At first, I honestly thought it was a human, crouched on all fours, walking on their hands and feet. But its skin was a strange grayish-almost-white color and its limbs were too long and spindly to be human, or any sort of creature I recognized. To this day, I couldn't tell you what it was. I can only tell you that seeing it and knowing that it's out there... changed my life."

Santiago's testimony carries us all the way to Bog's Creek and leaves me feeling, if possible, even more unsettled. It isn't the idea of this supposed monster that sends a shiver down my spine, though I'll admit it sounds absolutely terrifying. It's his certainty, the conviction with which he recounts his experience. He's absolutely convinced he saw something that summer.

Sort of like Floyd Whalen.

"This is it," Jason announces, trudging down to the water's edge. While the shallow edges of the creek have frozen over, the deeper water in the middle of the stream continues to flow.

"So, how do you guys want to do this?" Santiago asks.

"I know we talked about doing an interview, but now that we're here, I'm kind of thinking we turn this into a full-blown investigation," Logan chimes in. "I mean, anyone can stand around and ask questions. Why don't we explore the area and while we do, Santiago, you can let us know what we should be looking for?"

"I'm game," Santiago agrees.

As the three of them traipse ahead through the frozen underbrush, Daniel stays behind with me while I struggle to maintain my footing in the dark.

"Are you doing okay?" he asks. Even though I can barely make out his features, I know he's amused. I can hear it in his voice.

"Oh, yeah," I answer. "I'm truly an outdoor girl at heart."

"Not sure I believe you."

"You shouldn't."

"Here," he says, offering me his arm.

"Thank you," I smile and slip my hand through the crook of his elbow. Even through his thick winter coat, he radiates warmth and I find myself tempted to huddle even closer to him. Somehow, I resist.

"So, I guess this isn't exactly what Hettie and your mom had in mind when they suggested we go out after the Carnival," he says.

"I've got to tell you, Daniel, it isn't exactly what I had in mind, either."

"Fair," he laughs. "Is there any way I could make it up to you?"

"Well, you already owe me a vanilla latte."

"How about dinner then? Maybe next week sometime?"

My breath catches in my throat.

I could be wrong, but it really sounds like he's asking me out.

Before I have a chance to answer, however, Jason shouts out from up ahead.

"I didn't know this was still here!" he exclaims.

Daniel and I exchange curious glances before hastening after our companions. It isn't until we catch up with them that I realize he's taken my hand.

"What is it?" I ask. From where I'm standing, I can't see anything beyond the trees a few meters in front of me.

"Eloise, check this out," Jason says, holding his tiny camera monitor up in front of my face.

At first, my eyes have trouble adjusting to the harsh brightness of the screen, but once they do, I'm able to make out the wooden planks and rustic window frames of an abandoned cabin.

"Oh my..." I whisper. "That's... very spooky."

"I thought they tore the camp down," Logan remarks.

"Guess not," Jason says. "Or at least not all of it."

"Well? What are we waiting for?" Santiago asks.

"What are we waiting for... what?" I ask.

He can't possibly mean that we should go breaking into this rundown, forgotten building. I may not have seen many horror movies, but I've watched enough *Lifetime* with my mom to know this scenario has murder-in-the-woods written all over it.

But of course, breaking into the cabin is exactly what Santiago intends to do, and Jason and Logan are only too eager to follow his lead.

"Do you know where we are?" Daniel asks me.

"There used to be a summer camp here," I answer. "My parents actually tried to send me when I was little, but I didn't like it. They had to come and get me after two days."

"What didn't you like about it?"

"I was afraid of the woods. So afraid that I made myself sick. I ended up being too much for my counselors to handle so they called my parents and sent me home." Not one of my prouder moments, I'll admit. But once a scaredy-cat, always a scaredy-cat.

"I didn't like the woods when I was a kid, either," Daniel admits.

"Really?"

"I don't like bugs. Or poison ivy."

"That's funny because you look like you would be an outdoorsman."

"Is it the beard?" he asks.

"That, and you're tall and strong and you have a general sense of... you know... ruggedness." Oh my God, I am not good at this.

Thankfully, Daniel laughs.

"I'll take that as a compliment."

By now, we're close enough that I can see the details of the cabin with my own eyes. The building itself is overgrown with dead vines and the wood is stained from years of exposure to the harsh elements. The front porch looks rickety and unstable and I'm certain that if we were to search, we'd find discarded nails buried beneath the snow.

"This is *awesome*," Logan breathes.

"Think we can get in?" Jason asks.

"Only one way to find out," Santiago says.

Then, with Jason filming his every move, Santiago steps up onto the porch with the sort of self-assuredness that tells me he's not at all concerned about its structural integrity. We all watch with bated breath as he makes his way to the front door, which opens for him with rather unsettling ease.

"No way!" Logan exclaims as he and Jason scramble after Santiago.

Their idol, however, stops them in their tracks.

"Before we all go storming in, I just want to make sure it's safe," he tells them.

With that, he disappears into the dark, leaving behind a very anxious Logan and Jason.

That's when I hear it: a rustle in the distance. Someone shuffling through the snow. Frantic, I whirl around and attempt to pinpoint the location of the sound. Whatever it is sounds too large to be a deer, or even a bobcat or a wolf. It might be a bear, but it's highly unusual for them to be out this time of year.

Could it be human?

"Are you okay?" Daniel asks me.

"I thought I heard something," I answer, still on high alert.

"Probably a fox or something."

I don't care if he's right or not. I've had just about enough of this adventure.

"Hey guys, I think we should head back," I tell them.

"What, are you crazy? We just got here!" Logan protests.

"I know, but it's already much later than I intended to stay out. I need to get home to Isaac," I argue as Santiago reemerges.

"Guys, you've got to see this," he says.

Jason and Logan don't need to be told twice. Immediately, they hurtle up onto the porch and into the cabin, camera in tow. Daniel stays behind with me.

"We don't have to stay," he tells me. "They probably wouldn't even notice if we left."

I'm sure they wouldn't. And it would be so easy to turn away, take his hand, and run. But now my mind is reeling with morbid curiosity, and I know it won't let me rest or even relax until I know exactly what Santiago found inside that cabin.

Slowly, carefully, I step up onto the porch, which feels like it may give way beneath my weight at any moment. I make it to the door, but I stop there, resting my hand on the splintery outer trim.

At first, I don't see anything out of the ordinary. It's just an empty room.

Then my eyes fall on Logan, Jason, and Santiago, all huddled around something in the far corner of the building.

"What is it?" I rasp.

Logan looks back at me, a wild, almost feral glint in his eyes.

"Proof!" he exclaims.

Then, he shines his flashlight down to the cabin floor, illuminating a compilation of empty chip bags, discarded wrappers, and rotting fruit.

Logan's proof... is garbage.

"So really, that's all it was?" Daniel asks me once again as we turn onto Hettie and Theresa's street. In the midst of all the trash and chaos, I'd almost forgotten that Daniel didn't have his car and that getting him back to Hettie and Theresa's was my responsibility.

Not that I have any objections.

"That's literally all it was," I tell him. "I mean, the way they were acting, you'd have thought they'd discovered a message written in human blood. But no. It was just a pile of litter that a raccoon probably stole out of a wastebasket."

"And yet, they're convinced it's proof that the Bogman is truly out there."

"I guess so. Honestly, I've given up on trying to figure out what exactly goes on in their heads," I remark as I slow to a stop in front of Hettie and Theresa's house.

Unlike my tiny neighborhood at the edge of the forest, Hettie and Theresa live in a slightly more cultivated community. The houses are larger, the roads are nicer, even the trees seem tamer. For the record, I suspect these are all Hettie's preferences. I think that if Theresa had had any say in where they settled, they'd be living in a treehouse on some secluded island on the other side of the world.

"Well, I'm just glad that this night ended on a lighter note," Daniel admits.

"I am, too," I smile.

He smiles back at me, his eyes soft and warm. Suddenly, I'm very aware of just how close he is... and how alone we are. This is the first time, in fact, that it's ever really been just the two of us.

And now, I'm so nervous, I can hardly think straight. Daniel seems to sense it.

"So uh... I guess I'll see you Monday," he says.

"Yeah," I reply breathlessly. "Yeah, see you then."

"Oh, and thanks for the ride," he adds, climbing out of the car.

"Don't mention it."

"Good night, Eloise."

"Good night."

With that, he slams the door shut and walks briskly up to his aunts' house. I've just shifted my car into gear when I notice something on my passenger seat: a black leather glove. It must have fallen out of Daniel's pocket.

Quickly, I turn off my car's ignition and reach for the glove. Then, I leap out of my car and call out, "Daniel!"

He stops in his tracks and turns around as I sprint up the walkway after him. His legs are so long, he ends up meeting me halfway.

"You forgot your glove." I hold it out to him.

He doesn't take it immediately. He simply stands, staring down at me with a curious expression, almost like he's trying to solve a riddle. Feeling self-conscious, I realize that losing a glove probably isn't the most pressing issue, especially for someone I'm going to see again in two short days.

Blushing, I clear my throat and try my best to explain myself.

"I know I probably could have just given it to you on Monday, but it's supposed to get even colder this weekend, so I thought... you know, that you should have it."

Finally, he reaches out to take the glove, gently brushing my hand with his. I expect him to pull away but instead, he lingers, his fingers toying ever so slightly with mine. Instinctively, I take a step closer to him.

"Thank you," he mutters, his voice low.

Then, in the quiet stillness of the night, beneath the pale light of a million winter stars, his mouth finds mine. It's a gentle kiss; one that demands nothing. As swift and sincere as snowflakes on the wind.

And it's everything my heart could ever hope to want.

Chapter Fourteen

"I'm telling you, it was magical. In fact... it may have been the best night of my entire life."

"Wow."

"I mean, it was like I knew, I just *knew* that every moment had been leading up to it."

"I'm happy for you."

"See, I know you and I know you're not taking me seriously right now, but what I'm feeling is real. I actually think I might be in love."

"With... the Bogman?" I deadpan.

"Not with the Bogman himself, just... what he represents," Jason explains.

"And what does he represent?"

It's Monday morning and Jason has been talking my ear off since he walked into the bookstore. Which, incidentally, has lost power due to all the heavy snowfall we've been having recently. So now I'm cold, I'm in the dark, and I'm listening to Jason sing the Bogman a love ballad.

Today is going to be great.

"It's like Santiago said. Curiosity. Discovery. The idea that we don't know everything about the world we live in is... actually very liberating," Jason says. "I just can't wait to edit our footage. I think

Logan is actually planning on dropping in later to try and get some of it done this afternoon."

"Without electricity?" I ask.

"Oh, right," Jason mutters as though he's just realized the power is out. "Well, maybe, it'll be back on soon."

"We can only hope. We really can't do a whole lot of business without it."

"So, are you going to close the store?"

"Probably. But I'm going to stay here just in case the power comes back."

"Do you want me to stay, too?" That's Jason's polite way of letting me know that he'll stick around if I absolutely need him to, but he really, really wants my permission to take the day off. Probably so he and Logan can go find a functioning power outlet to work on their Bogman movie.

"I was actually hoping you might be able to run a few errands for me while I try to get in touch with the power company. I'll see if they can give me an estimation of how long the outage will last. If it's all day, then there's really no point in you being here."

"Sweet!" Jason exclaims. I raise an unimpressed eyebrow. "I - I mean... I hope the power comes back soon. Really soon! Like, in thirty seconds."

"Nice try. I'm going to write you up a list of what I need you to do."

It really isn't all that much. Mostly, I just need more firewood. I have enough to get me through the morning, but if I'm going to be here a while, I'm going to want to keep the fire burning.

I may also see if I can get him to run to the grocery store for me.

Once he's out the door, I make it my mission to contact the power company. Unfortunately, every other business owner in Downtown Cedar Ridge must be on the same mission, because an automated answering service answers both times I try to call. Maybe once Jason gets back, I'll make the rounds around Main Street to see if any of my neighbors have any information.

Or, you know, maybe I'll make Jason do it. It's cold outside.

Setting my phone aside, I kneel down to grab what remains of our firewood when the shopkeeper's bell rings. Curious, I glance over my shoulder, although I have a feeling I already know who it is.

Sure enough, Daniel appears moments later and suddenly, I'm finding myself feeling very giddy and light-headed.

"It's kind of dark in here, huh?" he asks.

"Yeah. I'm uh... afraid you won't be getting much work done this morning," I reply.

We haven't actually spoken since Friday night and we didn't even acknowledge the kiss. After it was over, we just sort of smiled at each other and said goodnight again. And that was it.

Now we're alone in this cold, dark bookshop and I can't help but wonder what he's thinking.

"That's fine," he assures me. "Do you need some help?"

"Oh. Sure. That would be great."

Casually, he sheds his jacket and drops his backpack into his usual armchair before kneeling down next to me. His proximity is electrifying and I am all too aware of just how close he is to me. So close that I can count the threads of his old, worn flannel shirt. So close that I'm breathing in the fresh mahogany scent of his cologne. So close that I could simply rise up and kiss him... if I were bold enough.

But I'm not, even after what happened Friday night.

"Is this all the firewood you have?" Daniel asks, setting the last log on the hearth.

"For now. Jason went out to pick up some more."

"Did he and Logan get some good footage the other night?"

"He says they did," I answer as our rather modest fire begins to flicker.

"Think he'll let us see it?" Daniel asks, rising up to his full height. Then, he offers his hand to help me up as well.

"Thank you." I smile once I'm on my feet. "And I'm sure he will. In case you hadn't noticed, Jason is not a shy person."

"No, he's not. But you know, I sort of admire that."

"I do, too," I admit. "Some days, I almost envy him. It must be nice to be that brave."

"You don't think you're brave?"

"Oh, I know I'm not."

"Why do you say that?" Daniel asks in earnest.

"Because... I'm afraid of my own shadow. I don't like taking chances or putting myself out there... I prefer to play it safe. I always have."

"That may be, but you've also built a whole life for yourself and your son. You took over a business, which you run with hardly any help. And you were prepared to face the Bogman in his own territory," he adds with a grin.

"That was peer pressure," I remind him.

"Nah. That was all you," he says as he takes a step closer to me and in doing so, closes the gap between us. Again, I'm struck by how tall he is. And how *warm*. God, if I could sink into him...

As though he's read my mind, he moves even closer and wraps his strong arms around my whole body. Engulfed in his embrace, I lift my hands up and grasp the soft fabric of his shirt. I can feel his heart beating beneath my fingertips as I pull him ever nearer.

"What if I dared you to be brave right now?" he murmurs through the empty stillness.

It takes little more than half a second for me to realize what he's asking. It's in that same second that I find myself wrapping my arms around his broad, sturdy shoulders. Then, I rise up on my toes and let my mouth hover over his. He leans forward, brushing his lips over mine, teasing me, tempting me until finally, I capture him with a kiss; a kiss which he returns wholeheartedly.

Suddenly, every inch of me is awake, alive, and alight with a million sensations. I feel Daniel's chest rising against mine as he breathes me in. I taste the hint of fresh spearmint on his tongue. I feel every flicker of every flame dancing in the fireplace as he kisses me over and over and over...

The next thing I know, Daniel is easing himself down onto the closest couch. Somehow, my body knows how to follow. As he settles in, he gently pulls me with him until we're perfectly entwined; our legs interlocked, my arm lying across his chest. Then, he raises his free hand and runs his fingers up through my hair as he guides my mouth back to his.

This kiss is slower, more intimate. Like a secret whispered through the shadows. After it ends, he drapes his arm back around my waist, exhales, and presses his forehead to mine. Then, he closes his eyes and pulls me in even closer. The way he's holding me... it's almost as though he finds comfort in my touch.

Then it hits me.

He's seeking the same solace I am. Of course he is.

Daniel is strong. He's a parent, a guardian, a protector. But he's also a man who knows what it's like to have his entire world ripped out from under him. To feel lost and vulnerable and helpless.

It's funny. In my fantasies, I've cast Daniel as this romantic, heroic figure; my own personal knight in shining armor. When I daydream, I always imagine he's the one saving me. But here in our silent sanctuary, I realize I want to be the one who rescues him. I want to protect him, comfort him, heal him...

I want to love him.

Deftly, I lift my hand up to his face and let my fingers toy with his beard. He takes another deep breath. Then he's kissing me again, this time with a newfound fervor, and I find myself praying that he'll never, ever stop -

Ding.

The sound of the shopkeeper's bell barely even registers with me. Daniel, on the other hand, hears it loud and clear.

"S'there someone here?" he asks, sounding confused, even a little dazed.

I have to think for a moment. *Is* there someone here? No one's *supposed* to be here. We don't have power. The store is closed.

"Okay El, I got your firewood. And your weird microwave pasta."

Oh, my God.

"*Jason!*" I hiss.

"I'm just gonna drop the groceries on the counter, okay?" Jason calls

Frantic, I move to untangle myself from Daniel's embrace. I've literally just leapt to my feet when Jason appears, bearing a bundle of firewood.

"Yeah. Yeah, that's great. Thanks," I breathe, trying to sound as casual as possible. "So uh... I guess the supermarket is still fully functional? Electricity and everything?"

"Yeah, and it's like the only place in Cedar Ridge. Speaking of, did you ever find out when ours is coming back?" Jason asks, setting the firewood down next to the hearth.

"Uh... no. No, they were busy every time I tried to call." Which was twice, but whatever.

"Well, I mean, of course they're probably swamped with half the town being out of commission. It's probably going to take a while. On that note - "

"Yes, you can have the rest of the day off," I answer before he has the chance to ask.

"You're the greatest." Jason grins. Then, he turns to Daniel. "Mr. Whitt - Daniel, I don't know if you'd be interested, but Logan and I are going to be editing some of our footage from Friday night and if you'd like to see it, I'd be happy to send it to you via DropBox or like... Facebook."

"In case you were wondering, that was Jason's not-so-subtle way of asking you to add him as a friend on Facebook," I tell Daniel.

"Was not," Jason insists. "Though if you *would* like to add me, I'd be totally honored."

"Actually, I'm not on Facebook," Daniel admits. "I would like to see your footage sometime, though."

"Really? I - I mean great! Thanks! I'll get that to you just as soon as I can!"

"Don't rush," Daniel advises him.

"No. No, of course not. Thank you, Sir," Jason beams. "Well, if you don't need me for anything else, then I am out! See you tomorrow! If we're open, that is."

"We're going to be open," I tell him.

"What if we still don't have power?"

"Then there's a whole storage room we can clean out and organize."

"Oh, joy," Jason grumbles on his way out the door.

And just like that, Daniel and I are alone again.

"Well uh..." I clear my throat. "I guess we're closed."

"So what are you going to do?" Daniel asks.

"I'll probably head home and see if I can get some laundry done. Maybe if I'm feeling adventurous, I could even vacuum."

"Want to come back to my place instead?" The question is innocent, his tone perfectly casual. And yet, somehow, I've forgotten how to breathe. "I can make you lunch. Show you around. Not to brag or anything, but I've got a pretty great view of the mountains - "

But before he can finish, I wrap my arms back around his shoulders and cut him off with a kiss.

"That sounds *much* better than vacuuming."

Chapter Fifteen

Daniel lives in a beautiful house about fifteen minutes outside of Cedar Ridge, even higher up in the mountains and surrounded by an enchanting frozen forest and miles upon miles of winter wilderness. While most homes in town are rather old and quaint, Daniel's is a work of modern architectural art. Elegant in its simplicity with window walls, slanted rooftops, and geometric structural design, it almost looks more like a luxury resort than a private residence.

"Well, this is it. Home sweet home," Daniel says.

"Wow..." I breathe.

"Told you the view was pretty great."

"It really is. And it's so open and bright. But..."

"But..?" he asks as he unlocks the front door.

"Don't you sort of feel isolated out here?"

"Maybe a little. But after living in New York City for almost a decade, I embrace the solitude. Besides, I've got Addie with me."

"That's true," I smile and follow him across the threshold.

Inside, the house is just as spacious and grand as one may expect, though Daniel and Addie are very clearly still in the midst of moving in. Cardboard boxes of all sizes line the farthest wall of the living room and the shelves and tabletops are empty. There is a very large television, however. And a couch. If Isaac were here, he would approve.

"So, it's still a work in progress," Daniel admits, taking my coat and draping it over a chair. "I wanted to make sure to unpack all of Addie's stuff first. After that, I sort of lost momentum."

"Trust me, I get it," I assure him. "I think I slept on a bare mattress for a solid month before I mustered up the will power to unpack my bedding."

"Okay, I was able to manage that. The rest of it though..."

"Do you need any help?"

"That is *not* why I brought you up here today," he laughs.

"No, I know," I blush. "But the offer stands."

"I appreciate it. But I don't want to put you to work."

"Oh, don't worry. I'd let you do all the heavy lifting. Or I'd outsource it to Jason and Logan. Though you probably don't want those two knowing where you live..."

"No, probably not," Daniel acknowledges with a grin.

"In all seriousness though, I know how challenging it can be, packing up your whole life and starting over. So if there's any way I can help make it easier, just let me know."

"You already have. You've made me feel welcome, you've given me a place to work... You've made Cedar Ridge feel like home."

I'm so incredibly touched by his sentiments, that for a moment, my own words fail me.

"I don't think that was me," I murmur bashfully.

"It was," he says with absolute certainty.

Then he reaches up, cups my face with his hand, and presses his lips gently to mine. As the kiss deepens, I realize how very easily and quickly things could escalate here in the privacy of his home. And as much as I want him, I'm not sure I'm ready.

"Daniel, wait," I gasp, breaking away.

"You okay?"

"Yeah. I'm sorry, I... I don't know if... It's just that I haven't..." I don't even know what I'm trying to tell him. He waits patiently as I take a deep breath and try again. "My marriage... ended very badly. And... I haven't been with anyone... or even dated really at all since. And I'm afraid..."

"No, no. It's okay. You don't have to explain anything to me."

"I know, but I want to. I mean, I want you to know..."

"Okay," he says, taking a seat on the couch. "So, tell me."

Oh God, where to even begin?

Feeling cold and clammy with anxiety, I sit down next to him and try to organize my fleeting thoughts.

"My ex-husband was... troubled," I finally say. "He grew up in a wealthy family, but it wasn't at all a stable environment. His father was never around. His mother was an alcoholic. And Lance struggled with substance abuse as well.

"When we met in college, I was immediately smitten. He was handsome. He was smart. He was a little shy, but once I got him to open up... I couldn't get enough of him. It didn't take me long to fall in love with him... or to figure out that he was damaged. But at the time, I thought that just made our relationship all the more romantic. I was going to be the one who saved him, the one who made his life happy and perfect and worthwhile.

"It wasn't until we got married that I began to understand just *how* sick he really was. There were days he was so out of it, he could barely string two words together. There were nights I'd have to scream and shake him just to make sure he hadn't passed away in his sleep. Then there were the times... granted, they were few and far between... that he was sober. And he was mean and nasty and... he never hurt me, but he threatened to. And he blamed it all on me. For not taking better care of him. For not caring enough to get him the drugs he needed. For everything that had ever gone wrong in his life..."

"Jesus," Daniel murmurs.

"I was working up the nerve to leave him when I found out I was pregnant. To tell you the truth, I seriously considered not telling him; just packing my bags and running. But I did tell him. And Daniel... he was overjoyed. It was like for a split second, I caught a glimpse of the man I had fallen in love with. He made me all sorts of promises. He'd get clean. He'd go to rehab. He'd be the perfect husband, the perfect father. And I wanted to believe him. So, I stayed.

"For a little while, things were good. Lance was very supportive of me during my pregnancy, and he was elated the night Isaac was born. I remember thinking finally, finally things were going to be all right.

"But then Lance relapsed. At first, I think he tried to hide it from me. To this day, I tell myself it was because he wanted so desperately to be a good father. But I think he was afraid. I think he knew that he was losing me. Whatever the reason, after a while... he just became so much worse. It got to the point that I was afraid of him... afraid of what he might do to me... or worse, to Isaac. And I couldn't... I *couldn't* let anything happen to him."

"Of course not. No, you did what you had to do," Daniel agrees. "If you don't mind me asking, is he... still a part of Isaac's life?"

"No," I answer. "I thought I wanted to give him the opportunity, but after Isaac and I moved out, he began to harass me. He'd call me constantly or drop by several times a day. He'd follow me whenever I left the house. Finally, I threatened him with a restraining order. And that's when he went to his parents. He tried to convince them that I was the one who was unstable... That they needed to help him take Isaac away from me. Obviously, that didn't happen, but we did end up in court."

"I'm guessing you got full custody?" Daniel asks.

"And my restraining order," I add.

"And he's respected it?"

I nod.

"It's been almost four years now since I've seen or heard from him. But he still haunts me. After everything... I'm still so afraid. And that's why I haven't let myself get close to anyone."

It's then that Daniel takes my hands and begins to trace small circles on my skin with his fingers. I expect him to offer words of comfort, maybe even a kiss and a promise of assurance that I'm safe.

Instead, he says, "You know, I actually just went through a similar custody battle. With Addie's grandparents."

"*What?*" I'm not going to lie to you. I'm stunned. "But... but that doesn't make any sense. You're her father."

"I'm a name on her birth certificate. That's about all the credit that they're willing to give me," Daniel explains. "I told you before that I missed out on a lot of Addie's childhood. Well, as far as they're concerned, I abandoned her. And looking back, I don't necessarily disagree with them.

"You see, Addie's mom Lisa and I didn't have the most conventional relationship. We'd barely known each other three months when she got pregnant with Addie and we eloped right before she was born. I tried to convince myself that we were doing the right thing, but I knew going in that I wouldn't have been marrying her if she hadn't been pregnant. Lisa knew it, too. And she resented me for it.

"When we broke up... I can't say anyone was really surprised. A few of our friends were actually relieved. But Lisa's parents weren't happy, and they made it very clear that they blamed me for everything that had gone wrong in the relationship. I was self-absorbed... over-ambitious... inattentive to their daughter's needs... And by packing up and moving clear across the country, I played right into that narrative.

155

"At the time, I argued that my move was strictly business, that I would have more opportunities in New York. And that was somewhat true. But I won't deny there was a part of me that wanted to get as far away from Lisa and her parents as possible. I thought we would all be better off... and that maybe they would be happier... if I wasn't around as much."

"Oh, Daniel..." I don't know what else to say. His confession is heartbreaking.

"After Lisa..." He can't bring himself to say the word, but I know what he means. "After the accident, her parents fought tooth and nail to keep Addie. They took me to court and argued that I had been absent practically her entire life, that it would be cruel to tear her away from the family she knew and loved. They claimed that by moving away, I had lost my right to her."

I want to agree that that's ridiculous, that as a father, of course he has every right to his child. But in that moment, I can't help thinking of what would happen to Isaac if I were to pass away. He'd *have* to stay with my mom and Lenny. I wouldn't want Lance to have him, not in a million years.

Granted, comparing Lance and Daniel is like comparing apples to oranges. With all his struggles, Lance isn't fit to be a father. At least, he wasn't when I knew him. Daniel, on the other hand, is willing and able to do whatever it takes for Addie. Clearly, he's capable of financially supporting her. And from what little I've seen of them together, he seems most attentive.

"I'm sorry," I whisper. And I mean it. I am sorry. For him. For Lisa's parents. And especially for

Addie. "Do you mind if I ask you a personal question?"

"Go for it."

My heart beats wildly and I pray I'm not about to offend him.

"Did Addie have any say in it? In... what happened to her?"

"Not officially," Daniel answers. "She never testified or anything like that. I did ask her, though, what she wanted. And she said that she..." For the first time since I've known him, Daniel's voice breaks. "She didn't want me leaving her again."

Oh, Addie. Oh, that poor, sweet girl.

And Daniel... How I wish I had words of comfort for him. I wish I could take away every heartache he's endured and fill the empty spaces with joy and love and warmth. But all I have to offer is a gentle touch and a kiss.

And for the moment, it seems to be enough.

"I'm glad you're here," I finally whisper. "I'm glad both of you are here."

"I am too. And I'm glad *you're* here," he replies, his mouth hovering mere inches above mine. "You're not the only good thing to happen to me in the past few months, but you are my favorite."

Then he leans down and kisses me again. I feel myself trembling in his arms. Perhaps it's his gift for words or the tenderness of his embrace, but no man has ever made me feel so cherished.

His lips linger a few moments more before he gently pulls away. I lift my hand up to his face, stroke his beard, and steal one more kiss. Then he smiles.

"You know, I think I promised you lunch," he says.

"You did." And now that he mentions it, I realize I'm starving.

"What would you like? I've got... soup. I think. I know I have sandwich makings. Oh, and I've got an entire shelf full of instant macaroni. I think some of it is even *Star Wars* shaped."

"You know what's funny is Isaac *refuses* to eat macaroni that isn't shaped like macaroni," I tell him.

Daniel shrugs.

"Kid knows what he likes."

"I guess he does," I laugh. "I, on the other hand, have no aversion to Yoda-shaped pasta."

"Is that what you want?"

"Sounds good to me."

"Then I'll go fire up the stove," Daniel grins.

Then, with one last kiss, he rises up and makes his way into the kitchen.

"Hey, do you mind if I use your restroom?" I ask him.

"Not at all. The guest bathroom is just down the hall and to your left."

"Thanks."

I lift myself up off the couch and head to the hallway, but right as I'm about to round the corner, something stops me in my tracks. Instinctively, I turn to look at Daniel, but he's busy rummaging about the cabinets. He isn't paying me the slightest bit of attention.

So why do I suddenly have that *feeling?* That cold, dreadful feeling that something just... isn't right?

I must be imagining it. I have to be. After all, we're very alone up here in the mountains. True, we passed a few other residences along the way, but Daniel's house is very secluded. There's no way someone could have followed us up here without us noticing.

Unless... I find myself thinking as my gaze falls on the acres of dense, wintry woods surrounding Daniel's property.

No. No, that's absurd. There is no one out there.

To prove it to myself, I march back across the living room and plant myself in front of the west-facing window wall.

Outside, the woods are as still and serene as a painting; the very picture of wild, frozen perfection. Frosted pine trees worship the winter sky as the light of the noonday sun casts blue shadows across the mountain range. It's a beautiful, peaceful sight, one that soothes my frazzled nerves and fills me with a sense of clarity and calm.

I was right. There's no one.

We're alone.

And we're safe.

Excerpt from *Knick Knack*
By D.H. Whittaker

When it came to misfortune, the residents of Fortune, Texas had adopted a rather strange philosophy: Blame it on the Knick Knack.

No one really knew what the Knick Knack was supposed to be or where the legend had even originated. They had just all come to accept that the Knick Knack was responsible for every unfortunate happenstance to plague the tiny town of Fortune.

When the barbershop on Main Street caught fire and burned to the ground? Must've been the Knick Knack.

Whenever a car stalled or an engine wouldn't start? Damn that rascally Knick Knack.

If a library book just happened to go missing? That old Knick Knack is at it again!

But while the older generations shared a laugh and a pint over their fabled trickster, Fortune's children lived in fearful fascination of the dreaded Knick Knack and they took delight in coming up with the scariest stories to frighten their friends and classmates.

"I saw it the other day! Down by Willa's Creek! It was tall and gangly like a scarecrow and it had yellow fangs that dripped with blood!"

"Well, my granddaddy told me that it lives in the backwoods, just beyond that old vacant lot on Vine Street. It doesn't like the sunlight, which is why it stays in the shadows. But at night, when we're all asleep, it comes out and walks up and down the road looking for something - or someone - to eat."

"That's stupid. I heard that it's a shapeshifter! It can change into anything, even people you know! And if you let it in... it never leaves."

And so the stories went, on and on, night after terrifying night. It seemed as though every child in town had a tale to tell.

Every child, that is, except Dwayne Cecil.

Dwayne and his family were new to Fortune, and although the town had welcomed them with open arms, the fact of the matter remained that they were outsiders. And Dwayne was often reminded of it.

It didn't bother him. Not really. After all, his new peers were happy to include him in their gatherings.

He only wished he could come up with a story of his own. A story so gruesome and garish that it would scare the living daylights out of his new friends... and impress the living hell out of Sweet Pea Hutchins.

Yes, it was her real name, but the girl known as Sweet Pea was anything but. Cool and conceited with a terrible mean streak, Sweet Pea Hutchins was the daughter of the Mayor and just about as close to royalty as you could get in a town like Fortune. And Dwayne was determined to be the one who won her over.

He just had to get creative.

Chapter Sixteen

Something's happened.

Reports started circulating late last night, but it isn't until after I see Isaac off to school this morning that I finally hear the news.

There's been a disappearance.

Yesterday afternoon, a young man vacationing at the ski resort went out for a hike and he never came back. His girlfriend, who is here with him, is absolutely frantic. She's heard all the stories, of course, of a monster in the woods. But she didn't believe in them until Jake went missing.

Jake. That's his name. Jake Kingsley.

His girlfriend's name is Hillary Lyons.

My heart is anxious for both of them.

"... twenty-six-year-old Jake Kingsley was last seen at approximately 4:24 on Wednesday afternoon. Witnesses report he was dressed in a white ski jacket with red and black stripes across the chest. He was also wearing a black knitted cap and black Ray-Ban sunglasses with red lenses. He is five-foot-eleven and weighs one hundred and eighty pounds..."

Local officials are theorizing it may have been some sort of animal attack. If that's the case, it's not very likely that we'll find him alive. Or find him at all.

I'm holding out hope, however, that he's simply stuck somewhere. Maybe he made his way into town and couldn't get back. Our roads are rather treacherous this time of year, especially for those who aren't used to driving in the mountains.

Wherever he is, I just hope he's safe. And warm. I hate to even think it, but harsh weather and freezing temperatures can be just as deadly as any beast, real or imaginary.

The good news is we have electricity again. That should at least make it a little easier for the local authorities and anyone else who may be working to find Jake.

It comes as no surprise that news of his disappearance has already spread like wildfire by the time I make it into town. Everyone is shaken, and reasonably so. After all, stuff like this just doesn't happen here, despite what Floyd Whalen would have us believe.

"It's him. I knew this would happen!" I overhear him barking at two innocent passersby in that gravelly voice of his. "That Beast's come back with a bloodlust and he's out to slake it."

Eager to avoid him, I quickly seek sanctuary inside my store. Not that he doesn't come wandering in every so often, but blessedly, those instances are few and far between.

I've just shed my coat and stashed my purse behind the counter when the shopkeeper's bell rings and Daniel appears.

"Hey," I greet him breathlessly. I haven't seen him since our rendezvous at his house, but we've texted a little bit every day. Unfortunately, given the rather tragic circumstances surrounding the community, it doesn't feel right to flirt or to throw myself into his arms.

No matter how much I may want to.

"Hey," he echoes.

"You heard the news." I don't have to ask. I can see it on his face.

"Yeah. Poor kid," he mutters. "How are you holding up? Are you doing okay?"

"I'm worried, but I think we all are."

"What do you think happened?"

"I don't know. To tell you the truth, I don't even know what to hope for. I mean, the most likely scenario is that he's lost or injured somewhere out in the woods, but if that's the case, then I just... I don't see how he could have survived."

"You never know," Daniel tries to reassure me, but his tone falls flat and his eyes are full of doubt. Then, he holds out his hand and says, "Come'ere."

I obey, taking his hand and allowing myself to fall into his warm, comforting embrace. He's so strong and here in his arms, I feel so safe. Like nothing in the world could touch me.

"It'll all be okay," he promises, pressing his lips to the top of my head.

God, I want to believe him.

Just then, the shopkeeper's bell rings again and Jason scurries into the store. I'm so startled that I leap at least half a foot backward, right out of Daniel's arms.

"Sorry I'm late," Jason apologizes. "I couldn't find my keys this morning and I didn't have time to look for my spare, so I had to call my mom for a ride to work which was equal parts humbling and humiliating. Then right as I was about to walk in, Logan called to let me know that there's going to be a search party for that missing tourist tonight and wanted to know if I could make it out."

"That's right, I heard something about that," Daniel says. "Are you going?"

"Probably. That is if someone doesn't mind giving me a ride. I'd ask my mom but something tells me she wouldn't be crazy about the idea of me running around the woods after dark. Especially since we don't know what's out there."

"Like the Bogman." The words escape my lips before I can stop them. I don't want to bring it up. I don't want to dwell on it. But it's a thought that's been haunting me all morning, even before I heard Floyd Whalen bellowing in the street.

"Exactly," Jason says.

"Come on," Daniel scoffs. "People aren't actually thinking that a monster dragged this kid off into the woods, are they?"

"I think they think it's a possibility," Jason argues. "Don't you?"

Daniel sighs.

"I think there's a time and a place for stories and legends. Like last week at the Carnival. But this is a man's life we're talking about. We can't just - "

Ding!

The shopkeeper's bell rings for the third time this morning, interrupting Daniel. This time, a man appears. Although he's never visited the store before, I recognize him immediately.

It's the man who approached me at the Carnival. The one who claimed to be an author.

I'd been so distracted by power outages, lost tourists, and my feelings for Daniel that I'd completely forgotten about him and his promise to stop by and deliver a few books.

Clearly, he suffered no such lapse in memory.

"Hello again, Eloise," he greets me like an old friend. I can't say why, but it makes me a little uncomfortable.

"Oh. Hello," I reply.

"I'll let you get to work," Daniel murmurs to me. Then, he takes my hand and gives it a light squeeze before retreating into the lounge.

Jason, on the other hand, stays right where he's planted.

"You know each other?" he asks. He's visibly confused and rightfully so.

"We met briefly at the Carnival last week," I explain. "Jason, this is... um... You'll have to forgive me, I'm not very good with names."

"That's all right. Cortland Hill," he introduces himself.

"Nice to meet you. So, have you come to sell us some books?" Jason asks, eyeing the cardboard box in Hill's hands.

"Actually, I was hoping you might sell them for me. I kinda wrote 'em," Hill grins, feigning humility.

"No way! Another author," Jason comments.

"I'm not the only one?" Hill asks lightly.

"Well, actually we - "

" - Have a local writers' group full of aspiring authors." I cut Jason off before he can drag Daniel into this conversation. I can't say for certain that Daniel wouldn't want to meet a fellow author, but for the moment, I'm not taking any chances. Not when there's a chance that this man may recognize him as D.H. Whittaker.

"Oh, do you?" Hill asks.

"I have a friend who's a member. I'd be happy to put you in touch with her," I tell him.

"I appreciate that. Thank you."

"So, what kind of books do you write?" Jason asks.

"Thrillers mostly. A touch of horror, a touch of paranormal, even a little sci-fi. You may have heard of this one," Hill says, passing Jason one of his paperbacks.

"*Tomorrow's Mercenary*," Jason reads.

"It's one of those dime-a-dozen apocalypse novels, but it's done pretty okay. A couple of bestseller lists, an award nomination here and there," Hill informs us. Again, I get the impression that he thinks he's being modest.

"Sounds right up my alley," Jason grins. "I'm all about the end of the world. In fiction, that is."

"I'd be glad to sign it for you if you'd like to buy it now. In fact, that's one of the things I was hoping to discuss with you, Eloise."

"That's right. The book signing." I'd been hoping that he wouldn't bring it up. "I'm afraid with everything that's been going on, I haven't had a chance to check my schedule."

"Yes, that power outage threw everyone off a bit," Hill says.

"And the disappearance," I add. Hill's face falls, just a little. "I don't know if you heard, but a tourist went missing yesterday."

"Yeah, I did hear about that. It's a real shame," he says.

"There's going to be a search party tonight if you're interested," Jason tells him, but I wish he hadn't. Jason is far too friendly.

"I'd love to be an extra set of eyes, but unfortunately, I'm on a deadline and I've still got a ton of research to do," Hill says. "Speaking of, you wouldn't happen to have any books on the Bogman, would you?"

"Is that what your new book is about?" I ask.

"Well, not the Bogman specifically, but I've always been pretty fascinated by life in small towns and how their local legends come to be. They make for great stories."

"They really do," Jason agrees. "You know, I don't think we have any books, but my buddy Logan and I are actually in the process of filming a documentary on the Bogman. I'd be happy to share some of our resources with you."

"Oh hey, that'd be great," Hill smiles. "In that case, you get a copy of this book for free."

"No, you don't have to do that. I'm happy to help."

"And I'm happy to have you read my work," Hill says, whipping out a pen to sign Jason's copy of *Tomorrow's Mercenary*. "I hope you'll let me know what you think."

"Yeah, absolutely," Jason tells him.

"And Eloise? May I leave these with you?" Hill asks, indicating the rest of his books. He has about half a dozen titles in total and has brought three or four copies of each.

"Yeah, sure," I reply.

"And don't worry about the signing. I'm sure we'll be able to work something out."

Super.

"Well, I think I've taken up enough of your morning," Hill continues with a smooth grin. "It was nice to meet you, Jason."

"You too, Cortland. Thanks for stopping by," Jason replies.

"Oh, it was my pleasure," Hill says. "Until next time, Eloise?"

"Yeah." It's the only response I can muster.

Then he's gone and I can finally breathe a sigh of relief.

"He seems nice," Jason says. "And how cool is it to have another author in town? I wonder if Daniel has heard of him."

"I don't know."

"You okay?"

"Yeah, I'm fine. I just..."

"What?"

"He doesn't seem... *off* to you?"

"No, not really," Jason responds, gathering up the books that Cortland Hill left behind. "Why? Do you think he does?"

"I guess not. I don't know."

Jason shrugs.

"Well, he seemed cool to me. I'm looking forward to reading his books."

And with that, he makes his way to the back of the store, leaving me alone with my muddled thoughts.

Acting purely on instinct and a strong desire to be near Daniel, I slip into the lounge where he sits, staring at his computer screen and absentmindedly stroking his beard. He seems so engrossed in his work that I almost reconsider. I don't want to disturb him. He looks up, however, when he realizes I'm there.

"Everything okay?" he asks, setting his laptop aside and rising to his feet.

"Do you know a Cortland Hill?" I ask in response.

"Name doesn't sound familiar. How come?"

"He's the guy who was just here," I answer. "He's an author too."

"Oh. Well, I'll have to check out his work."

"You'll have the opportunity. He just left about half his inventory here."

"You don't sound too happy about that," Daniel observes.

"No, no. It's fine. I don't mind selling books for authors. I've done it before. It's just..."

"What?"

"I don't know. Something about him is just... sort of weird. Like the way he talks to me. It's like he thinks we've known each other for years."

"You mean you haven't?" Daniel's brow furrows.

"No! I don't know this man at all. I met him once before, last week at the Carnival. And we talked for thirty seconds, maybe a minute."

"God, the way he approached you, I thought he was a neighbor or maybe a family friend," Daniel tells me. "If I'd known he was a stranger, I wouldn't have left you alone."

"It's all right. I mean, I had Jason there. And he doesn't seem to think there's anything to worry about."

"He's probably right," Daniel says. "There are a lot of writers out there who are a little socially awkward. Don't get me wrong, they're great people. But they tend to spend a lot of time inside their own heads."

He's got a point. I have a six-year-old aspiring director on my hands and he spends more than a fair share of his time daydreaming.

Maybe I'm overreacting. It wouldn't be the first time.

"You're not wrong…" I acknowledge.

"Well, even if I'm not, don't hesitate to come and get me if you ever feel uncomfortable. Okay?"

"Thank you," I smile.

"Don't mention it."

Then, he takes my hand, pulls me close, and lowers his lips to mine as though kissing me were the most natural and wonderful thing in the world.

Chapter Seventeen

The search for Jake Kingsley is set to commence at 7 o'clock. Volunteers are to meet at the Cedar Ridge Ski Resort at 6:30 to sign in and to receive our assignments.

When Jason first mentioned the search party, I had no intention of participating. Never mind the fact that it's a Thursday night and I have a business to run. It's also freezing outside. And I don't go into the woods unless I have to.

I also have a young son to think about.

I need to be there for him. To cook him dinner. To make sure his bath water isn't too hot. To see that he remembers to brush his teeth. To tuck him into bed and kiss him goodnight.

I told myself that he was every reason I couldn't go out there tonight.

But then, a dreadful thought occurred to me.

What if it was him?

What if Isaac was the one lost out there in the woods? I would want every person capable of holding a flashlight and traipsing through the snow to be helping me look for him.

That's when I realized that he's every reason I *need* to be out there tonight.

A mother's son is missing. And I have to help her find him.

My own mother agreed and promised to stay with Isaac until I come home. We've all already eaten dinner and now my mom and Isaac are upstairs working on his math homework. All that's left for me to do is wait for Daniel to come and pick me up.

When he suggested we ride up to the resort together, I was all too eager to accept. Not just because I enjoy spending time with him, but because my poor car is so old and run-down, I'm not sure if it would survive a journey even further up into the mountains.

However, I harbor no such reservations concerning the shiny new SUV that Daniel arrives in. I couldn't tell you its make or model, but it's charcoal gray and it looks expensive.

Locking the front door behind me, I hoist my backpack full of emergency survival gear over my shoulder and climb into Daniel's passenger seat.

"What've you got there?" he asks me.

"Flashlights, water bottles, Goldfish crackers, fruit snacks, a portable phone charger, a first aid kit, and disinfecting wet wipes." Okay, so maybe it's more like emergency survival gear for moms. But it's better than nothing.

"Damn. I hope I get you as a search buddy," Daniel grins, leaning over and kissing me swiftly on the mouth. Then, he shifts his car into gear and we hit the road.

"So who's staying with Addie tonight?" I ask.

"I actually dropped her off at Hettie and Theresa's on the way here. Since I didn't know how late we'd be out there, she's going to spend the night. I'll pick her up for school first thing in the morning," he answers. "How about Isaac?"

"My mom will stay with him until we get back. And if it's too late for her to drive, she can sleep in my room and I'll camp out on the couch."

"We won't make it too late," Daniel promises.

"It doesn't matter," I assure him. "I just hope we find some answers."

"I do, too."

The Cedar Ridge Ski Resort is a beautiful, rustic building that's been a part of local culture since the 1950s. Along with being a haven for winter sports enthusiasts, it also functions as a luxury spa. It even has a heated outdoor pool, which I've always been keen to experience. It's a little sad, really. I've lived a mere stone's throw away from this spectacular resort my entire life, and yet, I've never seen it with my own eyes.

Until now, that is.

Once Daniel and I have signed in with the search party organizers, we make our way to the gathering of volunteers outside the resort's grand entrance. Looking around, I spot several of my friends, neighbors, and fellow business owners, all bundled up and waiting patiently for further instruction. As tragic as it is to be gathered under these circumstances, it warms my heart to see so many members of our community coming together for a young man they don't even know.

"Eloise!"

I turn at the sound of my name to see Jason approaching. And joy of all joys, he's brought Logan along.

Be gracious, I tell myself. *He's here to help. It's actually very honorable of him.*

"Hey guys," I greet them.

"Quite the turnout, huh?" Logan asks. "The Bogman really knows how to shake things up."

I choose to ignore that remark.

"Okay, everyone, listen up!" Our chief of police, Emma Jean Wilde, announces from the wraparound porch of the resort. "Our objective tonight is to cover as much ground as possible. Now, since we don't want anyone else getting lost out there, I want all of you to have at least two teammates who know where you are at all times. Each team will be assigned to a specific section of the woods. Once you have your assignment, you will be given a map and a black Sharpie so you can mark off precisely where you've searched. There will be some overlap. That's okay. We need to be thorough.

"Finally, we will be giving each team a radio. If you happen upon anything troubling or suspicious, I want you to call me or one of my officers immediately. Don't try to investigate anything yourself. Again, safety is our number one priority. Now, does anyone have any questions?"

"I've got one. Are they planning on feeding us at all? Because I'm *starving*," Logan grumbles.

Daniel casts a stealthy glance in my direction. Heaving a sigh, I reach into my backpack and pull out a bag of Goldfish.

"Here," I mutter, offering him the snack.

"Oh hey, thanks, Ms. Keller!" Logan exclaims. "Wow, you really are a mom, aren't you?"

I'm not sure how he can take a word like *mom* and make it sound like an insult, but before I get the chance to respond, a new voice calls out to Jason and Logan.

Moments later, who should appear but Santiago Edwards in all of his green-haired glory. Like the rest of us, he's dressed in hiking boots and a heavy winter coat.

"Hey, the gang's all here!" Santiago exclaims, eyeing Daniel and me. "Didn't expect to see you folks out here tonight. Especially you, Eloise. No offense."

Okay, I'm just about done with these twenty-somethings and their adolescent wit.

"Hey, man! Glad you could make it," Logan grins, greeting Santiago like a long-lost brother. I suppose it shouldn't surprise me that they get along so well.

"Thanks for letting me know. This is going to make for some *great* footage," Santiago replies.

"I'm sorry. Footage?" I must not have heard him correctly. One glimpse at the sleek black video camera in his hand, however, and I realize there was no misunderstanding.

"You're filming this?" Jason asks, sounding as put off as I feel.

"Hell yeah!" Santiago exclaims. "I've been studying cryptids and investigating monster sightings for almost ten years now, but this is the first time I've been around for an active missing persons case."

In that moment, I'm struck utterly dumb. Jason seems to have fallen mute as well.

Logan... Well, if I know Logan, then he probably finds no fault in Santiago's reasoning.

Daniel is the one who finally speaks up.

"You don't think that's a little insensitive? A man is missing, for Christ's sake."

"They've got news crews here," Santiago points out. "What's the difference?"

"The difference is that they're here to provide a service," Daniel says. "To keep people informed. To keep them safe."

"Yeah, and that's what I'm here for, too. That's why I do what I do. To educate people about these creatures. And to help prevent future attacks."

"But we don't even know that it was the Bogman," Jason argues, finally finding his voice. "I mean, sure, I think it's a possibility. In fact, I'm probably more open to it than most. But even if it was him, that's not why we're here tonight."

"Jeez, man, lighten up," Logan scoffs. "Come on, we know how serious the situation is. We're one hundred and ten percent committed to finding this guy. But I don't see why we can't shoot and search at the same time."

"Because it's completely inappropriate," I spit before I can help myself. "This isn't about your ability to multitask. It's about basic human decency. You're taking a potential tragedy and exploiting it... for what? For dramatic effect?"

"God, if I'd known I'd be taking this much shit tonight, I'd've brought a shovel," Santiago remarks. "I'm not trying to exploit anyone or anything. I'm trying to raise awareness. Look, I don't know how to break it to you, but you live in a small town. That makes whatever happens here small news. But if I get

177

out there and share this story with my followers, then we get people involved all over the country. Hell, we get them involved all over the world. I guarantee you in a matter of days, we'll have donations, money, supplies, pouring in."

"You say that like you don't think we're going to find him," I remark.

That's when Santiago heaves a frustrated sigh and runs his free hand through his hair.

"Of course I think we're going to find him. But the guy's been gone over twenty-four hours now. Statistically speaking, the chances of him being found are just going to keep getting lower and lower the longer he's missing. That's why it's important to get this information out there as soon as possible, just in case we *don't* find him tonight."

"Fine then. Get it out there. But can't you do that without the camera?"

"Oh my God, this is beginning to feel like an interrogation," Santiago laughs, but it's a laugh of pure exasperation. "Daniel, you know me. You know I'm a good guy, right? Help me out, here."

"You are a good guy, San. But I'm with Eloise on this one. Filming here tonight is inappropriate. Come on, you don't see me out here taking notes for my next novel, do you?" Daniel asks.

"I already told you I'm trying to help."

"And as Eloise pointed out, you can do that without the camera."

Finally, *finally*, Santiago backs down.

"Okay, you know what? Fine. You win. I'll put the camera away," he says, slipping the device inside his equipment case. "But if we come across *anything* that looks even remotely substantial or compelling,

I'm whipping this baby back out and I am documenting the hell out of it."

"Be our guest," Daniel tells him as two young volunteers approach us with our assignment and supplies.

Jason agrees to man the radio while Daniel and Logan each take a heavy flashlight. Since Santiago is still carting around his camera bag, that leaves the map to me. It covers roughly eighty-six acres of forest, which they've divided into twelve sections. We've been assigned to Section Three along with two other groups. If I'm reading this correctly, it takes us off the designated hiking trail, down and around a creek bed.

"Remember everyone," Chief Wilde calls out. "Stay safe and stay together."

Then, armed with a flashlight of her own, she leads the first wave of volunteers into the dark, dense, and desolate woods.

Chapter Eighteen

"Jake!"

"Jake!"

"Jake Kingsley!"

The shouts and desperate calls of the search party echo through the night as our team trudges ever farther off the beaten path and into the untamed depths of the forest. Although I'm still not keen on venturing out into the woods after nightfall, this time, somehow, it feels different. Like I'm no longer at the mercy of the trees and shadows, but rather out to conquer them. Or at least discipline them for all the trouble they've caused.

Of course, it helps to know that I'm surrounded by over a hundred brave men and women and that we're all united by our shared desire to save a young man's life.

"Jake?" I call. "Jake, are you out there?"

"Hey, Jake!" Jason hollers from somewhere off to my right.

A brisk winter wind is our only response.

Shivering, I gravitate closer to Daniel.

"You okay?" he asks me.

"Just cold."

Immediately, he wraps an arm around my shoulders and pulls me as close to his warm body as our heavy coats will permit.

"We won't stay out too much longer," he promises. "To tell you the truth, I'm not sure there's anything out here to find."

"I hate to say it, but I'm beginning to think the same thing." It's true. We've been searching almost three hours now with no sign of Jake Kingsley. "But if he isn't here... where is he?"

"You know, I've been thinking about it. About the best possible scenarios. There aren't many," he admits. "But there is a chance he just... up and left. I mean, it would be a shitty thing to do to his girlfriend, to just take off and leave her here. But at least it would mean he's still alive somewhere."

"Over here!"

The shout comes from several meters ahead of us. Immediately, Daniel and I break into a sprint. We follow the voices down to a frozen creek bed, where a woman who looks to be about my age is shining her flashlight across the frozen creek and onto two downed logs that extend out over the ice.

"What is that? Do you see that?" she's asking the man standing next to her.

"Stay here," he says. Then he takes two cautious steps out onto the slick, solid surface of the creek.

He's just reached the other side when Santiago comes flying through the underbrush, camera in hand and already rolling.

"What is it?" he breathes.

"We don't know," Daniel answers.

"Hey! Did you find something?" Logan hollers from somewhere behind us.

"Just get over here!" Santiago yells back.

I feel my breath catch in my throat as the man investigating the fallen logs kneels down and picks something up out of the snow. From here, it's hard to make out, but whatever it is reflects the beam of someone's flashlight. Like a mirror. A strange red mirror.

Then, he glances up at the logs themselves.

"What the hell...?" I hear him murmur from across the creek.

"What is it?" his companion asks.

"I don't know..." he replies. "It looks like... scratch marks. And... oh, God..."

"What?" the woman presses.

"I think... I think this is blood."

Blood.

My stomach turns at the sound of the word. Desperate, I reach out for Daniel, who steadies me.

Santiago, meanwhile, is already sprinting across the ice. He's just reached the other side when Jason and Logan burst onto the scene.

"What's happening?" Logan asks.

"Did you find him?" Jason wants to know.

"No. But he was here," the man answers definitively.

"And he wasn't alone," Santiago mutters, inspecting the supposed scratch marks.

Part of me wants to go over and examine the logs myself. But the other part is terrified of what I might find.

"How do you know?" I ask, my voice trembling. "I mean... how do you know he was here?"

The man doesn't answer. He simply lifts his hands up for all of us to see. It takes me a minute to register what I'm looking at, to understand the significance of a pair of sunglasses. But then I catch that flash of red again and I remember.

Black sunglasses.

Red lenses.

The very same that Jake Kingsley was wearing yesterday when he went missing.

Over the next two hours, officers and volunteers alike scour the land near and around where the sunglasses were found. Those with sharp eyes are told to keep watch for more strange scratch marks in the trees or blood on the snow, but there's none. A few hunters are able to distinguish a path of tracks a few meters away from the two fallen logs, but it leads them nowhere. With no new sightings or discoveries, the volunteers are dismissed shortly after midnight.

Daniel and I drive back to my house in silence. We're both famished, exhausted, and struggling, I think, to process everything that's happened tonight.

We didn't find him. After five hours of relentless searching. Jake Kingsley is still missing. And yet, he was there. We know that now. Beyond the shadow of a doubt, we know that Jake was in those woods.

"*And he wasn't alone.*" Santiago's words echo in my mind and they chill me to the bone. He sounded so certain. That may be what frightens me the most. That sense of certainty.

Because if Jake is still out there, it means that whoever - or *what*ever - was with him is still out there, too.

"What a night, huh?" Daniel asks as we pull to a stop in front of my house. It's completely dark, no lights lit save for the lamp on the porch. It looks so haunting in the dark.

"Yeah," I reply listlessly.

"You going to be okay?"

"Yeah. I have to be." This time, I sound more confident, though I don't necessarily feel it. "Do you um... want to come in? I can make you something warm. Tea or coffee, maybe? Or soup?"

I'm almost afraid he's going to think me too forward, especially considering the evening we've just endured. But, to my great relief, he smiles.

"Soup actually sounds great," he tells me.

As he follows me along my short walkway and up the steps leading to my front porch, I realize this will be his first time inside my house, and I can't help but wonder what he'll think of it. It's comfortable and cozy, but it isn't very big and it certainly isn't new. It's not all that tidy either, come to think of it.

"I apologize in advance for the mess," I murmur as I attempt to unlock the front door with trembling hands.

"Not important," he assures me.

Once we're inside, I turn a few lights on in the living room before immediately excusing myself to check on Isaac. He and my mom are both fast asleep in my bed. I decide not to disturb them.

Quietly, I make my way back downstairs, where I find Daniel browsing my bookshelves.

"You've got some good books here," he says.

"Thanks. I wish I could tell you I've read all of them."

"Have you gotten around to this one yet?" he asks lightly, holding an older hardback novel up for me to see.

Oh, Lord. It's Jason's copy of *Underworld*. I completely forgot I still had it.

"I tried that one," I admit, blushing furiously.

"And?" Now he's grinning.

"Well... I like the author," I offer.

"I guess that's good to know," he laughs. Then, he slips his free hand around my waist and lowers his mouth to mine.

Despite my weariness, his kiss sends my heart into a frenzy. Slowly, I lift up my arms and wrap them around his shoulders as a million and one new and contradicting emotions engulf me. Desire. Fear. Comfort. Blessed relief and at the same time, an unsettling sense of remorse for the young man we failed out in the woods. After five hours of trudging through the bitter cold, I am profoundly aware of just how fortunate I am to be safe and warm inside my home. To have my mother and son here.

And to have Daniel here.

It's funny. I'd have thought a man like Daniel, successful and celebrated, would seem out of place in my small, simple world. But somehow, he fits right in.

"You know," he murmurs, pressing his forehead to mine. "We still haven't been on a proper date."

I can't help but smile a little. With everything that's been happening, going on proper dates, unfortunately, hasn't been much of a priority.

"Well, there's nothing stopping us from having one right now," I reply softly.

Then, with one last kiss, I lead him into the kitchen, where I retrieve two small firewood-scented candles and a couple of crystal wine glasses I inherited from my grandmother.

"So... I don't actually have wine," I admit. "But I do have apple juice. Or I could make you some coffee."

Daniel laughs.

"That's okay. I'll probably just sip on some water."

He helps himself as I empty a can of chicken noodle soup into a pot and set it on the stove. While I wait for it to heat up, I reach into the bread box and retrieve a few pieces of ciabatta. Then, just to make things fancy, I pour a little olive oil onto a dish and sprinkle in a dash of rosemary.

"Wow, you're trying to spoil me," Daniel grins.

"Don't get used to it," I warn him. "Most nights, it's the microwave around here."

"Better than my house. Unless Hettie and Theresa come over and cook for us, we order out."

"Do they come over a lot?"

"A couple of times a week."

"I know they love having both of you here," I smile.

"You know, they're actually planning to stop by Saturday. Why don't you and Isaac join us?"

"Really?"

"Yeah. We can make dinner, play in the snow, have a game night," he says. "What do you think?"

"I think it sounds wonderful," I reply.

We eat our soup in a comfortable silence and by the time we've both finished and rinsed out the bowls, it's nearly two in the morning. However, neither one of us is ready to say goodnight. So I fetch a few spare blankets and pillows from my upstairs closet while Daniel sets a couple of fresh logs in the fireplace. As the flames flicker to life, I arrange the blankets, comforters, and couch cushions into a makeshift bed on the floor.

"You sure this is okay?" Daniel asks, pulling me into his arms.

"Mmhmm," I breathe. "I want you to stay."

Reassured, he relaxes and presses his lips to my forehead. Then, he takes my hand and laces his fingers through mine. It occurs to me then just how long it's been since I've had someone to hold me on a cold January night, to have a strong, steady heartbeat to listen to while I fall asleep. For the first time in a very long time, I feel blissfully and utterly complete.

"You know, I just thought of something," Daniel murmurs, sounding sleepy.

"What's that?" I wonder.

"What if your mom wakes up and catches us?"

"Believe me, she'd be thrilled."

"Oh, would she?"

"She thinks I'm a spinster," I explain with a yawn.

Daniel laughs beneath me.

"I think you still have a few years before you qualify," he teases. Then, his tone turns serious. "You aren't planning on adopting any cats, are you?"

"I can't. Isaac's allergic," I sigh.

Daniel chuckles again, but his silent laughter gives way to a stifled yawn.

"I don't know how much longer I can stay awake," he admits.

"Then rest," I whisper, drifting on the edge of sleep myself.

Slipping into subconsciousness, images of sparkling ice and dazzling blue stars begin to dance in my mind. I see Isaac playing in the fresh snow and Daniel reading a book by a strange silvery fire. But there's something else. A figure, a fleeting shadow, passing through a maze of white willow trees.

No. No, they're not trees. They're curtains.

I'm at home.

In my living room.

And the shadow is outside my window.

Alarmed, I gasp and bolt upright, startling Daniel.

"Everything okay?" he asks.

I don't respond immediately. My attention is fixed on my moonlit, bright, and blessedly empty living room window.

Was there something there? Or was it just a dream?

It had to have been a dream. It couldn't have been real. Why would anyone be walking around my front porch at this time of night?

You've had a long day, the soft and often unheard voice of reason reminds me. *You're exhausted, you're emotional, and you're still scared for Jake. And now you're letting your fear get the better of you.*

"Eloise?" Daniel whispers.

"I'm sorry," I finally answer. "Bad dream."

"It's okay," Daniel assures me, coaxing me back down into his embrace. "You're okay."

For the moment, I choose to believe him.

Chapter Nineteen

I stumble through my last workday of the week in a sort of sleep-deprived stupor. And it isn't just me. Everyone seems a little out of sorts. Daniel doesn't even come in to write. He sends me a text message explaining that after dropping Addie off at school, he decided to take the day off and catch up on his beauty rest.

I'm not kidding you. That's exactly what the message says.

hey. think i'm gonna take the day off. gotta catch up on my beauty rest.

Far too tired to think up a witty comeback, I reply, *Not fair.*

To which he immediately responds, **sure it is. you don't need beauty rest.**

Oh my God, that is so corny. But I'd be lying if I said it didn't make me smile.

Saturday morning, I awake feeling refreshed, rejuvenated, and eager for an afternoon with Daniel, Addie, and the crazy aunts, as Daniel lovingly refers to them. He texts me shortly after ten, letting me know that Hettie and Theresa are planning to arrive around 3:00 this afternoon.

Can't wait! Can Isaac and I bring anything? I ask him.

maybe dessert? this may come as a shock to you, but theresa doesn't believe in sugar.

Total shock. Never would have guessed, I reply. Then I ask, *What does Addie like?*

cookies, ice cream, cake... she's not picky.

Good to know. Because Isaac is. I think he'll be happy with cookies, though.

sounds perfect.

So, after a late breakfast and an hour of Saturday morning cartoons, Isaac and I make a quick trip into town for cookies. Our local grocery store isn't all that big, but the produce is always fresh and the baked goods are always top-notch.

"Mom, are we going to make the cookies?" Isaac asks.

"I don't know if we'll have time, Sweetheart. Is it okay if we just buy some?"

"I guess," Isaac replies, heaving an outrageously dramatic sigh.

"What kind do you want?"

"Um... Chocolate chip. No! Peanut butter. Wait.... um..." I can see the little wheels in Isaac's head working overtime as he struggles to choose a favorite cookie.

"Since it's a special occasion, why don't you pick two?" I suggest.

"Um okay. Chocolate chip. And frosted." In six-year-old vernacular, *frosted* translates to iced sugar cookies.

"Are you sure?"

"Yes. No, wait! M&M's!"

"You want chocolate chip *and* M&M's?"

"Um... no."

"Tell you what. Why don't we go grab a few other groceries while you think about it. Then, once we're done, you can make your decision. Does that sound good?"

"Yes," Isaac answers with certainty.

If there's one thing I've learned in my time, it's never let a trip to the grocery store go to waste, especially when you're a single parent. I don't care if I don't think I need anything. I guarantee you I will find something to buy.

This time, it's toothpaste, Flintstones vitamins, and waffles.

We've just tossed the vitamins into the shopping cart when we turn a corner and very nearly collide with a fellow shopper in the frozen foods aisle.

"Whoa!" he exclaims.

"Oh! Excuse us, I'm so..." But my words catch in my throat and my apology dies on my lips as I find myself staring into the amber eyes of Cortland Hill.

"Eloise!" He smiles that unnervingly familiar smile. "This is a nice surprise."

"Um, yeah." He's harmless. I know this. And yet, I still find myself fighting a wild impulse to shield Isaac from him. "What um... what brings you out this morning?"

"I'm just here to grab a few microwave meals. I've been so wrapped up in researching the new book, I keep forgetting to feed myself!"

"Oh. That's not good." I try to laugh, but I'm afraid my attempt is a feeble one.

"Maybe you could take me out to dinner sometime. Make sure I remember to eat."

Um. Okay. That is *very* direct. And completely unexpected.

"Actually, my evenings are pretty busy. Don't have a lot of time to go out," I reply.

"That's understandable. You've got this little guy to take care of," he says, turning his attention to Isaac. I can feel my stomach tying itself into cold knots as he asks, "What's your name?"

"Isaac."

"It's a pleasure to meet you, Isaac. I remember you from the Carnival."

"I had a snowman on my cheek," Isaac reminds him.

"That's right! You did! And your mother had those beautiful, shimmering sparkles."

"Good memory," I remark.

"It's a gift," he winks.

Again, I recoil.

"Okay, well, it was nice running into you, but we actually have to get going. Come on, Sweetheart."

I take Isaac's hand and attempt to pull him away, but Hill stops us.

"Before you go, I was wondering if there might be a good time to come in and discuss that book signing next week."

Of course. Suddenly, all his flattery makes sense. He's not interested in me at all. He's interested in what I can do for him.

Thank God.

"Um, any time, really. Business tends to be a little slower in the mornings."

"Then I'll drop by first thing Monday."

"Sounds good," I tell him.

"Have you read any of the books I left with you?" he asks.

"To tell you the truth, I'm not much of a horror fan. I think my assistant Jason is reading them, though."

"Huh. Well, if that's the case, maybe I should consider dabbling in something a little friendlier. Maybe romance." The way he smiles at me makes me deeply uncomfortable.

"Never too late to try something new," I remark briskly. "Now, I'm sorry, but we really do need to be going. We have plans this afternoon. Come on, Isaac."

"Enjoy your weekend, Eloise! You too, little man!" Hill calls after us as we make our way further and further down the frozen foods aisle. And as far away from him as we can get.

Shortly after 3:00, Isaac and I arrive at Daniel's masterpiece of a house, where Hettie and Theresa's old Cadillac is already parked in the driveway.

"Whoa!" Isaac exclaims as I help him climb out of the car.

"Pretty neat, huh?"

"It looks like Elsa's ice castle!"

"I don't think it's quite *that* extravagant," I laugh.

"Do you think Adelaide likes *Frozen*?"

"I don't know. Why don't you ask her?" I suggest as the front door to the ice castle opens and Daniel steps out onto the porch.

"Hey!" He greets us with a broad smile.

"Hello, Mr. Daniel," Isaac replies.

"You can just call me Daniel, Isaac. What have you got there?" Daniel asks, eyeing the bakery package in my son's hands.

"Cookies. They're chocolate chip and peanut butter. But we bought them at the store. Mom didn't make them."

Called out by a first grader. This afternoon is off to a great start.

"That's okay. I bet they still taste pretty good," Daniel says.

"Probably much better than if I'd made them," I quip.

Daniel laughs and invites us inside where Hettie and Theresa are busy unpacking and organizing an assortment of herbs and spices. Addie, meanwhile, sits drawing at the kitchen table. Isaac's face lights up the minute he sees her.

"Hi, Adelaide!" he exclaims.

Addie looks up.

"Hi," she replies shyly.

"Oh, Isaac! Eloise! You made it!" Hettie exclaims, dropping everything to greet Isaac and me with big hugs. "I cannot tell you how happy we were when Danny told us you two would be joining us this afternoon."

"We're happy to be here," I grin. "Aren't we, Honey?"

But Isaac is already halfway across the room and peering over Addie's shoulder. Well, sort of. He's not quite that tall just yet. But he is staring quite intently at Addie's sketch.

"What are you drawing?" he asks her.

"My manga," she answers.

"I like to draw," Isaac tells her.

"Do you want some paper and pencils?"

"Yes, please!"

With that, Isaac discards the cookies right onto the floor and makes himself at home next to Addie.

"Isaac!" I groan.

"Don't worry, I'll get them," Hettie says, making her way back into the kitchen.

"He's not annoying her, is he?" I ask Daniel once we're alone.

"Addie? Oh, no. As long as she's drawing, she's in Heaven."

"They have that in common. Though with Isaac, it's more storyboarding."

"That's kind of what she's doing with her manga. It's going to be a full book eventually."

"Guess she takes after her dad that way," I grin.

"Nah. She's a lot smarter than I ever was."

"That's Isaac, too. He's so smart. And so ambitious. So much more than I've ever been. Honestly, I have no idea where he gets it."

"God, we sound a lot like parents, don't we?" Daniel grins. "What do you say I give you a tour of the rest of the house? You didn't get to see all of it the other day."

"Yeah, that sounds great," I blush. "Unless Hettie and Theresa need some help with dinner."

"Not a bit! You kids go have fun!" Hettie insists.

As Daniel guides me through the house, I can't help but notice there are far fewer boxes lining the halls. He's also hung up some new artwork. I actually recognize a few of the paintings as Theresa's. She loves painting trees, mountains, and streams and her work is always vibrant and colorful with just a touch of magic.

After a quick walkthrough of the ground floor, I follow Daniel up a short flight of stairs for a tour of the guest bedroom (which, apparently, Hettie and Theresa have already claimed for themselves), the media room (with an even larger television than the one in the living room), and Daniel's home office. His office, I must say, is truly a wonder to behold. The farthest wall is a built-in bookcase, filled not just with a magnificent collection of novels, but with awards, photographs, and literary knick-knacks. His desk is a little cluttered, but it faces a floor-to-ceiling window overlooking a beautiful range of mountains.

"Daniel... this is incredible. And this view..." I sigh. "Why do you spend so much time at the bookstore when you could be here?"

He shrugs.

"I like the view better at the bookstore."

Then, without skipping a beat, he slips his hands around my waist and kisses me. Suddenly, I'm feeling as silly and giddy as a besotted teenager.

Once the kiss ends, Daniel takes my hand and leads me out of his study and up one more short flight of stairs.

"Your house is like a labyrinth," I observe. "Or a glass funhouse."

"That sounds like an interesting concept for a book," Daniel remarks as we reach the final landing. "So, that's Addie's room," he says, indicating the first door at the right side of the hall. "And the door next to it is her bathroom. I can't tell you how tidy they are, though, so we might skip those for now."

"That's fine," I smile. I have a feeling he's protecting his daughter's privacy more than anything. And I appreciate him for it.

That just leaves the door at the far end of the hall.

Daniel's bedroom.

Like the rest of the house, it's very bright and open with floor-to-ceiling windows and an elegant simplicity in its decor and design. The king-sized bed in the middle of the room is rather poorly made, but it looks so comfortable that a few crooked pillows are easily overlooked. And the tables on either side of the bed are empty, except for a reading lamp and a picture of Addie.

"My room really isn't all that much," Daniel admits. "Now, the bathroom, on the other hand..."

"I'm sorry. The *bathroom*?" Where exactly is he going with this?

"Just go look," he tells me.

With a skeptical glance, I cross the room and open the door to the adjoining bathroom. Inside, I see an ordinary toilet, sink, walk-in shower... and a bathtub the size of a Jacuzzi. In fact, I think it may very well *be* a Jacuzzi.

"What in the..." That's it. Words have officially failed me.

"Like it?" Daniel grins.

"I do, it's just... I've never seen one of these before. Not in someone's home, anyway. And definitely not in Cedar Ridge."

"I usually try not to go too crazy with money... but sometimes, a man's got to buy himself a hot tub."

That's when I absolutely lose it. I dissolve into a fit of hysterical giggles.

"That... is the most ridiculous thing I've ever heard."

"Come on. You wouldn't treat yourself to one of these babies if you had the chance?" Daniel asks, his eyes alight with his own amusement.

"Well... maybe. If I knew I had enough set aside for food. And house payments. And Isaac's college fund. Then I *might* consider investing in my own personal indoor hot tub."

Daniel laughs. Then, he takes my hands and gently laces his fingers through mine.

"You want to try this one out?"

Now, I'm blushing. Furiously. *Crimson*.

"What?" My heart is fluttering so fast, I'm barely able to breathe, let alone speak.

"Not now, of course. But... it's worth mentioning that Hettie and Theresa offered to take the kids to the movies later. Give us some time together, just the two of us. But that's only if it's something you would be comfortable with. I don't want to pressure you or make you think that I'm coming on too strong."

With that, I feel my every inhibition wash away. For so long, I've kept my heart and body under lock and key, terrified of what might happen if I opened myself back up again. To trust. To be vulnerable. To be loved. But now, every wall I've spent the last four years constructing is crumbling into dust. And suddenly, I know I'm ready.

"You know... it's been a while since Isaac's gone to see a movie," I finally say. "Let me go ask him what he thinks."

Daniel smiles. Then, he pulls me back into his arms and seals the deal with a kiss.

Chapter Twenty

We spend the better part of the next hour trying to convince Isaac and Addie to go out and play in the snow with us. But all either of them wants to do is sit and sketch.

"We can't go play in the snow now, Mom! Adelaide is teaching me how to draw Hamilton! Look!" Isaac exclaims, holding up a cartoon portrait of a cutesy colonial soldier who, upon closer inspection, does bear a striking resemblance to Lin-Manuel Miranda as Alexander Hamilton.

"Wow. Addie, that is *really* good," I tell her.

"Thank you," Addie blushes.

"It's manga," Isaac explains. "Mom, can I have a manga?"

"Sure. I'll look around and see what we have at the store," I tell him. "But, in the meantime, are you sure you don't want to go build a snowman?"

"No. It's okay."

"There's a lot more snow out there than at home."

"Eloise, Dear, I don't think it's going to happen," Hettie tells me. "But you can always come and help Theresa and me in the kitchen."

We've decided to eat dinner early, around 5:00, so that Hettie, Theresa, and the kids will have plenty of time to make it to the movies. I don't know what they're going to see, but I can tell you Isaac was far more enthusiastic about sitting in a dark movie theater with his new friend than playing in the snow with his mom. I'm trying not to take that personally.

After a homestyle dinner of fresh salad, steamed vegetables, scalloped potatoes, roast chicken, and whole wheat dinner rolls, Theresa and Hettie stuff the kids into their coats and load them up in their car.

"Now, don't you two worry about the dishes. We'll get to them tomorrow," Hettie assures us with a wink as they make their way out the door. "Have a good evening."

Once they're gone, Daniel and I look at one another.

"She's been planning this, hasn't she?" I ask.

"Since the moment I told her I was moving here," Daniel affirms.

"Well... I'm glad she approves."

"Are you kidding? She's crazy about you. Seriously, if something happened between us and things didn't work out, she'd kick me out of the family and adopt you."

"I doubt that," I laugh. Although I appreciate the compliment.

"It's true. Not that I want to test that theory..." he says as he steps forward and gently tucks a stray lock of my auburn hair behind my ear.

Following his lead, I rise up on my tiptoes and brush his lips with mine.

For a short while, we stand holding each other in silence. Then, he takes a slow, deep breath.

"Are you all right?" I ask him.

"Yeah," he assures me.

"Are you nervous?"

"A little," he admits. "Do you remember the other day when you said that you hadn't done this in a while?"

"Yes."

"It's been a while for me, too. Probably not quite as long. But... it's been a *very* long time since it meant anything. And... I guess I just want you to know that I'm... I'm not just here for a good time, you know? I want you to know that this means something. *You* mean something."

In that moment, I have no words for him. I have no thoughts. I can only kiss him.

Then, I take his hand and silently lead the way upstairs.

Falling into bed with Daniel, I finally let myself appreciate just how damn sexy he is. True, I've always thought he was handsome and yes, I've fantasized about him since the beginning. But I never dared to dream that he might be mine. *Really* mine. And now that he is, I don't know if I'll ever get enough of him.

Every time he kisses me, every time he moves me, I feel overpowered. But in the best possible way.

Afterward, I drape myself over his bare chest and run my fingers through his beard.

"You okay?" he asks, gazing at me with sleepy blue eyes.

"I'm wonderful," I smile.

"You really are," he replies with a flirtatious smirk.

"I was afraid I'd be out of practice," I admit.

"You were perfect," Daniel assures me, running a hand up through my gloriously untamed hair. Then, he trails his fingers down my back and begins tracing small circles on my skin.

"How about you?" I ask him, savoring his touch.

"Me?"

"Yeah. Are you okay?"

"I'm better than okay," he answers, pressing his lips to my forehead. "This... is the happiest I've been in a long time."

"Really?" I find that hard to believe. Not that he doesn't sound sincere. But this is a man who's lived the kind of life that most only ever dream about. I can't imagine his immense success hasn't kindled at least a little joy over the years.

"Really. Don't get me wrong, life has been good to me. Probably a lot better than I deserve. But when I moved away from Addie... I lost sight of what really mattered. I let myself get caught up in everything that life threw at me. I took the book deals and the accolades and the money... and for a while, I had myself convinced that it was everything I could ever want. But it was just... meaningless," he explains. "But these last few weeks here with Addie, with Hettie and Theresa, with you... I can't imagine life gets any better." With that, he pulls me close and presses his mouth to mine, but he abruptly pulls away mere moments later. "Unless, that is... you want to continue this in the hot tub."

Once again, the notion of the hot tub is so absurd that I have to laugh.

Though I have to admit I *am* curious. So I wrap myself in a discarded sheet and follow him into the bathroom.

"You know, I think Isaac could actually swim in this," I remark as Daniel fills the tub with hot water.

"Mock me all you want. Once you experience it, you're going to wonder how you ever lived without it."

"It's funny. If you had asked me what I thought I might find in the home of the master of modern horror, I never, in a million years, would have guessed a hot tub."

"The master of modern horror?"

"It's what Jason calls you."

"Ah," Daniel says. "So, does he know about us?"

"No. I mean, he thinks I have a crush on you. He's been teasing me about it since before he even met you."

"Oh yeah?" Daniel's eyes sparkle in the dim lighting. "Do you have a crush on me?"

"No, not at all. I'm here for the hot tub."

"Makes sense."

Once the tub is nearly full, he shuts the water off and offers me his hand.

"Ladies first," he grins.

Feeling only slightly self-conscious, I let the bed sheet fall to the floor. Even though he's already well acquainted with the way I look, it's still a strange sensation, allowing myself to be so exposed. After pregnancy, childbirth, and six years of parenting, my body is far from perfect. I carry excess weight in my thighs and my lower stomach, and my once-petite breasts now bear the scars of stretch marks. Yet Daniel still looks at me like I'm beautiful.

Taking his hand, I step up and ease myself into the blessedly warm water. The tub itself is so deep that the water goes almost all the way up to my shoulders.

"So, what do you think?" Daniel asks, slipping in beside me.

"I feel like I'm at a spa," I reply with a laugh.

"It gets better," Daniel grins. Then, he flips a switch and suddenly, the water in the tub is swirling with streams of bubbles.

"This is... unreal," I laugh.

"You love it, don't you?"

"I could get used to it," I reply, keeping it coy.

"Oh, right," he scoffs playfully. Then, he grabs me around the waist and pulls me right up onto his lap.

Draping my legs over his, I clasp one hand around the back of his neck and guide his mouth to mine.

Kissing in a hot tub is a whole new sensation for me. Lance wasn't exactly the romantic type. He loved me, at least I think he did, but he was never able to express his emotions in a healthy way. He seemed to think showing affection was a sign of weakness. There were nights that he couldn't even touch me unless he was intoxicated.

But Daniel... the way his hands explore and caress my body as I sink further into his embrace... his sense of intimacy is effortless. He isn't afraid to share himself with me. And I'm not ashamed to want every inch of him.

After we've dried off and changed back into our clothes, Daniel retrieves a couple of blankets from his closet.

"So, do you want to build a fire?" he asks me.

"I'd love to," I smile, imagining how cozy his living room might feel by firelight.

To my surprise, however, he doesn't take me downstairs. We detour on the second floor, making our way out a sliding glass door and onto a balcony. The view out here is absolutely breathtaking. The winter night is calm, quiet, and bathed in the soft, mesmerizing glow of moonlight on the snow. And the mountains. Oh, the mountains. From here, they seem to stretch on into eternity. And they very well may.

"Not bad, huh?" Daniel asks, kneeling down onto the floor. It's only then that I notice the patio furniture and fire pit.

"It's beautiful," I sigh. "I feel like I could touch the stars out here."

"That's one of my favorite things about Cedar Ridge. In the big city, there's so much light pollution, you can't see anything. The sky is just... so still and empty," he says, striking a match and tossing it into the fire pit. As the flames flicker to life, he rises up to his feet and walks over to me. "I didn't want that for Addie. I wanted her to grow up in a place where she could really see the stars."

"Well, I think you came to the right place."

"I think we did, too," Daniel agrees. Then, he kisses me softly on the mouth before saying, "I should've asked earlier, but do you want anything? Coffee? Wine?"

"You don't have any s'mores makings, do you?" I grin.

"I... might have stale graham crackers..." he grimaces playfully.

"Maybe I'll just take a glass of wine, then."

"Red or white?"

"Red. White wine always tastes like summer to me."

"Cabernet? Merlot? Pinot Noir?"

"Surprise me," I tell him. I don't want to admit that I don't actually know the difference. I don't drink wine very often, and when I do, it's usually the cheapest bottle I can find.

"Be right back," Daniel says, wrapping one of the blankets around my shoulders.

With a sigh and a smile, I turn my gaze back toward the miles of snow-covered mountains and attempt to process everything that's happened in the past couple of hours.

This is real, I tell myself. *This isn't a dream or a fantasy or a really, really amazing book. This is actually happening.*

I'm trying my best not to lose my head. After all, Daniel and I really haven't known each other all that long. We haven't even discussed what it is we're looking for. And maybe we don't need to. Not yet, anyway. Perhaps, for the moment, all we really need is to enjoy this.

Whatever this may be.

Excerpt from *The Possession*
By D.H. Whittaker

It couldn't be true.

No. Not after everything they'd been through together.

Carter couldn't be dead. It just didn't make sense.

Tanner Bray paced anxiously back and forth, from one cold stone wall to another, wracking his brain, desperate to make sense of the last twenty-four hours. Desperate to even remember.

It had started out like any other investigation. Carter filming, documenting. Tanner leading the way, calling out to any spirits, earthly or otherwise, that may be present. And if local folklore was to be believed, there were plenty of spirits haunting the abandoned remains of the Green Springs Psychiatric Hospital.

Tanner had never been afraid of what couldn't be explained. He walked willfully into the dark depths of the unknown. And he had convinced Carter to do the same.

Carter. His lifelong best friend. The eternal optimist.

He's dead, *a cold, bitter voice reminded him.* He's dead. And it's your fault.

"No!" Tanner cried out.

It couldn't have been his fault. Tanner may have led Carter into the pits of hell, but he would have thrown himself into the flames before letting anything happen to his friend. He would have died trying to protect him. There had to be some mistake. Maybe the cops had it all wrong. Maybe it wasn't Carter's body that they'd found. Maybe he had run... run far away from whatever it was that had taken hold of Tanner. Maybe he was home safe right now, at that very moment...

Home.

God, what would his family have heard? Would they know where he was? Would they know what had happened to Carter?

Would Carter's mother know?

No. No, not Joy. Anyone but her.

Carter was her whole life. Her only child.

Tanner felt a physical pain twisting in his gut as he imagined her anguish. The thought of sweet Joy crumpled and broken, weeping for her boy... it was more than he could bear.

Overcome by guilt and grief and everything in between, Tanner fell to the floor and vomited.

"Hey! You'd better clean that up in there!" a guard spat at him through the steel bars of his desolate cell.

Tanner grimaced and retched again.

Once the heaving finally subsided, he reached up and wiped the sick away from his mouth with the back of his hand. The sensation of the vile, sticky substance on his skin triggered a sort of visceral reaction and he quickly succumbed to a severe panic attack.

The blood. *He shuddered violently at the mere memory. The blood had covered him. He could still feel it dripping down his face, soaking his shirt. He could see it staining his fingers a deep, rusted red.*

The blood. Carter's blood.

It couldn't be true.

But it was.

On a bright and cloudless day, within the decrepit and decaying walls of an abandoned hospital, Tanner Bray had murdered his best friend.

Chapter Twenty-One

I'm still smiling when I drive into downtown on Monday morning. Although I didn't get to see Daniel yesterday, we've been in constant communication since our liaison Saturday night. It really hasn't been anything serious. Mostly pictures and a flirtatious joke here and there. Still, every time his name flashes across my screen, my heart flutters.

I sober up almost immediately, however, when I catch a glimpse of the Missing posters plastered on every window of every shop on Main Street.

Jake Kingsley.

It's been almost five days now and there's still no sign of him. After the initial search, the authorities called in a professional search and rescue team, but they were also unsuccessful. Now, it seems the media's getting involved. I'm in the process of unlocking the bookstore when I notice a camera crew getting ready to film in front of one of the souvenir shops. Incidentally, the same shop that specializes in Bogman merchandise.

I try not to think about them - the media or the Bogman - as I flit through my Monday morning chores. Alas, when Jason arrives a few minutes later, it's all he can talk about.

"Did you see the news crew?" he asks, his eyes wide behind his glasses.

"Yeah, I did," I answer as I straighten out the Young Adult shelves.

"This is going to be huge. I mean, it's already huge. And you know, of course I don't mean that in a good way. But everyone is going to be talking about this!"

"What do you mean?" I ask. I thought everyone was already talking about it.

"I thought you said you saw the reporters."

"I did. So?"

"Eloise, that isn't our tiny local station reporting down there. That's a *national* news crew."

"Wait, *what*?"

"Yeah! They've got a helicopter out there and everything!"

Okay, now this is a surprising development. Nothing, and I mean *nothing* has ever brought national news crews out to Cedar Ridge. Even the Bogman didn't get original coverage. All the news stations that circulated the story of that first sighting used recycled footage from our local media.

Curious and slightly confused, I make my way over to the window behind the cash register. Sure enough, a jet-black news helicopter hangs low in the sky, hovering over the town.

"What is going on around here?" I mutter under my breath.

"They're here for Jake Kingsley," Jason answers, gazing out the window with me.

"I know, but hundreds of thousands of people go missing every year. You only hear about a handful on the national news."

"It must be Santiago," Jason says. "He's been sharing the story and posting updates on all his social media platforms trying to raise awareness."

"Oh. Well, that's good of him."

"Yeah. Hey, maybe Mr. Whittaker should say something. You know, reach out to his readers."

"I don't think he's really a social media guy," I respond. "Besides, he isn't D.H. Whittaker here, remember? He's just Daniel."

"Yeah, I know. But come on. Don't you think people are going to find out sooner or later?"

"Maybe, but for Addie's sake, I know he's hoping it's later."

Ding.

The shopkeeper's bell rings and my heart skips a beat. I turn, expecting to see Daniel. Cortland Hill smiles back at me instead.

"Bit of excitement happening this morning, isn't there?" he remarks.

"Oh, hey Cortland," Jason greets him. "Good to see you again."

"Likewise," he replies. "How are you liking *Tomorrow's Mercenary*?"

"I'm only a few chapters in so far, but it's good," Jason answers. Unfortunately for Mr. Hill, I've known Jason long enough to know that's his way of saying it isn't one of his favorites. Jason is a self-proclaimed certified fanboy. When he legitimately enjoys something, he raves about it. Tirelessly. Endlessly. On and on and on.

"Thank you. I'm glad you're enjoying it," Hill beams before turning his attention to me. "So, are you ready, Eloise?"

"I'm sorry?"

"To discuss the book signing."

"Oh, right. Of course," I laugh nervously.

"I was thinking either this Friday afternoon or maybe sometime early next week. Of course, it's whatever works for you. But I thought scheduling it later would give you a little extra time to really get the word out, maybe come up with some fun little advertisements."

"Yeah, that's... good thinking. But..." I hesitate, uncertain of how he might react to what I'm about to tell him. "The truth is, Mr. Hill... I've been giving it some thought and... I'm not sure now is the best time to be scheduling a book signing. Not right away, at least. It's just with everyone so on edge and with a young man still missing, I'm not sure it would be appropriate."

For the first time, the smile fades from Hill's face as he considers what I've just said. Before he can respond, however, the front door opens and Daniel steps inside.

"Hey," he greets me with a broad grin.

"Hi," I reply, suddenly feeling very pink around the cheeks.

"Brought you a treat," he announces, handing me a reusable souvenir cup from The Mountain Cafe. And it just so happens to be full of sweet, steaming coffee.

"You're the best," I smile.

It's only then, as I accept the gift, that I realize Hill's gaze has shifted and is now fixed on Daniel.

"Sorry," Daniel apologizes. "Didn't mean to interrupt."

"Not a problem," Hill assures him with a suave smile.

"Um, Daniel, this is Cortland Hill," I say.

If Daniel recognizes the name, he hides it well.

"Good to meet you," Daniel says, shaking Hill's hand. "You new in town, too?"

"Just passing through. I'm here to research the new book I'm writing."

That's when I notice the slightest shift in Daniel's demeanor.

"A writer, huh? Tough gig," he remarks.

"Not for all of us," Hill counters. "In fact, Eloise and I were just determining what date would work best for a book signing."

"Oh. Well, good luck with that," Daniel says. Then he turns to me. "You okay? Do you need anything?" I'm pretty sure this is his way of asking me if I'd like him to stick around.

"I uh, I think I'm okay," I tell him. "But thank you. And thanks for the latte."

"Don't mention it," he replies. Then he takes one last look at Hill before disappearing into the lounge.

I watch him retreat, wishing I could follow. Wishing that the rest of the world would just fall away.

"He seems nice," Hill comments.

"He is," I say. "Anyway, as I was saying - "

"Listen, I know you have your concerns. It's understandable. This town has been through a lot this past week. But you see, that's why I think now is the perfect time to do this. We all need something to take our minds off of what's happening, and I think a book signing is just the ticket. Give the people of Cedar Ridge something to smile about. Something to look forward to."

I stare at the man standing before me, momentarily at a loss for words. I understand taking pride in your work, but Cortland Hill must really think the world of himself if he believes a book signing is all it will take to make everyone forget about Jake Kingsley and the Bogman.

"That... is very gracious of you," I manage to say. "But I still don't think it's a very good idea. I'm sorry. It's not at all personal. It's just... I know this town. If I were to host any signing or special event in the middle of a crisis... it would reflect badly on everyone involved. I don't want that for you."

Finally, Hill nods.

"I appreciate that. And I understand." He smiles, but it doesn't quite reach his eyes. Then he clears his throat and says, "Well, I think I've taken up enough of your valuable time. If you'll excuse me..."

With that, he ducks out the front door, leaving the shopkeeper's bell ringing in his wake.

Daniel reappears almost immediately.

"Everything okay?" he asks.

"Yeah," I answer. "I told him that with everything going on right now, I didn't think the signing was a very good idea and... I think he was disappointed."

"But he was the guy, right? The one you asked me about last week?"

"Yeah. That was him. What'd you think?"

"Seems a bit full of himself, but he wouldn't be the first to let the power of the pen go to his head. I mean, some of us think we're so great, we buy ourselves hot tubs."

Oh my God, I *knew* he'd bring up the hot tub!

"The hot tub... was a good investment," I comment casually as my cheeks flush a brilliant pink.

"Glad you approve," Daniel grins. Then, he leans forward and across the counter until his lips are a mere whisper away from mine. For a moment, I wonder if he's teasing me. Then he asks, "Is this okay?"

I close the distance between us in response.

Of course, Jason chooses this precise moment to come bounding back to the front of the store.

"Hey El, I've got a question..." he begins, but his voice trails off as soon as he sees Daniel and me. "Oh," he says once he's taken a moment to process what he's just witnessed. Finally, a sly grin spreads across his face. "So uh... this is a thing now, huh? You know, you two?"

"You said you had a question?" I ask.

"Well yeah, I did. But now I need to know exactly when all this officially started."

"Why?"

"Because if it was any time before last Monday, then Logan owes me twenty bucks."

"You're joking," I deadpan.

"Not in the slightest. Now, if you would please disclose the information so I can collect my winnings?"

I'm tempted to lie. I don't want to reward Jason for making stupid bets about my love life. Then again, I don't want the twenty bucks to go to Logan, either.

"Why don't I tell you after you tell me what you wanted to ask?" I suggest.

"Oh, right," Jason says. "You know how all these reporters are here and everything? Well, I was right. They're here because of what Santiago shared. Now ABC is requesting an interview with him and he's invited Logan and me to be a part of it too since, you know, we're filming the documentary and everything."

"So, are you asking me for time off?"

"Actually... I was going to ask if you wouldn't mind... if we filmed the interview here."

I blink.

Jason, Logan, and Santiago Edwards, plus a bustling camera crew and nosy reporters. Talking about the Bogman. In my store. My sweet little sanctuary.

It sounds like a damn nightmare.

"Before you say no," Jason continues, "I want you to consider why we're doing this. It isn't to promote the documentary. It isn't to make the Bogman mainstream. It's to try and save Jake Kingsley."

As soon as he mentions Jake, my resolve begins to weaken.

I don't want a noisy news crew setting up shop in my bookstore. But I *really* don't want Jake Kingsley to spend another night in the unknown.

"Okay," I finally agree.

"Yes! Thank you, Eloise. You're the best," Jason exclaims. "Now uh... about my twenty dollars?"

"Yeah, no. I think we're just going to keep our personal business to ourselves. What do you say, Daniel?" I ask.

"Do we get a cut?" he wants to know.

"You're a world-famous multi-millionaire and you want to know if you get a cut out of my twenty dollars?" Jason asks.

Daniel shrugs.

"I've got a kid to put through college and a new girlfriend to impress. Every little bit helps," he reasons.

I'm not too proud to admit that hearing Daniel call me his girlfriend sends me soaring straight to cloud nine.

Of course, I come crashing right back down when Jason says, "Please. You're literate and you know her coffee order. She's sold."

"Okay, I'm not *that* easily won," I argue, though I have no evidence to support this claim.

"She also really appreciates a good internet connection," Jason adds.

"Don't you have like, floors to sweep or something?" I ask.

"Actually, I need to call Logan back and let him know we're a go for the interview. Then I'll sweep the floors," Jason promises as he sprints off to retrieve his phone.

"And clean the windows while you're at it!" I call after him.

If he wants to have reporters and cameras in here, this whole store had better be sparkling by the time they show up.

Chapter Twenty-Two

Jason, Logan, and Santiago schedule their interview for 8 o'clock Tuesday morning. On the bright side, this means they should be finished by the time the store opens at 9:00. On the not-so-bright side, I have to get to work an hour earlier than usual which means my mom has to stay with Isaac and see him off to the school bus. She doesn't mind, of course. Still, I hate that I have to ask.

Now, as ABC's Beth Goldberry and her two cameramen set the stage for the interview in my lounge, I text Daniel and warn him to stay away. I don't know if Beth or her crew would recognize him as D.H. Whittaker, but I'd rather not take any chances.

"All right, boys, I think we're ready to get started," Beth says, taking a seat in what I've come to think of as Daniel's armchair. Santiago, Logan, and Jason all sit on the couch, which they've moved so that it's positioned right next to Beth. "Everyone ready? Any last-minute questions?"

"I think we're good to go!" Santiago answers with a bright, winsome smile. For the first time in the few days I've actually spent with him, he's dressed in a black button-down shirt and a red tie. Combined with his green hair, his outfit sort of makes him look like he's auditioning for a Christmas pageant. Logan and Jason are also dressed in their best.

"Then let's begin," Beth says. Then, she locks eyes with her cameramen and waits for their cue. "Since the very beginning, humankind has sought to make sense of the world around us. Our thirst for knowledge, our quest for deeper understanding has taken us from the farthest reaches of our galaxy to the foreign frontier of the ocean floor. But what if we've missed something? Something that may dwell just beyond the borders of our own backyards? Citizens of Cedar Ridge, a small town nestled in the Blue Ridge Mountains of North Carolina, may be about to find out.

"I'm joined by renowned cryptozoologist Santiago Edwards and local filmmakers Logan Taylor and Jason Harberger to discuss the disappearance of a young man... and the monster they believe is responsible.

"Santiago, let's start with you. You're known in paranormal circles for your work investigating claims of legendary creatures all across the globe. What drew you here to Cedar Ridge?"

"To answer honestly, I was invited. You see, I was a guest speaker at a winter festival a few weeks back and I really hadn't intended to stay for more than a day or so. But then a friend of mine introduced me to Logan and Jason here and when they told me about the documentary they're working on, I became invested. Ask anyone and they'll tell you they've heard of Bigfoot and Nessie. But the Bogman is relatively new to the cryptozoological scene. And I wanted to learn more about him."

"And what have you learned so far?" Beth asks.

"Its history. Its first sighting. We actually sat down with a few eyewitnesses who were willing to share their stories with us. And of course, Logan and Jason here have conducted quite a bit of impressive research on their own."

"Logan, Jason, the two of you have lived here in Cedar Ridge your whole lives," Beth says. "Tell me a little about life here in town and the kind of impact recent events have had on you and the community."

It goes on like this for a while. For the whole interview, basically. And by the time it ends, I'm feeling more than a little irritated and confused.

"Well, I thank you boys for your time, and thank you, Ms. Keller, for providing us with such a lovely setting," Beth smiles as she and her cameramen show themselves out.

"My pleasure," I reply listlessly, though I'm fairly certain they don't hear me.

"Oh man, this was great! Eloise, thank you so, so much for letting us use your store," Santiago beams.

"Yeah, Ms. Keller. You're the best!" Logan adds.

"El? Everything okay?" Jason asks.

"I guess I just don't really understand. What was the point of all that?" I ask.

"What do you mean? You know what it was for," Santiago answers. "To spread awareness."

"And to help find Jake Kingsley," Jason adds.

"Yeah, you keep saying that, but you guys talked for almost an hour and I didn't hear his name come up once," I point out.

"That's because it's not our place, Eloise," Santiago explains. "Come on, I don't think you need me to tell you that we're not authorized to discuss active missing persons cases. All we can do is offer our insight and expertise on what we *do* know. And that's this town... and the Bogman."

I sigh. I don't want to admit it, but he's got a point. They have absolutely no business talking about Jake Kingsley on international television. In fact, it could have easily done more harm than good.

"You're right," I acknowledge. "I'm sorry."

"Hey, nothing to be sorry for," Santiago tells me. "You were thinking of Jake."

"Thanks."

"Sure thing," Santiago smiles. "Now, I guess Logan and I had better clear out so you and Jason can get this place up and running."

"I don't want you to feel like you have to leave. You're welcome to stay," I tell him. Although I've had nearly all I can stomach of monster talk for one day.

"That's sweet of you, but we really should be going. We've still got a few hours of footage left to edit. Let's go, Logman."

"Logman?" I ask.

"Like Logan and Bogman. Get it?" Logan asks me.

"Ah. Clever."

"Thanks again, Eloise!" Santiago calls. Then he and Logan are gone.

I wait a beat before turning to Jason, who's busying himself getting the furniture in the lounge back to its original set-up.

"Those two seem awfully chummy," I remark, stepping forward to help him with the couch.

"Be careful. This is heavy," Jason warns me. "And yeah, they've been hanging out a lot."

"Working on the documentary?"

"I guess. Santiago's actually crashing at Logan's place though, so they've probably played their fair share of video games, too."

"Wait a minute. Why is Santiago staying with Logan? Doesn't he have a hotel room or like, an Airbnb or something?" I wonder.

"He had a hotel for that first weekend he was here, but then when he decided to stick around, Logan invited him to stay with him."

"Huh. I would have thought he'd prefer to stay somewhere a little... I don't know, nicer." Not that I have any idea what sort of conditions Logan lives in. For all I know, he may own a house as grand as Daniel's. But somehow, I doubt it.

"He probably can't afford to," Jason states matter-of-factly.

That surprises me.

"What? I thought he was kind of a celebrity."

"In cryptozoological circles. But he's not mainstream famous or anything. I mean, yeah, he has his YouTube channel and his podcast which are both *awesome*, but even with all his subscribers and listeners, he probably doesn't make the kind of money that other internet celebrities do."

"Oh." I'll be the first to admit I don't know a thing about YouTube or making money with social media, but it sounds complicated.

"Anyway, thanks again for letting us shoot here. We really do appreciate it," Jason smiles.

"Any time," I reply, even though I don't necessarily mean it. Don't get me wrong. I adore Jason and would do anything for him.

But I'm still not crazy about the cameras.

Even though Beth and her crew have cleared out by the time the store opens, I receive a text message from Daniel shortly after 9:00 letting me know he's decided to lie low for the rest of the day.

but, he adds, **what would you say to dinner later? you, me, and the kids?**

I'd love that, I reply.

Without Daniel, the workday passes a little slower than usual, but finally, my eight hours are up and I hustle home to let Isaac know we're going out. I know he'll be thrilled. We rarely go out to eat, mostly because it's more affordable to make meals at home. But he absolutely loves being out in the world and eating food that well... isn't mine.

Sure enough, he's exceptionally excited to go out for dinner. But he's even more excited to see Addie and to show her his new *Wizard of Oz* manga.

By the time we make it to Mona's at 6:30, Daniel and Addie are already sipping sodas in a booth by the window. They've gone ahead and ordered us a couple of drinks as well. As soon as Daniel spots us, he rises to his feet.

"Hey," he smiles. "Glad you could make it."

"I'm glad you suggested it," I reply, accepting a brief, friendly hug. Isaac and Addie know we're friends, of course, and Addie's probably old enough to suspect we're something more. But I don't think either of us is ready to have *that* talk with the kids. Not yet, anyway.

"Adelaide, Adelaide! Look at this!" Isaac exclaims, sliding into the booth and waving his manga in the air.

"That's awesome," she smiles.

"You know, Addie, I have to thank you," I say, taking my seat next to Isaac. "Isaac's never really been much of a reader, but he's had his nose stuck in that manga since I brought it home for him."

"That's something I love about it," she explains. "Reading was sort of hard for me growing up. But with manga, I really, really enjoy it."

"That's the key, isn't it? You've got to find something you love," I say.

Addie nods in agreement.

"You know, this place has been around since I was a kid," Daniel tells his daughter. "I used to visit Aunt Hettie here every summer. And every time she let me decide where we ate dinner, I'd always pick Mona's."

"I love Mona's," Isaac announces.

"Yeah?" Daniel asks him.

"It's my favorite."

"What do you recommend?"

"Um... the cheese pizza," Isaac answers very seriously.

"I like pepperoni and sausage," Addie says.

Isaac scrunches up his nose. To me, he's the most extraordinary boy in the world, a walking miracle. But in so many ways, he's just your typical six-year-old who will only eat cheese pizza.

"So, how was your day?" Daniel asks me while our kids launch into a colorful debate over pizza toppings.

"Not bad. The lounge seemed rather empty, though."

"I do take up a lot of space," he grins playfully.

"Oh, please. No, you don't," I laugh.

"I don't know. Last summer, after the *Knick Knack* movie premiere, some twenty-year-old gossip blogger wrote a whole Buzzfeed article about me and my 'dad bod.' Then she posted like, sixteen of the most unflattering pictures of me that she could find. My agent tried to assure me that she meant it as a compliment, but I don't..."

Although I'm highly amused by Daniel's story, I'm afraid I miss the end of it. Not because I've intentionally tuned him out, but because the warm and welcoming atmosphere inside our favorite pizza place has suddenly shifted.

It's back. That same dreadful feeling that's been haunting me for weeks. Something isn't right.

Anxious, I glance around the restaurant. It's busy, especially for a Tuesday evening. I know most everybody here. I see Dave and Cynthia Miller and their four kids at their usual table near the kitchen. I see Reverend Filsinger and his wife waiting for their order at the To-Go counter. Everyone is minding their own business. Everything is as it should be.

Then, I catch a glimpse of familiar amber eyes watching us with keen interest from across the room.

Cortland Hill.

He doesn't seem at all embarrassed to have been caught staring. Quite the contrary. Instead of turning away, he holds my gaze and smiles, almost as though he's sharing a secret with me.

"Eloise?" Daniel's voice startles me. "Everything okay?"

I don't respond immediately. I don't know what to say.

As I mentioned before, almost every person in this room is a friend of mine, or at least a more-than-casual acquaintance. That's the thing about living in a town like Cedar Ridge; it isn't unusual to run into people you know. In fact, it's nearly impossible not to. And Mona's is the best pizza place in town. So you see, it isn't at all strange that a single man like Cortland Hill should happen to be dining here tonight.

But if that's so, then why does his presence leave me feeling so uncomfortable?

Maybe I'm just overreacting. I probably am. Arrogant though he may seem, Hill's really never given me a reason not to trust him. True, he absolutely has an ulterior motive in attempting to befriend me, what with his book signing and all, but that doesn't give me permission to pitch a fit or get him thrown out of a public dining establishment. He's just here to eat. Same as anybody.

"Yeah," I finally answer, taking one last look at Hill. "Everything's fine."

Chapter Twenty-Three

It's been one week to the day since Jake Kingsley disappeared and despite the search and rescue team's best efforts, his whereabouts remain a mystery. A mystery that, thanks to Beth Goldberry and Santiago Edwards, the entire nation is watching unfold. This morning, there are even more cameras and reporters crawling the streets, requesting interviews, and stirring up all kinds of rumors and speculation.

Now, with so many eyes on our tiny town, emotions are beginning to run high.

"They ain't gonna find him," an older man I recognize as Jim Darcy grumbles to a reporter just outside the coffee shop. "Kid goes missin' this long? In these mountains? He either don't wanna be found or there's nothin' left *to* be found."

"Well, I heard he was involved in some sort of scandal," Rhonda Mann, a middle-aged woman chimes in. "Selling stolen electronics. He was supposed to be meeting with his supplier when he went missing."

"No. It was him. The Bogman," another woman insists. "My daughter's seen him. She and her boyfriend were building a campfire out in the field behind his house when they heard something groaning and growling in the woods. They turned around just in time to see him, watching them."

"Oh, come on, Tessa. You sound as crazy as old Floyd Whalen!" Jim scoffs.

With the media lurking around every corner, it comes as no surprise that Daniel once again opts to work from home. I understand, of course. But I still find myself feeling slightly disheartened.

After work, I take a quick detour to the grocery store. While I have a few friends who've mastered the art of shopping only once a week, I'm afraid I lack the organizational skills required to plan out seven days' worth of meals and necessities. So, it's off to the supermarket several times a week I go. Today, I'm here for milk, eggs, toilet paper, and laundry detergent. I also text my mom to find out if she needs me to pick anything up for her or Lenny. While I wait for her reply, I make my way to the back of the store to grab the milk and the eggs.

I'm in the process of examining the expiration dates on Isaac's favorite chocolate milk when an all-too-familiar voice calls my name.

"Eloise!" My stomach sinks and my heart begins to thud as Cortland Hill strides toward me, a broad grin etched on his face. "You know, if I didn't know better, I'd think you were following me."

"What are you doing here?" I'm well aware of how rude I sound, but I can't help it. I was able to accept last night as a mere coincidence. I was almost able to forget about running into him on Saturday altogether. But this is too much.

"Shopping," he answers simply. "We seem to be on the same schedule. Kind of spooky, isn't it?"

"Yeah, spooky," I echo and attempt to turn away from him.

He doesn't let me.

"Hey listen, I know you're probably in a hurry to get home to Isaac, but I just want you to know that I'm sorry about last night," he says.

"What about last night?"

"I should have come over and said hello instead of watching you from afar like some awkward would-be Romeo. But I truly didn't expect to see you there. I guess you kind of caught me off guard."

"That makes two of us." I can't help but notice my tone still sounds rather accusatory.

"Well, maybe you'll let me find a way to make it up to you." The sentiment is friendly enough, but the way he says it... it almost sounds like a threat.

I take an automatic step backward.

"You know, I really need to be going. Good evening, Mr. Hill."

And then, milk and eggs forgotten, I hasten as quickly as I can without making a scene down the aisles, out the front door, and into the bleak, wintry twilight.

When I get home, I find my mother and Isaac in their usual spots on the couch and in front of the television. One look at my face, however, and Mom immediately knows that something isn't right.

"Eloise? Are you okay? Where are the groceries?" she asks as I toss my coat and purse aside and onto the nearest chair.

"I didn't get them," I answer shortly.

"Why not? Did something happen?"

"Sort of." I want to talk to her about my strange encounters with Hill. I *need* to talk to her. But I can't let Isaac overhear. I don't want him to worry. And he would definitely worry. "Hey, baby." I kneel down to give him a kiss on the cheek. "Did you have a good day?"

"Uh-huh."

"That's good," I smile, running my hand over his soft curls. He barely even reacts. He's too busy drawing to pay me any attention. "Hey listen, I need to have a grown-up talk with Grandma in the kitchen. So, why don't you go wash up for dinner?"

"In a minute," he replies, still engrossed in his artistic endeavor. Honestly, I could probably tell my mom everything right here, right now and he wouldn't absorb a word. But I'm not taking any chances.

Once we're in the kitchen, I set about gathering pots and pans to create a little extra clamor while my mom watches me, anxiously awaiting an explanation.

"All right, Eloise, tell me. What's going on?" she asks. "Is it Daniel? Are you having issues?"

"No, it isn't Daniel. He's great," I assure her. "But there is this... other guy."

My mom gasps.

"Oh, Eloise, that isn't wise. Not in a town this small."

"No! Mom!" I groan. "I didn't mean another guy like *that*."

"Oh, thank Heavens," my mom sighs. "Not that I ever expected that of you. But it would have made things very awkward between Hettie and me - "

231

"Mom."

"I'm sorry, I'm sorry. Please, go on."

Briefly, I recount all of my meetings, planned and unplanned, with Cortland Hill. I tell her about the way he approached me at the Carnival and his determination to arrange a book signing at the store. Finally, I tell her about the unnerving way we keep running into one another and his unsettling insinuations that we should spend more time together.

"Well... maybe he just likes you and doesn't know how to show it," my mom suggests.

"Mom, come on. We're not in middle school. This guy... there's something off about him."

"You said that Daniel met him, right?"

"Yes."

"And Jason?"

"Yes."

"What do they think?"

"I don't think Jason cares much for his books, but he seems to think he's pretty okay. Daniel thinks he's just your typical writer who spends too much time in his own head."

"So, neither of them gets a bad vibe from him?"

"No, but Daniel doesn't know he was at the restaurant last night. I never told him. I never told him about the first time running into Hill at the grocery store, either."

"Why not?"

"Because until this evening, I was able to convince myself that each time was just an ordinary small town happenstance."

"And you're probably right," Mom says. "How long did you say he's been here?"

"I don't know exactly," I reply. "The first time I met him was at the Carnival, but the way he talked, it sounded like he'd been here a while. At least long enough to know who I was and where I worked."

"Well, he's an author. I'm sure he asked around about all the local bookstores. And if he hasn't been here that long, chances are he hasn't had the opportunity to get to know too many people. You're probably one of the few he thinks of as a friendly face."

I sigh. Everything she says makes perfect sense.

"I hadn't thought of it like that," I confess. "I guess with everything going on, with all the media and the - "

Suddenly, realization dawns on me, cutting me off mid-sentence. My mom's brow furrows with concern.

"What is it?"

"Jake Kingsley," I mutter, more to myself than in response to her question.

"What about Jake Kingsley?"

"What are the odds that a man goes missing right after Cortland Hill moves to town?"

"What? Eloise - "

"No. Mom, hear me out. I know everyone is theorizing that Jake was attacked by some kind of monster or wild animal... but what if it was a person? And he just made it look like an animal attack. And - And! Oh!" My mind is spinning so quickly that my tongue can't keep up. "The first time I met Hill, he told me he was here researching his new book, which he described as something of a Bogman retelling. That's why he came here! To immerse himself in the small-town-stalked-by-a-monster culture. But what if *he's* the monster? And he's responsible for all of this?"

"Eloise." My mom looks at me with hard, disapproving eyes. "That is a *very* serious accusation to make."

"I know, but Mom, it makes sense. It would explain everything."

"Sweetheart, listen to yourself. Do you really believe that this man would take another man's life... for a book?"

"Maybe he didn't take his life. They haven't found a body. Hill could just have him tied up somewhere," I argue. "And get this. He came to the store the day after Jake disappeared. Hill, I mean. He wanted to talk about setting up that book signing. He didn't seem at all concerned that a person was missing. In fact... he didn't seem to understand why the rest of us were bothered by it at all. Now either he lacks empathy, which would also be very concerning, or he knew there was no reason for the rest of us to be worried in the first place."

My mother shakes her head.

"Eloise, you know I love you. And I will always support you, no matter what. But... I think you're sensationalizing something that probably has a very simple explanation. And after what you went through, it's understandable - "

"Mom, this has nothing to do with Lance. It's about connections. And I know it sounds crazy, but I really think that Cortland Hill and Jake Kingsley are connected."

Finally, my mom sighs.

"Well, look, if it will make you feel better, why don't you go and talk to Emma Jean? Don't make any outright accusations, but let her know your concerns and if she asks you for names, you can give her Cortland's. But make sure you clarify that you do not have any solid evidence. You just wanted to bring this to her attention. If you want, I could even give her a call and let her know you're coming." Mom and Police Chief Emma Jean Wilde have been friends for years. Of course, Mom has been friends with most of the people in this town for years.

"Thanks, but it's all right. I'll just drop in tomorrow morning before work," I tell her. "Would you mind too terribly seeing Isaac off to the bus again?"

"Not at all. I'd do anything for that boy," Mom says. "And I'd do anything for you."

It's true. Every time I've needed her, my mom has gone above and beyond to be there.

I can only hope that one day, I'll be able to make it up to her.

Chapter Twenty-Four

The Cedar Ridge Police Station is a quaint brick lodge two streets over from my book shop. Ordinarily, it's rather a quiet scene, but now that the media has gotten involved with Jake's disappearance, the station is swarming with reporters, search and rescue teams, and volunteers hoping to lend a helping hand.

It's so chaotic that, for a moment, I wonder if I'll be able to see Emma Jean at all. Shortly after giving my name to the receptionist, however, I'm escorted back to her office.

"Eloise, come in," Emma Jean calls from her desk. "I hope you weren't waiting too long. As you can see, it's a bit of a madhouse around here."

Emma Jean is a strong, wild-haired woman in her early fifties who takes no nonsense and suffers no fools. Although she's never been anything but kind and courteous to me, I've always been slightly intimidated by her.

"I can. And I appreciate you taking the time to see me. I promise I won't keep you long," I tell her.

"Oh, it's not a problem. You're a welcome relief from all the psychics I've been interviewing for the past twenty-four hours."

"Psychics?" That's not at all what I was expecting to hear.

"Ever since the Jake Kingsley story aired on national news, we've had self-proclaimed clairvoyants and mediums calling in from all over the country, claiming that they've been visited by his spirit and giving us tips on where to find him. My question for them is if Jake is reaching out to them, why didn't he tell them to call sooner? Like before the story went national?" Emma Jean sighs.

"That's... so strange," I remark.

Emma Jean shrugs.

"Their hearts are in the right place. So, what can I do for you?"

"Well, I..." I hesitate. After hearing about her dealings with so-called psychics, I'm reluctant to be another voice shouting out theories with no real substance. But I'm already here and she's watching me with patient albeit steely eyes. "I was wondering if you were familiar with a man named Cortland Hill."

"No," she answers point-blank.

"He uh, he just moved here. Well I mean, I don't think he's moved here *permanently*. He's in town doing research for this book he's writing..." Quickly, every detail of every interaction I've had with Hill comes spilling out of me yet again. Emma Jean listens intently, her expression utterly neutral.

"So, do you think he's following you?" she asks once I've said my piece.

"Well, no. At least, I hope not. But I... I was thinking more of Jake Kingsley and how he went missing less than a week after Cortland Hill showed up," I reply. Then, remembering my mom's advice, I add, "I'm not making any accusations and I have nothing that really connects the two except for timing. I just... I guess I thought I would feel better if you knew his name. If you knew he was here. I'm sorry if I wasted your time."

"You didn't," Emma Jean assures me. "If someone's making you feel uncomfortable, then I want to know about it. Do you happen to know where he's staying?"

"That, I couldn't tell you. I'm guessing one of the motels."

"Well, I'll ask around. Tell my deputies to keep an eye out for anyone looking out of place. Since we don't know where to find him, there really isn't much we can do, especially when we don't have probable cause to make an arrest. But we can certainly ask him a question or two should he ever cross our path."

I nod.

"Thank you, Emma Jean."

"Any time, Eloise. You give my best to your mother."

"I will."

Leaving the station, I replay my discussion with Emma Jean over and over. By the time I make it to the bookstore, I'm so lost in my own thoughts that I almost run my car right into Jason as he's climbing out of his truck.

"Whoa!" he hollers.

"Jason!" I exclaim, leaping out of my car. "Oh my God, I'm so sorry! Are you okay?"

"Yeah, fine," he says, though it's plain to see he's still a little shaken. "Wait a minute. Are you just now getting here?"

"Uh, yeah. Running a little behind this morning."

"What were you doing? You - oh!" Suddenly, he gasps. "You were with Daniel, weren't you?"

"No, I wasn't with Daniel," I reply, unlocking the front door to the bookshop. "Actually, I was at the police station."

"The police station? Why? Did something happen?"

"Not exactly." I then proceed to tell Jason the same stories I told Emma Jean and my mom. I share the same theories, express the same concerns. The only difference is that this time, I'm confiding in someone who's actually met Cortland Hill.

"So wait, you're telling me that you actually went to the police with all of this?" Jason asks, incredulous.

"Well, yeah. Do you think that was a mistake?"

"I... don't really know what to think," Jason admits, running a hand through his dark curls. "I mean, I know you're not exactly his biggest fan, but do you really think he would *kidnap* someone?"

"I don't know. I don't know him! And besides, even if Emma Jean decides to pursue him, it's not like she's going to lock him up and throw away the key. If anything, she'll ask him a few questions and that will be the end of it." Unless he really is the one behind Jake's disappearance. Of course, that part, I keep to myself.

239

"I don't know, El," Jason sighs. "Do you have any idea how serious this is? You just gave an innocent man's name to the police."

"We don't know he's innocent. What about the way he keeps showing up? And how he barely even seemed to bat an eye over the fact that we have a tourist missing?"

"He probably - "

Ding!

Just then, the shopkeeper's bell rings, cutting him off and mercifully sparing me a lecture. I glance around and am delighted to see that my accidental knight in shining armor is Daniel.

"Everything okay in here?" he asks. I guess the tension between Jason and me is palpable.

"Everything's fine," Jason answers.

At the same time, I step forward and say, "I did something this morning. I went to talk to the police about Cortland Hill."

Daniel's brow furrows and his eyes immediately harden.

"What about him?"

And so, I tell the story yet again. Daniel listens intently, leaning against the checkout counter and every so often, stroking his beard. Jason, on the other hand, has apparently heard enough, because he stalks off to the back of the store as soon as I mention Jake Kingsley.

"... and again, I made sure she knew that I have absolutely no evidence to substantiate these claims. It's just... it's all a little too coincidental for me," I say, wrapping up my admittedly shaky testimony. "What do you think?"

Daniel takes a deep breath. I can tell he's trying to figure out how to speak his mind without hurting me. Or at least without telling me he thinks I'm flat-out wrong.

"You know, after he came into the store the other day, I actually did some research on him," Daniel tells me.

"What did you find?"

"Not much, to be honest. He's thirty-nine. He's from Mystic, Connecticut. He's written seven books that have done reasonably well, but he isn't a household name or anything. Though judging by the way he talked about his work and how persistent he's been to set up a signing, I'd say he really wants to be one. He wants that recognition, that sense of high esteem. That's why I don't think he has anything to do with Jake Kingsley's disappearance. He's not going to risk tarnishing his reputation. His career is too important to him."

I nod. Everything Daniel is saying makes sense.

"So... do you think I made a mistake?" I ask.

"No, I don't. Because even if he isn't involved in the Jake Kingsley mystery, I don't like the way he keeps finding you. Especially when you're alone or with Isaac," Daniel says. "You know if you ever need me, all you have to do is call. If you ever feel uncomfortable or threatened..."

"I know. Thank you."

With that, Daniel takes my hand and pulls me into his warm embrace.

"And hey, if it would make you feel better, you and Isaac can always come crash with Addie and me. We've got plenty of room. Lots of movies. Good food.

A hot tub..." Daniel teases, giving me a playful squeeze. I can't help but laugh. "On second thought, you should just come over anyway."

"Are we going to pawn the kids off on Hettie and Theresa again?"

"Hey, you know what? They love spending time with those kids," Daniel argues. Then, he cups my face with his hands, leans down, and kisses me.

Suddenly, I'm very tempted to lock every door and switch the sign in the window from **Open** to **Closed**. I'm considering sending Jason home, or at least out to run errands for a few hours. I'm totally content to lose half a day's worth of revenue as long as it means I get Daniel all to myself, even if only for a little while.

Although, now that he's mentioned the kids, there is something I want to ask him.

"I'm curious... What have you told Addie about us?"

"That we're friends. Though I've been thinking about it... trying to come up with the best way to break the news. I even asked Hettie and Theresa for their advice."

"What do they think?"

"Theresa says that we need to live our truths and follow our heart chakras or something along those holistic lines. But Hettie thinks we need to take a more sensible approach. She argued that while Addie does deserve to know the truth, we need to keep in mind just how much her life has changed in the past six months and how she might not be ready for... well..."

"For someone new in her father's life?" I supply.

Daniel doesn't respond immediately. Instead, he brushes a stray lock of my auburn hair away from my face and kisses me lightly on the lips.

"You're not just someone new. Addie really likes you. And she loves Isaac."

"Aw. Really?" I beam.

"Yeah. She likes teaching him to draw. I think she thinks of him as her protégé."

"That's adorable."

"My point is... I don't think it's going to be a difficult discussion to have with her. I just need to figure out the right time. In a lot of ways, she and I are still sort of getting to know each other. You know, she and her mom... they were so close. And they were always so open with one another. Addie told her everything. But she's not there yet with me. Our family counselor that we saw back in Irvine advised me to just give her time, let her get comfortable with her new circumstances." Daniel pauses to take a breath. "I know she'll be happy for us when we tell her. That's just the kind of person that she is. But I guess I just... I mean I don't want..."

Again, I know what he's trying to say.

"You don't want her to think that I'm more important to you than she is."

"It sounds so harsh when you put it that way," Daniel remarks.

"But it's true. And it's okay. She should be the most important person in your life. I know Isaac is the most important person in *my* life. And listen, I want you to know that I wasn't asking to pressure you or anything. I just wanted to know the protocol," I laugh.

Daniel smiles. Then he slips both of his hands around the small of my back and pulls me close.

"Thank God for you," he murmurs, pressing his lips to the top of my head. "I will tell her soon."

"There's no rush," I assure him. "I certainly haven't told Isaac yet. Of course, he's six and he thinks kissing gives you cooties."

"Uh-oh. Well, you're definitely infected then," Daniel teases.

I shrug.

"I can learn to live with them."

Then, I rise up on my tiptoes and gently guide his mouth back to mine.

Chapter Twenty-Five

It's pretty much impossible to calculate how quickly gossip spreads in a small town. It's equally impossible to pinpoint exactly when and where new rumors originate. All we can be sure of is that once a story hits the streets, it's bound to be the talk of the town within a few hours. And today's hot topic? Oh, it's a good one.

According to a "reliable source," the Cedar Ridge Police have identified a suspect in the disappearance of Jake Kingsley. It seems as though a distressed citizen took her concerns to Chief Wilde and her testimony was compelling enough for the department to look into it.

I think I'm going to be sick.

"You don't know it's him," Jason tries to reassure me. I guess he feels bad about our little tiff yesterday.

"But what if it is? And what if you were right?" I ask. "What if he really is just an innocent man who's stopping by to do some research and I just turned the whole town against him?"

"Hey, no one knows his name, right? They can't turn against someone if they don't know who it is. And who knows? The police might not even be able to track him down."

"I don't know if that makes me feel better or worse," I mutter.

It doesn't help that every person to wander into Blue Ridge Books this afternoon seems absorbed in their own questions and convoluted conspiracy theories all concerning the newly revealed person of interest.

First, it's a young couple browsing the new releases.

"So wait, if they've got a suspect, does that mean they don't think it was the Bogman?" the girlfriend asks.

"Oh, it was the Bogman. They're probably just saying that they have a person of interest so the press will get their noses out of their investigation," her boyfriend responds.

Ten minutes later, it's a trio of local ladies fresh out of the hair salon.

"I bet it's that man who works down at Finch's Deli. You know, the one they hired last month?" the tallest of the three says.

"The one with all the *tattoos*?" the one with golden blonde hair gasps as though she truly believes tattoos are the mark of the devil.

"The tattoos and the biceps," their third friend sighs.

"Really, Margie?" the tall friend asks.

"What? I've got a thing for bad boys," Margie shrugs. "Besides, have you really looked into his eyes? Those big, soulful brown eyes? Those aren't the eyes of a cold-blooded kidnapper."

Then there's the woman on her cell phone, talking loud enough for the entire store to hear.

"Well, if you ask me, the police are trying to cover their own asses. They're no closer to finding Jake Kingsley than they were when he went missing and they're hoping to mask their incompetence by conveniently letting it slip that they've identified a 'person of interest.'"

It's probably worth mentioning that as of this afternoon, the police have yet to release any sort of official statement regarding the witness or their so-called person of interest. Every story floating around Cedar Ridge right now is pure hearsay.

"Don't worry about it," Daniel advises, noting my uneasy demeanor. Or possibly my queasy green complexion. "If he's innocent, he shouldn't mind answering a few harmless questions. And if he isn't innocent, well, then you helped bring a criminal to justice."

I nod my head in response. I'm still not entirely convinced. And Daniel can tell.

"Hey listen, why don't we do something fun tonight? Just the two of us?" he asks. "I know we talked about getting together with the kids this weekend anyway, but tonight, I think we should just make it about us. We could get out of town for a little bit, maybe take your mind off things."

Alone with Daniel. Away from Cedar Ridge. It *does* sound very tempting.

"I'd have to ask my mom to stay late with Isaac..."

"Tell her I want to take you out and spoil you. She won't mind," Daniel winks.

"You're not wrong," I acknowledge. "Okay, let's do it."

"Great. I've got to go pick Addie up from school, but what do you say I swing by and grab you around six?"

"Sounds perfect," I smile.

As Daniel predicted, my mother is happy to stay and watch Isaac while we embark on our romantic getaway.

For my attire, I select a long-sleeved, beige sweater dress; stylish and simple. Paired with a brown coat I found at the thrift store and brown riding boots, I think I should be warm enough in the twenty-eight-degree weather.

Besides, it isn't as though this is a typical date. Tonight is meant to be more of an escape. But I do want to look nice, regardless.

Daniel seems to be of a similar mindset. My heart skips a beat when I see him dressed not in his typical flannel and winter coat, but in a nice white button-down shirt and black blazer. He's even traded in his well-worn jeans for a newer pair of dark denim trousers.

"So, are you ready?" he asks, opening the passenger side door of his SUV for me.

I kiss him swiftly in response.

Our journey out of Cedar Ridge is rather a short one. Less than twenty minutes after pulling out of my driveway, we arrive in the equally small town of Banner Elk. Although similar to Cedar Ridge in many ways, there always seems to be so much more to do in Banner Elk. They have an arts center that allows for professional theater productions, an Alpine coaster (incidentally, the only one in North Carolina's Blue Ridge Mountains), they even have wineries. And as it just so happens, Rustic Villa Winery and Restaurant is our destination this evening.

It's a beautiful establishment, with white twinkle lights hanging from every rafter and bouquets of pale pink and white flowers on every table. It's the sort of place that would be perfect for a party or a celebration.

If only that's why we were here tonight.

"So, are you feeling better?" Daniel asks, watching me take in the atmosphere.

"I am," I reply. "Thank you for this."

"Oh, it's my pleasure. To tell you the truth, I probably needed this about as much as you did."

"Really?"

He nods, scratching at the back of his head.

"This new book I'm writing is a killer," he admits. "I don't usually struggle with writer's block, but with everything that's been going on... I don't know, I guess I've been a little distracted."

"Is part of that my fault?" I ask.

"Yes," he grins. "But in the best possible way."

We spend the rest of our time at the winery engaged in light-hearted conversation, mostly about our kids, and about how nice it is to have a change of scenery. We sample a small selection of Rustic Villa's wines; Merlot, Sangiovese, and Seyval Blanc to name a few. Then, after a dinner of salmon and seasoned vegetables, we indulge in a delectable slice of New York style cheesecake, topped with fresh berries for dessert.

Our evening draws to a close far too quickly, but as much as I love spending time with Daniel, I'm eager to get back to Isaac. And to relieve my mom of babysitting duty.

We drive in a comfortable silence through the black shadow of night. Out here in the wilderness between towns, Daniel's headlights are our only source of illumination. Somehow, their brightness makes the world around us seem that much darker. In a strange way, it's sort of peaceful. And yet, at the same time, not being able to see beyond the reach of the headlights is dizzying, almost disorienting.

"I'm glad you're the one driving tonight," I confess.

"Why is that?" he asks.

"The older I get, the less confident I feel driving in the dark," I reply. "That... and I may have had just *one* too many sips of wine tonight."

"Oh yeah?" he grins. "You feelin' a little tipsy?"

"Just a *little*." I really hadn't even felt it until watching the road started making me woozy. "I really don't drink all that much. In fact, I think I've consumed more alcohol with you in the last week than I have... in about two years."

"You're kidding."

"Sadly, I'm not."

"Not even around the holidays?"

"Nope. I used to drink socially. But then after watching Lance and all of his struggles... I don't know. I guess it sort of lost its appeal."

"That's understandable."

"But tonight was *so* much fun," I exclaim, eager to lighten the mood. "And oh, the food was *amazing*."

"It really was, wasn't it? Especially that cheesecake."

"You know, maybe when it gets a little warmer outside we could - "

Screeeeeeeech!

Suddenly, without warning, Daniel slams on the brakes.

Everything that happens next happens in a blur.

I fly forward, my seat belt nearly strangling me as it holds my body in place. Daniel's SUV swerves and skids across the road. My heart lurches. I think I scream.

Then it's over and the world outside my window slows to a stop.

"Shit!" Daniel swears under his breath. "Are you okay?"

"I think so..." I reply, my voice trembling. "What happened?"

"There was something... I could have sworn..." Daniel scrambles to form a coherent thought.

"What?"

"There's something... *out there*."

As his words sink in, my blood begins to run cold.

"What are you talking about?"

"I don't know. Up ahead, something just... staggered out into the road."

Unbidden, stories of strange encounters in the middle of the night flood my memory. Images of a beastly figure trudging along the side of the highway flash before my eyes.

It's not real. It can't be real.

Panicked, eager to disprove each and every one of those witnesses and to soothe my own frazzled nerves, I glance around, scanning the darkness for any signs of movement.

There's nothing. Only the road, the snow, and the unending forest. I heave an uneasy sigh of relief.

"Maybe... maybe it's gone," I whisper.

Daniel doesn't look convinced. He's still keeping his eyes on the empty highway in front of us.

Then, I see it. At first, I think the night is deceiving me, that a phantom shadow is playing tricks on my vision. But then the thin, bedraggled figure stumbles out of the dark and into the harsh white beams of Daniel's headlights. And that is when my heart *stops*.

The being standing before us isn't the Bogman.

It isn't a bear or a coyote or even a deer.

It's Jake Kingsley.

Chapter Twenty-Six

"Where did you find him?"

"Did he tell you what happened?"

"It's Jake! Jake Kingsley! He's alive!"

"It's a miracle."

"He's going to be just fine."

The questions and declarations and well-meaning assurances echo through the pristine and sterile halls of Blue Haven Medical Center. I barely register them. All of my attention instead is focused on the young man lying in the hospital bed mere meters away from where Daniel and I stand. Although he's technically no longer my concern, I can't seem to keep my eyes off of him.

He looks so frail. Frail, and so very, very thin. His honey-colored curls are matted and thick with dirt and grime. His skin is pale, a sickening off-white, almost grayish pallor, and he's covered in superficial scrapes and bruises. By the grace of God, however, he doesn't seem to be too badly injured. Just a little frostbitten and severely malnourished.

Maybe he really was just lost, after all.

"Hey," Emma Jean Wilde greets Daniel and me. She and a few of her officers spent about an hour or so talking to Jake after the doctors first took a look at him, but he was so exhausted, he couldn't keep up for very long. "How are you two holding up?"

"Tired," Daniel answers honestly. "But glad the kid is okay."

I can only nod in response. It seems I haven't quite found my voice yet.

"I'm sure you're both anxious to get home to your kiddos, but would you mind coming down to the station and answering a few questions?" Emma Jean asks.

I suppose I should have been expecting this. Still, my stomach twists itself into a tight knot as I imagine myself back in her office, this time under interrogation.

"You're not in trouble," Emma Jean assures us. I guess she saw the look of agitation on my face. "But I'm going to have to file a report and make an official statement, and before I can do either of those things, I need to make sure I have all the facts."

"Yeah, of course," Daniel says. "It's not a problem."

"I appreciate it."

We follow Emma Jean back to the police station in Daniel's car. Already, a small crowd of reporters, news anchors, and onlookers is gathering outside the building. Rumors must already be circulating. Thankfully, Emma Jean leads us around towards the back entrance.

"We'll sneak in this way," she mutters, careful not to alert any of the media to our presence. "I'll never get over how fast word gets around in this town."

Once inside, she leaves Daniel with her deputy while she escorts me back to her office.

"You're quiet tonight," she observes. "You doing okay?"

"I think... I think I'm just stunned," I answer honestly.

"Yeah. You and me, both," she admits. "We'd all written Jake Kingsley off as dead. We figured he'd had to've succumbed to the elements by now. And yet, there he is." Then, never one to beat around the bush, she asks, "So, what happened?"

"We were driving up 184. It was about 9:15. Maybe a little later - "

"Where were you coming from?"

"Banner Elk. We decided that we needed a getaway. Just the two of us."

"Okay. Can you tell me where on 184 you were?"

"God, I never pay attention to mile markers. Daniel has a pretty fancy SUV, though. It might have a GPS that could tell you. But from where we found him, it took us about twenty minutes to reach the hospital."

"Did he say anything to you? What sort of interaction did you have?"

"Not much," I answer, thinking back to those frantic first moments after I realized exactly what I was seeing. "He was pretty weak. He was sort of limping toward us and gasping, 'Help. Help me. Please.' Just over and over again. Daniel assured him that he was okay. That he was safe. I think he told Jake our names, but I was so shocked that I wasn't really making sense of anything. After we got him in the car, Daniel told me to call 911 and they instructed us to bring him straight to the hospital. The dispatcher said we could get him there faster than if she sent an ambulance to pick him up. And so that's what we did."

"Did he tell you what happened?"

"He seemed... pretty distressed. But I think he was so relieved to be found, to be safe, that he just passed out in the back seat. I kept my eyes on him the whole time to make sure he was still breathing. Whatever he went through, it drained him. I just... I don't know how he's still alive."

"I don't think he does, either," Emma Jean says.

"Did he... I mean... Did he tell *you* what happened?" I ask, though I'm not altogether sure I'm permitted to do so.

"He gave me a rather muddled account. I'm going back to talk to him tomorrow after he's had time to rest. All that matters now is that he's safe."

I nod in agreement. Then, a new concern crosses my mind.

"You're not going to tell anyone that we're the ones who found him, are you?" I ask.

"Not if you don't want me to," Emma Jean promises. "You want to remain anonymous?"

"If you don't mind. I know that I can't speak for Daniel, but I'm fairly certain that he wouldn't want his name getting out there."

"Any particular reason why not?"

"His job, mostly," I answer. It's not entirely untrue. "And you know, he just moved here a few weeks ago. He and his daughter are still getting settled and I really don't think he's going to want to draw a lot of attention to himself."

"That's understandable. I'll confer with him to be sure. But you don't want your name released either way?"

"No."

"It could help your business," Emma Jean grins.

"Well, you're not wrong," I laugh, grateful to her for lightening the mood. "But I think for Isaac's sake, and the sake of my sanity, I'd rather keep my name out of the headlines."

"Of course," Emma Jean complies. "Oh, and one more thing."

"Yes?"

"I looked into that guy you told me about yesterday. Cortland Hill? Of course, I didn't get too far and, as it turns out, that's all null and void now anyway. But I did manage to make quite a few phone calls."

"And?"

"No one's heard of him."

"What?" I can't have heard her correctly.

"I called every motel, every inn... I even checked with all the local Airbnb listings. There's no record of a Cortland Hill ever being in Cedar Ridge. Now, I'm not telling you this to scare you. It's very possible that he's staying with friends or that he's even got himself a room a town or two over. I just thought you'd want to know, especially since he seems to have taken something of a shine to you."

"No, yeah. Of course." I shake my head. My mind is swimming with questions and contradictions. "I'm glad you told me."

"Listen, if you see him again, be cordial, but don't encourage him. And don't feel guilty if you need to establish some boundaries. You know, a lot of times, people don't realize that they're crossing any sort of lines. And it's okay to tell them. In fact, he might even be glad that you did."

"Thanks, Emma Jean."

"Any time, Eloise. Now, let's get you and that boyfriend of yours out of here. I've still got a report to file and a news crew to satiate."

"Good luck," I grin.

"I'll need it," she mutters, leading me out of her office and down the hall to where Daniel is waiting for me near the back entrance. As soon as he sees me, he pulls me into his arms and squeezes me tight.

"You okay?" he murmurs.

"Mm-hmm," I sigh into his chest. "I just want to go home."

"We're going, Baby," he assures me. Then he addresses Emma Jean. "Are we free to leave?"

"You are. I just need to verify something that Eloise mentioned."

"Shoot," Daniel replies.

"She tells me she doesn't believe that you would want your name released to the press. Is this correct?"

"Yeah, if that's not a problem."

"It isn't. I just wanted to be sure before I release any sort of statement."

"Thanks, Chief. I appreciate it," Daniel says.

"Well, then, the two of you are good to go. Enjoy the rest of your evening," Emma Jean smiles. "And thank you. You guys did a really good thing tonight."

"It wasn't us," Daniel tells her. "We were just in the right place at exactly the right time."

"Well still, I thank you. And I know Jake's family and girlfriend will, too."

"We're happy we could help," Daniel says. "Have a good night."

Then, with one arm still wrapped around my shoulders, he turns and walks me out the back door and into the parking lot. After sitting in Emma Jean's small, stuffy office, the cold night air comes as such a welcome relief, I can't help but take a slow, deep breath.

It's over, I tell myself. *Jake is safe. We've done our part. All is well.*

"There they are!"

Before I have time to even react, a small hoard of photographers, reporters, and cameramen appears out of nowhere, snapping pictures left and right, shoving microphones in our faces, and asking us over and over again if the rumors are true.

"No comment, thank you." Daniel tries his best to move past the crowd without making a scene, but the mob is relentless.

"Just one moment of your time, please!"

"What are your names?"

"Is it true that you found Jake Kingsley?"

"Did he say anything about the monster?"

Overwhelmed by the flashing lights of a dozen cameras and the swarm of strangers surrounding us, I close my eyes and bury my face in Daniel's chest. He continues guiding me forward, shoving his way through the demanding throng of media vultures.

"Look, it's been a long night. We're tired. We just want to go home," Daniel reiterates. "Now, if you'll please excuse - "

"Hey, wait. I know you!" One of the news anchors gasps. Or he might be a cameraman. I don't know. My eyes are still closed. All I know is that in that moment, time seems to stand still.

"Please, this really isn't the time," Daniel protests, but to no avail.

"You're D.H. Whittaker, aren't you?" The same young man exclaims.

And then the chorus of inquiries begins anew.

"D.H. Whittaker? The horror author?"

"Oh my God. It *is* him! Mr. Whittaker, what brings you to Cedar Ridge?"

"Are you here working on a new novel?"

"What are your thoughts on the Bogman?"

"Is this your new girlfriend, Mr. Whittaker?"

Even though I'm not looking at him, I can feel Daniel growing more and more frustrated with each passing second. Thankfully, Emma Jean's deputy and a few other officers have caught on to the mayhem.

"All right, everybody! Break it up!" One of them shouts. "If you have questions, you may direct them at us."

In a world where Daniel was just another nameless witness, this might have worked. But as far as these news anchors and reporters are concerned, Jake Kingsley's rescue is now the second-hottest scoop that they'll be getting their sleazy hands on this evening. The *real* story that is sure to make all the headlines is that D.H. Whittaker, internationally-acclaimed bestselling author, is in Cedar Ridge.

And it's for that very reason I know that they're not about to let him out of their sight.

Excerpt from *Morphling*
By D.H. Whittaker

The job was ideal, really.

The hours were flexible. The pay was decent. And he never had to show his face. Best of all, it was an opportunity for him to do something he loved. Something that really gave him a rush. For years, Richard Sykes Gordon had sought his passion, his one true place in the world.

He'd finally found it at the Mills County Murder House.

The name was misleading, of course. No murders actually took place inside the once-abandoned three-story building. It was a haunted funhouse, a seasonal attraction designed for those seeking the thrill of that fear-induced high.

Richard knew the feeling. He'd been searching for that same sense of euphoria his entire life. Of course, in his case, the thrill didn't come from being scared. Richard Sykes Gordon liked to be the one doing the scaring.

No. He didn't like it. He craved it. He lived and breathed for it.

Late at night, while his beautiful wife slept peacefully at his side, he would often lie awake and imagine pulling a knife on an innocent passerby. Or he might picture himself following a vulnerable young woman down a darkened alley. That look of terror in her innocent eyes... The pleasure was almost more than Richard was able to withstand.

Not that he'd ever act on those fantasies. And even if he did, it wasn't as though his victims would be in any real danger. He simply wanted to scare them, to experience that sense of satisfaction and power. When it was all over, he'd let them live.

His new position as Ax Wielder #2 at the Murder House didn't give him quite the same freedom to really explore and express his impulses, but it at least provided him with an acceptable outlet. For that, he was grateful.

He knew his wife was grateful, too. Although she constantly professed her love for him, he knew it was all a farce. He saw the look of doubt and despair in her eyes every time he was dismissed by an employer. She couldn't even pretend to love him... not when he failed her over and over and over again.

This time, however, things were going to be different.

This time, he was actually going to enjoy the work.

Chapter Twenty-Seven

Man Missing For Over a Week Found by Renowned Horror Author!

Jake Kingsley is Alive... And You'll Never Guess Who Rescued Him!

D.H. Whittaker is Saving Lives in Cedar Ridge!

Cedar Ridge.

Yes, you read that right.

And yes, you have heard of it!

Located in the Blue Ridge Mountains of North Carolina at an elevation of 5,370 feet, it is actually one of the highest towns in the eastern United States. And with a population of just over 2,000 people, it's also one of the smallest.

So what in the world is an internationally-acclaimed bestselling novelist like D.H. Whittaker doing there?

If our sources are to be believed, Mr. Whittaker has abandoned his lofty, high-end apartment in the Upper West Side of Manhattan and relocated to the snow-covered sanctuary of Cedar Ridge to raise his young daughter, Adelaide. Adelaide's mother, retired model Lisa Bell, died in a tragic accident at her Irvine, California home six months ago.

But you know, a world-famous horror author moving to a small town in the middle of Nowhere, North Carolina isn't even the half of it. Because this particular author also happens to be a big damn hero.

For those of you wracking your brains, trying to remember why the name Cedar Ridge sounds so familiar, it's because a young man named Jake Kingsley went missing there over a week ago. His disappearance fueled a multitude of theories and rumors, most of which placed the blame on a mythical creature the locals call the Bogman.

Well, we can't tell you if an abominable snow monster had anything to do with the vanishing of Jake Kingsley. But we can tell you that thanks to D.H. Whittaker and an as-of-yet unidentified female companion, his whereabouts are no longer a mystery. Jake Kingsley has been found.

Even though the article doesn't mention me specifically, my phone has been ringing off the metaphorical hook all morning. And it probably goes without saying that, after our particularly harrowing night, I'm not feeling all that inclined to answer.

Naturally, Jason was the first to call.

"El, what the HELL is going on? You and Daniel found Jake Kingsley? How? What happened? Did he say anything? Where has he BEEN? Oh, and you've probably already heard, but one of the reporters recognized Daniel. Everyone is going to know who he is, if they don't already. I don't know what the damage is just yet. I'm seriously only awake right now because Logan won't stop texting me updates. Anyway, call me

back as soon as you get this. *Seriously, El, this is CRAZY."*

Then it was Lauren Greene, one of the moms who helped to organize the Winter Carnival. The one who invited Daniel to her writers' group.

"Hi, Eloise. It's Lauren. I may be crazy, but you know Hettie's nephew? The man we met at your bookstore? Well, I just read an article about Jake Kingsley and the famous author who found him and... I think it's him! Hettie's nephew! Do you know for sure? Are you friends with him? And if you are, is there any way you might be able to put me in touch with him? I would love to pick his brain about establishing a writing career. You know, finding an agent, getting my manuscript into the right hands, that sort of thing. Maybe he could read what I've got so far and give me some feedback? Let me know!"

I haven't mustered up the energy to listen to the rest of the messages. I'm sure they're all of a similar nature.

"Here, Sweetheart," my mother says, handing me a mug of steaming coffee. She's still here with Isaac and me this morning. After waiting up and listening to the whole story of Jake's rescue last night, she decided to stay. And I'll be forever grateful that she did. "How are you feeling?" she asks, joining me at the kitchen island.

"Drained," I answer with a dry laugh. "I think I'm still processing everything that happened."

"Oh, I'm sure you are," my mom replies, sipping at her own cup of coffee. "Do you want to talk about it?"

"I don't know what there is to talk about. I'm so happy that Jake's okay. But... I'm worried about

Daniel. And Addie. You know, all this media attention is exactly what he was hoping to avoid."

"Did you know? You know... that he was..."

"Yeah. I've known for a while."

"You never said anything."

"I was waiting for the right time. To tell you the truth, I'm surprised Hettie didn't tell you."

"Well, she did call to ask how you were doing."

"She did?" I ask. "What did you tell her?"

"That you were tired and overwhelmed, but that you'd be fine."

"Did she mention Daniel? Is he okay?"

"He and Addie are actually going to be staying with Hettie and Theresa until the media storm dies down a little bit. And Hettie wanted to extend that same invitation to you and Isaac."

"Oh." I think of Hettie and Theresa's house. It's bigger than mine for certain, but not nearly as spacious as Daniel's. Though it might be just roomy enough for four adults and two kids. Still, I couldn't possibly accept. "That's sweet of her. But I can't impose like that."

"I don't think she'd have offered if she considered you an imposition."

"I know."

"Well, at least call her and thank her for the invitation," my mom says. Then, she stands up and walks over to the sink to rinse out her coffee mug. "I probably need to be going. I have to make sure Lenny hasn't starved without me." She rolls her eyes playfully.

"Give him my love," I tell her.

"I always do. And you give Isaac all of mine."

Isaac isn't awake yet, which isn't unusual for a Saturday.

"I will," I promise.

After helping my mother with her coat, I walk with her to the front door and out onto the porch. It's an unusually quiet morning. The sky is a calm, overcast gray and the air smells like fresh ice crystals. It's all very comforting. I even manage a smile and a wave as I watch my mother drive away.

That smile quickly fades, however, when another car catches my eye; a navy-blue Chevy that I've never seen on my street. Not once. It's parked far enough away that I can't quite make out the face behind the steering wheel, but just close enough for me to notice the somewhat outdated black camera he has aimed directly at my house.

Well, that didn't take very long, did it? I suppose it should come as no surprise. For all I know, he could have been staked out here all night, waiting for a halfway decent shot. And now that he's seen me, it won't be long before others show up.

Ducking back inside, I scamper through the house, frantically closing every drape and every blind of every window, even the ones upstairs. Then, I retreat into my bedroom to search for my phone.

Once I've found it, I scroll through my contacts until Hettie's name lights up my screen.

"Hettie? Hey, it's Eloise. Listen, I was thinking I might take you up on your offer."

Within an hour, Isaac and I are pulling into Hettie and Theresa's driveway.

"I thought we were going to Adelaide's," he says.

"I know, Sweetheart, but something came up at the last minute. But she's here at Hettie's. In fact, you get to spend the whole weekend with her. Won't that be fun?"

"Hettie's house smells funny," Isaac declares, wrinkling his nose.

I sigh. I've tried my best to explain the situation to him, but I don't know how to tell him the whole truth without worrying him. I can't, for example, let him know that the reason we're spending an entire weekend in Hettie and Theresa's incense-infused home is that I'm afraid of camera-snipers aiming their telephoto lenses through his bedroom window.

"Come on, you'll have fun. You always do," I remind him.

He doesn't look convinced as I grab our overnight bags from my front passenger seat and scan the street for any unusual or unfamiliar vehicles. Finally, feeling mostly confident that we haven't been followed, I climb out of the car and quickly usher Isaac to the front porch.

Hettie's waiting for us at the door.

"Come in! Hurry!" She exclaims in a dramatically hushed voice. I can't say for sure, but I get the feeling she's secretly enjoying this. The way she's acting, you'd think she was housing a couple of jailhouse runaways. Wrongfully convicted, of course. You know, like in a *Lifetime* movie.

"Thank you for letting us hide out here, Hettie," I say.

"Oh, it's our pleasure, Dear. We've witnessed firsthand just how *invasive* the press can be. We don't want that for you. And neither does Danny," she says, leading us through the dining room where they throw all of their extravagant parties and into the living room.

Hettie and Theresa's house is just as warm and inviting as they are. Each wall is decorated with antique mirrors, old family photographs, and Theresa's oil paintings, and every piece of furniture is draped with a colorful bohemian throw blanket. In the far corner of the living room, Hettie and Theresa have arranged a small indoor garden of potted trees, shrubs, and succulents. Their world, for all intents and purposes, is a fairy tale.

Although Isaac is right. The incense does sort of smell funny.

"Hi, Isaac. Hi, Miss Eloise," sweet Addie greets us from the reading nook, which Hettie and Theresa have converted into an arts and crafts corner.

"Hey, Addie. What are you working on today?" I ask her.

"I'm designing a character for my new story," she explains.

"Will you show me how to draw Elphaba?" Isaac asks.

"Later, sweetheart. Let Addie work on her own projects," I tell him. "You brought your crayons, didn't you? And your notebook?"

"If he didn't, trust me, we've got plenty," Daniel announces, emerging from the hallway. "You doing okay?" he asks as soon as he sees me.

"Better now," I admit. "I'd really hoped this wouldn't be necessary. Not that I didn't want to spend more time with all of you. It's just..."

"The circumstances. Yeah, I get it," he agrees. Then he notices the bags in my hand. "Here, let me."

"Oh. Thank you."

I follow him back to one of the guest rooms. I suppose I'll be bunking with Isaac since spending the night with Daniel is sort of out of the question. But we can at least steal a moment or two alone now.

"How are you doing? Are *you* okay?" I ask him.

"Oh, yeah. I'm used to it," he answers. "Addie's the one I worry about, but she seems to be handling it okay."

"She looks happy today."

"She loves being here. It's like her very own magical playground. I just hope the cameras give us a break when she goes back to school on Monday."

I hope that, too. For all of our sakes.

"Maybe they'll be focusing more on Jake by then," I suggest rather optimistically. "Once he gets to feeling better, I'm sure everyone will want to talk to him." Then, wrapping my arms around his broad shoulders, I tease, "Maybe, just maybe, they'll forget all about you."

He grins as he presses his hands against the small of my back. I can feel his fingers toying with the waistband of my jeans as he lowers his mouth to mine. His touch is almost enough to make me forget everything; where we are, why we're here... I very nearly forget my own name.

"I wish we were alone," I whisper.

"Well, Hettie and Theresa offered to take the kids again. Said they could steer clear of town and any place they might seem too conspicuous."

"Ah, yes. Hettie with her fur and diamonds and Theresa with her peasant skirts and bohemian scarves. They're the most inconspicuous couple I know," I remark.

Daniel can't help but laugh.

"Point taken," he says. "So, should we tell them not to go?"

I sigh. I want to be with Daniel. But I don't want to risk exposing the kids - or the aunts, for that matter - to anything remotely like what Daniel and I endured last night.

"I think it's for the best."

Daniel nods.

"I think you're right."

Chapter Twenty-Eight

Hettie and Theresa do not agree. In fact, they're outright argumentative.

"They're kids! And it's their Saturday! We can't keep them cooped up inside on a Saturday!" Hettie exclaims.

"And what if you run into a reporter?" Daniel asks.

"They're not going to recognize *us*," Theresa reminds him.

"What if someone's figured it out and tipped them off?"

"Danny, you seem stressed. Would you like me to diffuse some lavender for you?" Theresa asks.

Daniel bites his tongue and fights back a grimace. I can't say for sure, but I'm fairly certain he's making a conscious effort to not roll his eyes.

Hettie, meanwhile, takes her nephew by the hands, forcing him to look at her.

"Listen to me. I promise we will not let anything happen to Addie or to Isaac. We just want to make sure they get some fresh air... and that you two get a moment to breathe. If it would make you feel better, we'll text you every thirty minutes. We'll send you pictures. You can track our phones if you'd like. But we're taking them out for at least a little while."

Daniel sighs. Then, he turns to me.

"What do you think?"

I hesitate. Then, I'm struck with a solution of sorts.

"Why don't we ask the kids what they want to do?"

Knowing Isaac and Addie, they may very well choose to spend the day inside. And perhaps they might have, had Hettie not offered to take them to The Playhouse Museum.

"The Playhouse Museum?" I exclaim. "But that's all the way in Boone!"

"Only a forty-minute drive," Hettie reasons. "Close enough for a day trip but far enough away that we won't attract any unwanted attention. And there's so much to do! There are indoor slides, games, a ball pit, a science lab, an art center... The kids will love it."

I'm sure they will. I've always wanted to take Isaac there. We were supposed to go for his fifth birthday, but he came down with an ear infection and we had to cancel our plans.

"Well... okay," I finally surrender. It's not like I can say no now without completely crushing my son's hopes and dreams. And you know, maybe it will be good for him and Addie to get away from their overly anxious parents and have some fun for a few hours. But *only* for a few hours. "Just promise you'll be back before dark."

"Oh Honey, we'll be back before dinner," Hettie assures me. "We're going to make you all something special: whole grain lasagna with fresh tomato sauce and spinach."

Okay, if Hettie's plan is to calm my frazzled nerves with the promise of home-cooked food, well, it's working.

Before they leave, I give Isaac an extra kiss and a hug goodbye.

"You be good for Hettie and Theresa, okay? And make sure you're never out of their sight," I tell him. "I love you."

"Love you, too," he responds semi-automatically. He's far too eager to get to The Playhouse Museum to indulge me for long.

After they're gone, I stand at the window and watch the road, just to make sure they're not being followed. Daniel seems to sense my agitation.

"They're going to be fine," he says, taking my shoulders and pulling me backward into his embrace.

"You really think so?"

"I do," he replies, gently twirling me around to face him. "Do you know what else I think?"

"What's that?"

"Hettie was right. I think you and I need to take some time just to breathe. To relax." He smiles and takes my hand. "Come on."

He leads me, not back to the bedroom as I had been expecting, but up two flights of stairs to a room I've never seen before. I realize, glancing at the low, A-frame ceiling, that we're in the attic. But it doesn't look like an attic at all. Instead of crumbling cardboard boxes and old devices collecting cobwebs and dust, the room is filled with a variety of pillows, cushions, and large fleece blankets. White twinkle lights hang from every wall and there's even a tiny bookshelf filled with a variety of classic novels and candles.

"Wow," I breathe. "This is my kind of attic."

"This is actually where I used to stay as a kid," Daniel explains. "I thought it was so cool, having all this space to myself. It was pretty creepy too, back then. Theresa used to collect all these ugly statues of like, pagan gods or something, and this is where she kept them. I would lie up here on my makeshift bed and imagine them coming to life at night, sneaking around the house, trying to read my mind..."

"Then why on Earth did you sleep up here?" I laugh.

"Because I liked it! I like being scared. It's what inspires my imagination."

"That... is twisted."

"Oh yeah?" Daniel asks. Then, with an impish grin, he scoops me right up off of the ground. I'm glad we're alone in the house because I can't stop the shriek that escapes my lips as he carries me across the loft and falls with me down onto a pile of soft, plush pillows. Gazing down at me, he traces my face with his fingertips and toys with wisps of my auburn curls. "What inspires you?"

That's an easy question.

"Isaac. The mountains. The smell of old books... And you."

He leans down and kisses me then. It's the kind of kiss that surely would have left me weak at the knees had I not already been swept off my feet. As we sink deeper into the sea of pillows and blankets, I raise up my arms and wrap them around his body, gripping him, clinging to him as though my very life depended on it. Again, I find myself overwhelmed by how much I want him, how much I crave his touch.

Afterward, he takes me into his arms and kisses my temple.

"I'm sorry I dragged you into all of this," he murmurs.

"What do you mean?" I ask, pulling away to look him in the eye.

"Having to hide from the cameras, being chased out of your own home by the media..."

"It isn't your fault. I mean, yeah, you being who you are has something to do with it. But this is only happening because we found Jake Kingsley alive. And you certainly shouldn't apologize for that."

"I guess I hadn't thought about it that way."

"I really hadn't either until just now," I admit. "I don't like the cameras, and I hate the idea of being talked about or followed. But it's a small price to pay for an innocent life."

"I'll have to keep that in mind," Daniel sighs. "I'm still just so worried about Addie. Some of these articles that are being written... they're rehashing everything that she went through last year. And I just don't understand it. Why include that in an article that's supposed to be about a kid who miraculously survived a week out in the frozen wilderness?"

I remain silent for a few moments. Now that he's broached the subject, there's something I've been wondering. But I haven't known quite how to bring it up... if I should even bring it up at all.

"Can I ask you a question? And if it's too personal, you don't have to answer."

"Sure," he replies.

"How did Addie's mom die?"

"Freak accident," he answers simply. "When she didn't show up to pick Addie up from school that day, the office called her grandparents. They came to get her and then they drove her to the house where..." Daniel trails off. I don't have to guess why.

"Please tell me that Addie didn't see her," I whisper, horrified by the mere thought.

"I wish I could," Daniel sighs and rubs his forehead. "She'd fallen down the stairs, in plain view of the front door."

"God, Daniel. I'm so sorry." I can't imagine what it must be like for a child to find her mother like that. Or for a parent to find their child... I don't even want to think about it.

"That's another reason I brought Addie here. I wanted to get her away from all those memories."

"I would, too," I tell him, snuggling even closer to him.

"Guess this isn't your typical, schmaltzy pillow talk, is it?" he asks.

"Not exactly, no. But I think it's what we need to talk about. And that's a lot more important than whispering sweet nothings and cozy clichés."

"You're incredible. You know that?" He asks, hugging me even tighter against his chest. "I'm not sure what I did to deserve you."

"You deserve everything, Daniel," I whisper, savoring the warmth of his bare skin and the strength of his embrace. "Absolutely everything."

We drift in and out of a dreamy haze for what may be hours. Then again, it may only be a matter of minutes. All I know is by the time we emerge from our passion-induced stupor, I'm completely famished.

"I know Hettie and Theresa are cooking for us tonight, but I've got to have something to tide me over," I tell Daniel as we make our way back downstairs.

"Hey, you don't have to explain it to me. I can always eat," he assures me.

In the kitchen, we help ourselves to a bowl of fruit and a few cubes of Theresa's dairy-free cheddar cheese.

"You know, I really wasn't sure what to expect from something called a cheese alternate, but it's not bad," I admit.

I'm just about to reach for another bite when the front door swings open and Hettie, Theresa, and the kids come scurrying in.

"Back so soon?" Daniel asks, checking the time on his phone. "You've barely been gone two hours."

"Addie was feeling a little anxious," Theresa explains.

"What do you mean?" Daniel asks.

"There was a man," Addie answers.

"A man?" Daniel echoes.

"We didn't notice him right away, so we don't know if he was there before we got there or if..." Hettie trails off.

"If he followed you," Daniel concludes.

Hettie nods.

"Addie's the one who noticed him. She said he'd been in the art gallery, then in the science lab, and then he showed up in the play area. He was standing so out of the way, I don't know if I would have paid him even the slightest bit of attention if Addie hadn't pointed him out. After she did, though, I decided to keep an eye on him. And sure enough, he pulled out a camera."

"Shit," Daniel growls under his breath.

"I'm sorry, Danny. We got them out of there as quickly as we could," Hettie apologizes.

"It's okay," he replies gruffly.

"Thank you for taking care of them," I say, kneeling down to look Isaac in the eye. "Are you okay, Baby?"

"Yeah. Can we go back soon?"

"Yes. We'll definitely get you back there soon," I promise.

"They had a music room!" he exclaims.

"Oh, now *that* is cool," I smile, thankful that he doesn't seem to have been all that aware of or affected by the paparazzi's presence at the Museum.

Although the incident does leave me feeling a bit unsettled, I try my best to remain calm and composed for what remains of the afternoon. And truthfully, being around Daniel and the kids helps. Even the crazy aunts are a source of comfort, although that could be due to Theresa's lavender or sage or whatever she has diffusing throughout the house. Whatever the reason, being here with all of them, it feels as though nothing out there in the world can touch us.

Then the text messages start flooding in.

Most of them are from Jason. A few are from my first grade group chat. One is from a number I don't even recognize. But they all say the same thing.

Jake Kingsley is awake, aware, and has given his account of what happened to his family and to police officers. According to him, he had just planned to go for a quick hike, no longer than an hour or so. He wanted to be back at the resort in time for dinner with Hillary. Then he heard what he thought was an injured animal in the woods. He considered turning back for help, but the sound was so close that he ended up running toward it.

What happened next, he said, is a blur.

He saw it. It rushed him. He hit his head. He isn't sure if he lost consciousness or not. But he remembers flying through the trees as though he were being carried. He remembers sharp claws ripping through his clothes and digging into his skin. And he remembers the smell, like rancid sweat and fresh earth.

Every word, every vivid detail leaves me with a hollow ache in the pit of my stomach.

Because if Jake Kingsley is telling the truth, then all those crazy cryptid conspiracy theorists were right.

There really is something out there.

The Bogman exists.

Chapter Twenty-Nine

By Monday morning, those in the media still haven't given up their pursuit of Daniel, but they at least don't seem quite as interested in me. I guess with a famous author running around town and a real-life monster dragging tourists off into the woods, a local bookshop owner just trying to make it through the day is kind of small peanuts.

And honestly, it's a relief. I want to be able to go out. I want to be at my store. Even with Jason here, following me around like a second shadow and asking the same questions over and over and over.

"Do you think Daniel will come back? I mean, now that everyone knows who he is, he's still going to stay in town, right? What does he think of the Bogman? Do you think he'd be willing to make an appearance on the documentary now?"

"Jason. I don't know. You're just going to have to talk to him," I repeat for what may very well be the dozenth time this morning.

"What about you? Do you want to be in the documentary?"

"Me?"

"Yes, you. You're part of the legacy. You rescued Jake, too."

"Sort of. I'm not even sure I would call it a rescue. More like a miraculous coincidence."

"Well, whatever you want to call it, you were one of the first people to see him after a week in the wilderness. You could talk about what that was like."

"It was surreal. And terrifying."

"Did he happen to say anything to you while he was in the car? You know, about..."

"No."

"And you didn't see anything?"

"Like what? The Bogman?"

"You say it like it would be hard to believe," Jason remarks.

"Yeah, well, it is."

"Are you serious? We've got an eyewitness, a guy who was actually abducted. How can you still be skeptical?"

"Maybe because I don't *want* to believe in it."

"I don't think believing in something is really a choice. You either believe or you don't," Jason argues. "I think what you mean to say is that you *do* believe. You just wish you didn't."

Ding!

The shopkeeper's bell rings before I have a chance to consider whether Jason has a point or not. And to my dismay, Logan is the one who comes shuffling through the door.

"Big. News," he announces without so much as a greeting. "Jake Kingsley has just been discharged from the hospital and he's agreed to a sit-down with us and Santiago for the documentary!"

"Wait, are you *serious*?" Jason exclaims.

"Bro, I am as serious as a freakin' heart attack. This is it. You, me, and Santiago, man. We've got it made!"

"And you're sure that Jake is up for this?" I ask.

Logan turns to look at me as though he hadn't even realized I was present.

"Oh hey, Ms. Keller! Glad you're here!" he grins.

"Where else would I be on a Monday morning?"

"Good point. Listen, I've got a favor to ask - "

"Let me guess," I interrupt him. "You want to use the bookstore for your interview with Jake."

"Solid hypothesis, but no. Don't get me wrong, your store is great, but it's way too public. We want to keep this on the down-low," Logan explains. "No, what I was hoping you might do is talk to your boyfriend and see if he might be willing to - "

"Don't bother. She already said no," Jason cuts in.

"Dammit," Logan grumbles. "Okay, then at least tell us when the two of you got together so one of us can claim our twenty bucks."

I don't even dignify that with a response. Instead, I turn and make my way to the cash register so I can be prepared for my real customers.

"I think that's a lost cause too, man," Jason remarks.

"Ms. Keller! Come on! You've gotta work with us here!" Logan groans. "Can you at least give Jason the rest of the day off?"

"What for?"

"'What for?' Do you even listen?" Logan asks. "For the interview!"

"It's today?" I ask.

"Perhaps you've forgotten, but Jake doesn't actually live here. Now that he's recovered, he wants to get the hell out of here. And after what he's been through, I can't say I blame him," Logan says. "So, what do you say, Ms. Keller? Can you spare my man, here?"

It takes everything in me not to heave an exasperated sigh. After a wonderful albeit hectic weekend at Hettie and Theresa's, I'm exhausted and could really use some help around the store. On the other hand, I know how passionate Jason is about this documentary, and this really could be huge for them. In fact, I know it will be huge.

As someone who wants to see him succeed, as his lifelong friend, I can't say no.

"Go on," I tell Jason. "I'll see if Blythe can come in for a few hours."

"El, you're the best!" Jason exclaims, scooping me up into a huge bear hug.

"Thanks, Ms. Keller. I knew you were cool," Logan grins.

Considering the source, I'm not entirely sure I take that as a compliment.

As soon as they leave, I pick up the phone and call Blythe. I hate to ask anything of anyone at the last minute, but I'm sort of desperate. And it's not only that. I also know Daniel won't be coming in today and I really don't want to be here alone. Not after everything that happened this weekend. I need a familiar face here to keep me calm. Balanced.

"Oh, Honey, of course I can come in!" Blythe says. "Just give me a few minutes to do my hair."

A few minutes in Blythe vernacular could mean anywhere from three short minutes to two hours. But at least I know she'll be here. Eventually.

While I wait, I decide to slip into the storage room to catch up on some inventory. I don't have any customers at the moment, but I keep an ear open for the shopkeeper's bell just in case.

It isn't long before it rings.

"In the back! I'll be right with you!" I holler.

"No need to rush."

The voice is so close and unexpected that I flinch and, in doing so, slam my knee against the back room's built-in shelves.

"Agh," I groan.

"I'm sorry. Didn't mean to startle you there," Cortland Hill apologizes from the doorway.

"Not to be rude, but customers aren't usually allowed back here."

"Well, as the owner, I'm sure you can make an exception," Cortland smiles, taking a step inside the storage room.

I recoil instantly.

"How can I help you, Mr. Hill?" I ask, my voice uncharacteristically standoffish.

"I just wanted to stop by and check in. I heard the news that Jake Kingsley's been found. That's wonderful." The sentiment is kind, his tone sincere, and yet, I don't trust him. "And how heroic of Daniel - I mean D.H. Whittaker."

Of course. That's why he's here. He's looking for Daniel.

"Yeah. It was a miracle."

"Oh, I think it was more than a miracle. I mean, what are the odds that he and his... *female companion...* would happen to be driving along the exact stretch of highway at exactly the right time of night to cross paths with a young man who, I'm fairly certain, had no idea where he was?"

Wait a minute. What is he insinuating? He obviously knows that I'm the woman who was with Daniel that night. It really isn't all that surprising. After all, the media swarm did publish their pictures of my rather distinctive hair. But he seems to be implying something else too. It almost sounds like he's accusing us of staging the entire rescue.

"Astronomical, I'd say," I reply lightly. "But it *is* what happened."

"No need to get defensive. I'm not accusing you of anything. Though if I were, I guess we could call it even."

With that, my heart begins to pound with dread and a deafening rush floods my ears.

"What do you mean?" I try to keep my tone conversational and nonchalant, but a tremor in my voice betrays me.

"I know you thought I was the one who kidnapped Jake. And I'll admit, my showing up the week before he disappeared probably seemed a little too coincidental. Hell, if I had been in your shoes, I may have suspected the same thing. I just don't know that I would have taken that suspicion all the way to the police."

"I'm sorry," I apologize without hesitation.

"I know you are. And I forgive you," Hill assures me. "Of course, if you wanted to make it up to me - "

"I could schedule you a book signing?" I ask.

"You could," Hill laughs. "No, I was going to say you could let me take you to dinner sometime."

Now I'm confused. He knows I'm with Daniel. Or at least, he knows I was with him on a Friday night. And although his persistence is sort of flattering, I can't help but feel that he has no real interest in me. That he's just playing some sort of game to which I've yet to figure out the rules.

"Mr. Hill - "

"Cortland."

"Cortland... I think you know that I'm not available," I tell him as gently as I can.

"Not even for *one* night?"

"No. I'm sorry."

"What if we just went out as friends?"

"*Are* we friends? I mean, after the police and everything, I'm surprised you even want to be in the same town as me."

"I want to give you the chance to get to know me better," he replies. "I mean, I can't have made the greatest first impression if your first instinct was to suspect me of kidnapping."

Well, he's got me there.

"Again, I really am sorry about that. I tend to be a little... overly cautious. And this time, I guess I let my fear get the better of me."

"And that's okay," he says, reaching out to touch my shoulder. Even though it seems like he's trying to comfort me, I automatically flinch away. "Come on. Just one night. I promise I'll be on my best behavior. I'll even wear a suit. What do you say?"

"Cortland... I hope you know that you seem like a very... *decent* man." I don't necessarily believe this, but it's the best I can come up with on the spot. "But I'm with Daniel." And even if I wasn't, I wouldn't be interested. But he really doesn't need to hear that. "I'm sorry. I just don't think it's a good idea."

It's then that my words finally seem to sink in. Hill's friendly grin vanishes from his face in an instant, and his once warm amber eyes are suddenly cold and resentful. It's almost as though he's morphed into a completely different person.

"I guess I'm not surprised," he sneers, his voice hard and callous. "After all, why would you want me when you've got D.H. fucking Whittaker?"

I'm so stunned by his anger and vulgarity that I'm rendered absolutely speechless.

"You know, I thought you were different, Eloise," he continues. "I thought you were the kind of woman who knew how to appreciate a man's inner value. But you're just another dimwitted, gold-digging slut."

With that, he storms out of the storage room and tears across the store, kicking over a rolling cart stacked with books in the process. I can only stand, frozen to the spot, and watch as he yanks the front door open so violently, I'm afraid he may pull it clean off its hinges. Just before he leaves, however, he stops and looks back at me.

"Oh, and one more thing," he hollers. "When he turns his back on you - *and he will* - don't expect any sympathy from me."

Then he disappears into a gust of wintry wind, leaving me shocked, confused, and utterly shaken.

Chapter Thirty

"So what, do you think he was threatening you?" Jason asks.

It's been roughly twenty-four hours since my encounter with Cortland Hill yet I can still hear his harsh words ringing in my ears as loud and clear as the shopkeeper's bell.

"I don't know if I would say that he was *threatening* me," I reply, kneeling down to help him restock and reorganize the books in the Young Adult section. "It was more like he was taking everything out on me. His anger, his jealousy, his loneliness..."

"You think he's lonely?"

"He sure seems like it. I mean, clearly, he wants someone to be with. I think I was just the first available woman he met and he sort of zeroed in."

"Probably doesn't hurt that you own a bookshop, either," Jason adds with a quick grin.

"I really thought that was all he was interested in. But now... I don't know. Now it seems like there may be something else. And whatever it is, I don't like it."

"Are you going to report him?"

"No. I'm not making that mistake again."

"Yeah, I guess you were sort of off the mark the first time."

"It's not even that." Although, it *would* be a little more than awkward to go traipsing back into Emma Jean's office with another complaint about the same guy I falsely accused just last week. "I don't know how, but he found out that I talked to the police about him."

Jason's face falls.

"Are you serious?"

"Yeah. And it gets even more unsettling. According to Emma Jean, she never talked to him. She couldn't find him. He's not staying in any of the motels, any of the inns... The guy is a ghost."

Jason stops to think while he straightens out a paperback set of the *Doll* trilogy by Miracle Austin.

"Well, did you ever stop to think that maybe Cortland Hill is a pen name? I mean, Daniel writes under D.H. Whittaker. Santiago's real name is Stuart. Maybe Hill's so hard to find because he's using a different name."

Oh, my God. Of course. Why *didn't* I think of that?

"Jason, you're a genius."

"I know. It's a burden," he sighs, feigning humility.

"Although, it still doesn't explain how he found out about me going to the police in the first place."

"It's a small town. And everybody was talking about how they'd identified a suspect," he shrugs. "Maybe he heard the rumors and put two and two together."

"Maybe," I echo.

"So, what does Daniel have to say about all this?"

"Oh, he doesn't know."

"You didn't tell him?" Jason asks.

I shake my head.

"He has so much on his plate right now with the media and worrying about Addie and the new book and... I just didn't want to add to all that, you know?"

"But don't you think he'd want to know?"

"He already knows he makes me uncomfortable. And if it happens again, then yeah, I'll tell him. But for now, I'm just going to let him focus on Addie. And on avoiding all the reporters who, by now, are probably camped out on his front lawn," I say. "And hey, speaking of interviews, how did yours go?"

Jason looks thrilled, almost giddy that I'm asking. I can tell he's been eager to talk about it all morning.

"It was *amazing*, El. I don't even know where to begin," he gushes.

"So, you believe his story? You think he really saw...?" I trail off, unable, or perhaps unwilling to say the words.

"I know he did. And I know you probably don't want to hear the gory details but - "

"No. It's okay. You can tell me."

Jason takes a deep breath. Then, he's grinning from ear-to-ear.

"He said it was like something out of the movies. He didn't even believe it was real at first. He thought it was a guy in a costume, with the gruesome teeth and the matted black fur. It was the eyes that finally convinced him that it wasn't his imagination running away with him. He said they were stained brown and yellow, like an animal's eyes. But the way it looked at him, like it was trying to understand or solve some sort of problem... That intelligence, he said, made it seem almost human."

Jason's story sends a chill down my spine. Still, I stand my ground.

"So, what happened?" I ask.

"When he realized what he was seeing, Jake said he wanted to scream. He wanted to run. But instead, he froze. Santiago asked him what he was thinking in that moment and he said he was hoping that if he didn't seem threatening, the monster would just wander off. But that creature - that *thing* - it had already seen him. And somehow, it knew."

"So it attacked."

"Yeah," Jason confirms. "He doesn't remember much after that. He hit his head pretty hard after it lunged. But the one thing he does remember, he says, is the smell. The putrid, sweaty, smell of fur and blood and dirt. He says he can still smell it, even after almost two weeks."

God, what a nightmare.

"How did he survive? I mean, how did he last a week in freezing temperatures?"

"He said he woke up in some sort of den. He thinks the monster must have made it. Originally, he tried to run, tried to stumble back to the trail, but he got so dizzy that he knew he wouldn't make it far. So he laid low and he snuck back to the den. And that's where he hid."

"And the... thing never came back?"

"He said he saw it a few more times, passing through the trees. But it stayed away from the den. Santiago guesses it probably has more than one."

"That's reassuring," I deadpan.

"He also thinks there's *probably* more than one Bogman." Jason draws out the last few words of his statement like he's reluctant to tell me. Probably because he knows it's something I don't want to hear. "I mean, it had to come from somewhere, right?"

"I'd really rather not think about that."

"Noted. But hey, if it makes you feel better, they seem to want to avoid us as much as we want to avoid them."

"No, that doesn't help."

"Well, then I've got nothing," Jason laughs.

It's only then that it finally hits me how monumental this is, not just for Cedar Ridge or the scientific community, but for Jason. For Logan and Santiago, too. This discovery, their documentary, and especially their interview with Jake could easily kickstart their careers.

"This is really going to change things for you, isn't it?" I ask Jason.

"Yeah. I think it is," he replies. He sounds anxious, yet excited.

"Guess I'm going to have to dust off the old **Now Hiring** sign when you go off and become an eminent and esteemed filmmaker."

"Well, you know, when that happens, I'm going to owe it all to you," Jason says.

"What are you talking about? You don't owe me anything."

"But I do. You've always believed in me, El. Even if you didn't necessarily understand my fascination with the paranormal, you've always encouraged me to pursue my passion. Most employers wouldn't have given me time off whenever I wanted to run around chasing monsters."

Listening to him, I feel my heart begin to melt. I never realized how much my support meant to him.

"I want your dreams to come true. And not just so you can buy me a new car when you get rich and famous," I tease.

"Hey, last time I checked, you've got a rich and famous new boyfriend who could probably buy you ten new cars."

"Yeah, but I wouldn't feel guilty taking advantage of *your* good fortune," I laugh. Then, something he said earlier suddenly hits me, evoking a very delayed reaction. "Wait a minute, did you say that Santiago's real name is *Stuart*?"

"Oh, yeah," he snickers. "He figured he'd only get so far in the paranormal world with a name like Stuart Edwards, so he changed it to Santiago. Apparently, his great-grandmother was from Spain so he thought he could get away with it."

"Fascinating," I remark.

"Do you know why Daniel chose the name D.H. Whittaker?"

"No. Do you?"

"No! That's why I was asking!"

"Really? You don't know? I thought you were his biggest fan!"

"I thought it was his real name!"

"Well, I guess I'll have to ask him next time I see him."

"When's that going to be?"

"Hopefully in the next day or two."

"You two are getting pretty serious, aren't you?" Jason grins.

"I don't know," I shrug. "I mean, it's not like we've had the most normal courtship."

"Yeah, that might be because you go around unironically using words like courtship," he quips. "I'm still holding out hope I get to be your dude of honor at the wedding though."

"*Dude* of honor?"

"Well, it'd be a little presumptuous of me to think I could be Daniel's best man. I mean, I might be the best friend he's got, but if I am, that'd be really sad."

"You're so strange," I sigh.

"That's why you love me," Jason grins.

Sure, it is.

As luck would have it, I'm going to get to see Daniel much sooner than I'd expected. Logan and Santiago invited him to stop by Logan's apartment this evening for a sneak preview of the interview before it "goes viral" and he accepted, but only on the condition that he could bring me as his date. Naturally, they agreed.

"Will you be there?" I ask Jason as we go about closing up shop for the day.

"Hell yeah, I'll be there. You think I would miss it?"

"No, I guess not," I laugh. "Hey, since we're not supposed to be there until 7, do you want to stop by my place after we're done here? We're having chicken tenders and smiley-faced french fries; both your and Isaac's favorite."

"Wish I could, but I've got a few errands to run. And I promised the guys I'd get there early to go over any last-minute edits. But I am definitely going to take you up on that soon. I miss just hanging out with you and Isaac."

"Yeah. It seems like it's been a while."

"Well, you've got a boyfriend and I've got a Bogman," Jason grins. "But hey, if we're done, I'm going to go ahead and get going. But I'll see you tonight!"

"See you tonight," I reply with a wave.

At home, I try my best not to hurry through dinner. It isn't usual for me to be rushing in and then rushing back out again, especially on a Tuesday night, but I promise both my mom and Isaac that I won't be late.

"I'm not even letting Daniel pick me up," I explain to my mom. "I'm taking my own car so that I can leave as soon as it's over."

"Don't worry about it. I'm just happy that you're finally getting out," my mom tells me.

"Well, like I said, I can't imagine this viewing party will last longer than an hour. In fact, I'm loath to even call it a party."

"Eloise. It's okay. Go out. Enjoy. Isaac and I will be fine."

"Thank you," I smile.

I make sure to kiss Isaac twice just in case I don't make it back before his bedtime. Then, I slip my coat back on and step out into the winter twilight.

Logan's apartment complex is less than a five-minute drive from my house. In fact, when I was looking for a place for Isaac and me to live, I considered renting an apartment there. Of course, in the end, I decided I wanted a house, and I've always been glad that I did. I'm even gladder now that I know how perilously close I came to having Logan Taylor as a neighbor.

I make sure to locate Daniel's car in the parking lot before knocking on Logan's door. Even though I know Jason said he'd be arriving early, I don't want to be the person who shows up before the guest of honor. I'm the second-string invitee.

Santiago is the one who answers the door.

"It's Eloise!" he hollers back into the apartment. To me, he says, "Come on in. Toss your coat anywhere."

Logan's apartment looks exactly how I might have imagined it had I ever stopped to wonder. The kitchen, it appears, hasn't been cleaned in at least a week. The plastic waste bin overflows with disposable red cups and empty pizza boxes and the countertops are cluttered with dirty plates and discarded paper towels. In the living area, a faded orange futon sits in front of a second-hand coffee table and a television that's hooked up to what looks like three different gaming consoles. The bookshelf at the far end of the room is rather bare, save for a few graphic novels and action figures, but the walls are lined with an impressive collection of vintage horror movie posters.

"So, what do you think of my humble abode, Ms. Keller?" Logan asks, emerging from the darkened hallway and carrying a laptop that has certainly seen better days. Daniel trails a few feet behind him.

"It's... homey," I answer as Daniel pulls me into a casual embrace.

"Pretty sure that's girl code for *filthy*," Santiago remarks, reaching his hand into a family-sized bag of Doritos. "Chip?" he offers.

"Oh, no thank you," I reply. Daniel declines as well.

"I'm glad I get to see you today." He smiles down at me.

"I am too. I can't stay too late, though. I want to try to make it home before Isaac's bedtime."

"What?" Logan yelps. "You mean you'd rather tuck your kid into bed than spend time with us?"

I honestly can't tell if he's joking or not, so I change the subject.

"Hey, where's Jason? He told me he was going to be here early."

"Yeah, well, he was *supposed* to be," Logan grumbles. "But apparently, he decided to flake out on us."

"That's not like him." Jason is one of the most dependable people I know. When he says he'll be somewhere, he'll be there.

"Yeah, tell me about it. Usually, when something comes up, he's at least considerate enough to text. I don't know. Maybe he lost his phone charger or something." Logan shrugs.

"Did he seem okay earlier?" Daniel asks me.

"Yeah, he was fine. He was really excited about tonight," I reply.

"Maybe he's having car trouble," Santiago theorizes. "Last time my car broke down, I was so preoccupied worrying about what was wrong with it that I didn't think to let anyone know what had happened."

"I'm going to try to reach him," I announce, scrolling through my contacts in my phone until I find Jason's name. I tap on it and wait for a dial tone.

My call goes straight to voicemail.

I try not to let my overactive anxiety get the better of me.

"Hey, it's Jason. Leave a message."

"Hey Jason, it's Eloise. I'm here at Logan's and he said he hasn't heard from you, so I'm just calling to make sure that you're all right. Call me as soon as you get this, okay? Or at least text me to let me know everything's okay."

"I'm sure he's fine," Daniel assures me, slipping his hand around the small of my back.

I let him guide me into the living area, where Logan has hooked his laptop up to the television. Jake Kingsley's haunted face stares down at me from the screen.

"Okay, we're just about ready," Logan announces. "Take a seat, take a seat."

Daniel and I sit with Santiago on the futon while Logan drops down onto the floor beside the coffee table.

"You guys ready for this?" Santiago asks Daniel and me.

"Yeah, let's do it," Daniel answers.

"Are you sure you don't want to wait for Jason?" I ask.

"I mean, we can, but you're the one who said you wanted to leave early," Logan reminds me.

"I know. It just doesn't feel right to watch without him."

"Fine. We'll wait. The rest of us have got all night." Logan shrugs.

"Actually, I want to get home at a reasonable hour, too," Daniel says. "It's a school night."

"Okay, then we're watching it now," Logan decides. Then he presses *Play*.

The interview begins with introductions and a brief history of the Bogman before Jake recounts his experience with the beast. Although it's plain to see the guys have taken great care with Jake, with the story, and with the production itself, my mind keeps drifting back to Jason. It just doesn't make any sense. He was so excited to share this interview with us tonight.

Obsessively, I check my phone every other minute. And not just the text messages or missed calls. I check Facebook to see if his account has been active recently. I check Instagram, which I rarely use, to see if Jason has maybe shared a story. I even check my email on the off chance he's tried to reach out that way.

Nothing. There's nothing.

The minutes tick by. I check my messages and missed calls and Facebook and email over and over and over again. The interview eventually ends.

Jason never shows up.

Chapter Thirty-One

It's Wednesday morning, the store is open, and I still haven't heard from Jason. No one has. Not even his mother. It probably goes without saying that she's frantic with worry. We both are.

"I'm sure he's fine, Sweetheart," Hettie assures me. After she heard about Jason, she dropped everything and drove down to the store to check on me and to see if I needed any help.

"I hope so. This is just so unlike him," I whimper, fighting back tears. "I keep replaying yesterday in my head, everything we talked about, everything he said. It doesn't make sense that he would just... disappear."

"You said that he was going to run some errands. Do you know what they were?"

"No. But his truck isn't here, so he must have at least made it away from Main Street." As I speak the words, I map out Downtown Cedar Ridge in my mind. Jason didn't specify the errands he would be running, but knowing him, there're really only so many places he might have gone. The grocery store. The liquor store. Maybe Radio Shack if Logan needed something for his computer or his editing software? I don't know.

Ding!

My heart leaps at the sound of the shopkeeper's bell. Hoping to see Jason, I whirl around only to find myself face-to-face with my stepfather Lenny and three of his hunting buddies.

"Lenny?" I ask, more than a little confused. Don't get me wrong, I love my stepfather. He's good to my mother and he's always been very supportive. It's just that he and his friends are more likely to frequent the bait shop than the bookshop. "What are you doing here?"

"Your mom called and told me about Jason. Me and the boys thought we'd stop by and see if there was anything we could do before we head out into the woods," Lenny explains.

"Got us a Bogman to hunt!" Earl, a tiny old man who always wears the same aviator hat, whoops with a staggering amount of gusto.

It probably goes without saying that most of our local outdoorsmen are Bogman enthusiasts.

"You're not really thinking of going after it, are you?" Hettie asks, toying with her strands of party pearls.

"Hell yeah, we are, Hettie!" Tommy, Lenny's younger brother, exclaims. "This damn beast's been terrorizing our town long enough! And if you'd've seen the boys' video, you'd be saying the same thing!"

"Wait, what video?" I ask.

"That interview they did with Jake Kingsley. *Miss Sally in the Morning* showed a clip of it on her show, so my wife pulled up the whole video for us to watch on YouTube," Scott, the fourth member of the hunting party, answers.

My mouth runs dry. They wouldn't. I know Logan and Santiago are unapologetically ambitious, and yes, their priorities can seem a little skewed at times, but *surely* they wouldn't go ahead and share the interview when their friend and colleague is *missing*.

And yet, they did.

Is this some sort of game to them? Do they not understand how serious this is? Jake Kingsley barely escaped the clutches of whatever's out there with his life. If Jason is the Bogman's latest victim, he may not be so lucky.

"What were they thinking, Hettie?" I ask once Lenny and his friends have cleared out. "Jason vanished into thin air and yet they still thought it would be appropriate to post that stupid video?"

"Now, now, Eloise. Think about it for a minute. Do you remember how much publicity those boys generated for Jake Kingsley last week? They were trying to help him. Maybe this is their way of trying to help Jason, too," Hettie suggests.

I'd like to believe that. And you know, maybe there is some truth to it. Santiago and Logan may have very well been acting out of genuine concern for their friend. The problem is, however, that I know they had made plans to share the video today long before Jason went missing. And his mysterious disappearance wasn't enough to derail those plans.

Suddenly, I'm blinking back tears.

"I hope so," I whisper, stifling a sob. "God, Hettie, what if something really bad has happened to him?"

"Oh no, Sweetheart, you can't think like that," Hettie says. "Jason has a whole town full of people who care about him and who are going to do whatever it takes to find him."

"It was upsetting enough to know a stranger was lost somewhere out there. But Jason... he's like my little brother. I can't lose him."

"You won't," Hettie says. "What do you say I stick around and help you out today? Would you like that?"

Sniffling, I nod.

"Thank you, Hettie."

She smiles and pulls me into a warm hug.

"Everything is going to be all right," she promises. "You'll see."

I move through the rest of the day in a sort of trance. We have a steady stream of customers, all offering their condolences and encouraging me to let them know if there's anything they can do. Everyone in town knows and loves Jason, but somehow, their sympathies and sincere expressions of grief only make me feel worse. Because Jason didn't deserve this. The whole town agrees that he didn't deserve this, that it shouldn't have happened.

So why *did* it happen? I'm not sure that we'll ever know. I can only hope we'll find some answers tonight. Emma Jean has been working tirelessly with her officers and with Jason's parents to organize a search party. That's where I'm headed now.

Another search party. I can't help but shudder. We shouldn't have to be doing this again. Especially not for Jason.

But it *is* for Jason. And that's why I need to keep it together. I can't fall apart. Not tonight. I have to be strong. Present.

Just as before, volunteers are asked to arrive thirty minutes before the search itself is scheduled to begin. This time, however, we're staying a little closer to home. Jason was last seen on Main Street, right outside of The Mountain Cafe, so we're meeting at Town Hall to sign in, to split up into teams, and to strategize.

Suddenly, I find myself fighting off a sickening sense of déjà vu.

By the time I arrive, Town Hall is already packed to the rafters with concerned citizens, eager volunteers, and determined local authorities. It looks as though the entire town has turned out to help find Jason. Glancing around, I spot Emma Jean poring over a series of notes with Jason's father. A few feet away from them, Logan and Santiago are doing their best to comfort Jason's inconsolable mother. Off to the side, I see a team of dads from Isaac's school rummaging through their backpacks. Some of them have even brought along their eldest children.

And then, there's Daniel.

Seeing his face, a lump immediately forms in my throat, and as he makes his way over to me, I once again find myself trying not to cry.

"You're here," I breathe.

"Of course I'm here," he says, taking my hand and gently pulling me into his arms. "Jason... he's a good kid."

"He really his," I whimper.

"How are you doing? Are you okay?"

"I'll be better once I know he's safe. How about you?"

"About the same," he answers.

"Are you... I mean... Are you *okay* being here? What if someone recognizes you? Or what if a reporter shows up and - "

"Hey, hey, shhh. It's all right," Daniel soothes me. "If it happens, it happens. That's not important right now. All that matters is finding Jason and making sure he's okay."

Too choked up to speak, I simply nod.

"All right, everybody! Can I have your attention please?" Emma Jean's amplified voice reverberates through the hall. She's positioned herself at the front of the room and is speaking into a wireless handheld microphone. "I know a few of you still need to get signed in, but I want to go ahead and get started." She takes a deep breath and deliberates a moment before she continues. "I never expected to be doing this again. Especially not for one of our own. I think most of us in this room know Jason Harberger. We watched him grow from a thoughtful and curious boy into a fine young man. And we are going to do everything in our power to bring him home safely."

The crowd murmurs their agreement as Emma Jean continues.

"It is for that reason that I've asked two of Jason's colleagues to speak here tonight. Now we don't know if his disappearance is in any way connected to what happened to Jake Kingsley, but if it is, these young men may be able to give us all a better idea of what we might be dealing with here. So please give your undivided attention to Santiago Edwards and Logan Taylor."

I expect Santiago and Logan to address the crowd with their usual confidence and robust determination, but that isn't what happens at all. Logan looks pale, almost ashen. His hands visibly tremble when he steps forward to take the mic. Santiago looks slightly less worse for the wear, but he's clearly agitated. He keeps shuffling his feet back and forth and he runs a hand through his green hair at least once every ten seconds.

I guess Jason's disappearance is affecting them more than they were willing to let on last night.

"Good evening, everyone," Logan begins. His voice sounds hoarse. Has he been crying? "I'm Logan Taylor. For those of you who don't know, Jason is my best friend. Like Emma Jean said, we don't want to take up too much of your time, so let's get down to the basics..."

"*Harumph*," a low, gravelly voice from somewhere behind me snarls.

Startled, I turn to see a frail, frazzled figure limping slowly through the crowded room. His head is cocked slightly to the right and his pale blue eyes are looking Logan and Santiago up and down with blatant distaste.

"Floyd Whalen," I whisper.

"Hmm?" Daniel asks.

"Right there." I nod in Floyd's general direction, but he's still on the move, crouched and slinking toward Jason and Santiago with a considerable amount of caution. In a way, he reminds me of an old, gray alley cat stalking prey he doesn't fully trust.

"Liars," Floyd Whalen grumbles as he pushes his way further into the crowd.

"What is he doing?" I hiss.

"Maybe he's trying to help," Daniel murmurs.

Maybe. But it certainly doesn't look that way.

By now, Floyd is drawing more and more attention to himself, pressing ever onward and sputtering even more nonsense. Finally, he breaks through to where Logan and Santiago are still attempting to share their insights on Jake Kingsley and the Bogman attack.

And Floyd is having none of it.

"Liars!" he exclaims again. This time, however, his guttural growl echoes through the entire hall. "Don't listen! Don't listen to them! They're cheats! Impostors!"

"I'm sorry, who the hell are you?" Santiago demands.

"I'm Floyd Joseph Whalen. I'm the guy who's calling you out on all of your *crap!*" Floyd spits back at him.

"Jesus," Logan mutters and buries his hands in his face.

"What? You thought you could get away with this? With your silly little made up stories?" Floyd demands. "Bullshit."

"Okay, could somebody please get him out of here? Chief Wilde?" Santiago asks.

Emma Jean and her deputy are on the scene within seconds.

"All right, Whalen, that's enough," she says. "Come with us."

"I ain't goin' nowhere until they admit it!" Floyd barks back.

"Admit what?" Santiago challenges him.

Floyd squares his jaw and looks him dead in the eye.

"That it was all a sham. That you made up the whole damn thing. That you two wouldn't know the Beast of Bog's Creek if it bit you on the ass!"

Chapter Thirty-Two

Logan and Santiago stand frozen and absolutely speechless as every soul inside of Town Hall waits for their response to Floyd Whalen's accusation.

It's Jason's father who finally breaks the silence.

"Is it true?" he demands.

"No!" Santiago tries to insist. But his voice breaks and his eyes betray him. "Why would you think that? Why would anyone think that?"

"Black fur," Floyd rasps.

"What?" Santiago asks.

"You boys... in your video... described a monster with gold eyes, gnashing teeth, and *black* fur."

"Yeah, because that's what Jake *saw*," Santiago argues. "That's the monster that freaking attacked him!"

"Then it wasn't the *Beast!*" Floyd growls back.

For a moment, I wonder what Floyd could possibly be hoping to accomplish by discrediting the two people in town who believe in the Bogman as much as he does. Then suddenly, I hear his voice in my head, describing his encounter with a monster as tall as two grizzlies. A beast with a pig's snout and long, glistening fangs. A creature with *russet* fur, matted with mud and blood.

Russet. Not black.

Logan and Santiago didn't stick to Floyd Whalen's story.

It's a minor detail. No one who watched the video would have given it a second thought. But Floyd caught it. And now he's taking them on in front of the entire town.

Santiago just scoffs.

"You're crazy. Tell him, Logan."

But Logan remains at a loss for words, looking for all the world like a man who's just realized he's made a profoundly grave mistake. Because the thing is Floyd Whalen *is* crazy. Everyone in Cedar Ridge knows he's crazy. And *why* do we all think that?

Because he's the only one who's supposedly seen the Bogman face-to-face. He's the only one who's been attacked. He's the only one who, if he was telling the truth, if the monster is real, would be able to catch them in a hoax.

And if the look on Logan's face is any indication, he just did.

"Logan?" Jason's poor mom whimpers.

That's when Logan finally breaks.

"I'm sorry," he chokes.

Several people gasp. Then everyone begins shouting at once.

"What do you mean? What are you saying?"

"But what happened to Jake?"

"Where's Jason?"

"Quiet!" Emma Jean bellows. Even without the microphone, her voice commands the attention of the entire hall. "Everyone, settle down!" Then, she turns to Logan and Santiago, her eyes ablaze. "You. Explain yourselves."

Santiago, realizing he's been defeated, draws in a shaky breath.

"It wasn't supposed to go this far. We just... wanted to generate a little publicity. Help the Bogman take his rightful place in mainstream cryptozoology," he tries to explain.

"Wait a minute. Are you saying that *you* kidnapped Jake Kingsley?" a young man in the crowd demands to know.

"No! Of course we didn't kidnap him," Logan answers adamantly.

"Jake is a friend of mine. He's an actor," Santiago explains.

"He was *in* on it?" I tremble.

"He figured it couldn't hurt his prospects if, you know, a few extra people knew his name," Santiago admits.

"But... his injuries... the sunglasses out in the woods..."

Santiago shrugs.

"What can I say? The guy's committed."

I can't be hearing this. It wouldn't be hard for me to believe that Logan and Santiago would exploit a man who'd spent several days lost in the woods. I wouldn't put that past them at all. But for them to orchestrate the entire thing? To inflict an actual nightmare on so many people? How could they do that? How could Jake agree to it? And Jason...

"What about Jason?" I ask.

"What?" Santiago responds.

"Jason! Did *he* know?" I'm openly crying now and I don't even know why. Shock? Disgust? Exhaustion? Perhaps a combination of the three?

"No," Logan says. "No, he had no idea. He thought it was real. We knew that he... that he wouldn't have approved."

"No, he wouldn't have. He would've *never* gone along with it," I sob.

"So, what is this? Another trick?" an older man in the crowd wants to know.

"No," Santiago swears. "We had nothing to do with this."

"But you *are* interfering," one of the younger police officers points out. "Not only are you brazenly wasting valuable time tonight with your lies, you got local and state police involved in your little publicity stunt. And you may not know this, but that is a criminal offense."

"What?" What little color remains in Logan's face drains from it completely and he takes an involuntary step back.

"Shit," Santiago mutters.

"You know, I think it would be better to continue this discussion down at the station," Emma Jean intervenes. "Now, I'd appreciate it if you two came willingly, but I will arrest you right here, right now if you feel like resisting."

Santiago and Logan both murmur their agreement.

Emma Jean turns to address her officers.

"Pearce, Tony, you're with me. I want the rest of you scouring every inch of this town for Jason Harberger. Search every alley. Plaster every window with posters. Make no mistake, we *will* bring him home safely. Now let's go!"

The search for Jason carries on well past midnight, but there's still no sign of him. And by the time Daniel walks me back to my car, I'm feeling drained, disoriented, and hopeless.

"Look at me," Daniel says, cupping my face in his hands. "Are you going to be all right?"

"Yeah, I'll be fine," I answer automatically, though I don't necessarily believe it. I'm not sure that he does, either.

"I can come back with you if you want," he offers.

There's nothing I'd love more than to have him with me. I want him to hold me, to love me, to make me forget about everything I learned tonight. And everything I might have lost.

"I do want that. But you should be home with Addie tonight." After an evening like this, we all need to be at home with the ones we love the most.

He nods. Then, he pulls me into his arms and presses his lips to my forehead. Settling into his embrace, I take a moment to close my eyes and just breathe.

"Where could he be?" I whisper before I can help myself.

"I don't know," Daniel admits.

"A small part of me feels like I should be relieved, you know? Knowing that it wasn't some bloodthirsty monster. But if it wasn't the monster, then what was it?"

"I wish I could tell you," Daniel murmurs, running a soothing hand up and down my back.

"I just... I can't believe that Logan and Santiago were ready to let us believe that they had all the answers... at Jason's expense. They were fully prepared to let us believe the lie, even if it meant leading us in the wrong direction."

"If it makes you feel better, I think they were struggling with it."

It doesn't. Perhaps it should, but the fact remains that they still did it. They still staged a young man's disappearance. They wasted time and resources and God knows what else... and for what? An interview? A few clicks on their YouTube channel?

I can't think about this anymore. I don't want to think about it.

"Thank you for being here tonight," I say, pulling away just enough to look into his eyes. "It really means so much."

"I wasn't about to let you go through it alone," Daniel replies, softly stroking my cheek with a gloved hand. Then, he leans down and kisses me. His mouth on mine is warm, comforting.

I love you. I don't speak the words, but I feel them dancing on the tip of my tongue. I love him. And yet, I can't bring myself to tell him. Not after everything we've been through tonight.

"We should probably be getting home," I murmur, my voice tinged with regret. The thought of leaving him, even for a short while, leaves me feeling cold and empty. But by now, we're the only two left on the street. It's too still out here. Too silent. And I can't help but fear that, if we stay out here any longer, whatever it was that took Jason might just come for us, too.

Daniel pulls me in for one last kiss before nodding in agreement.

"Promise to text me when you get there?" he whispers.

"I promise," I reply.

He waits until I've climbed into my car to begin making his way back to his own vehicle. I'm not sure where he's parked, but my eyes follow him until he's turned a corner onto another street.

Shivering I insert the key into my car's ignition and turn it. The engine cranks. But then, it sputters, coughs, and falls silent. I try it again. Same result.

No. Come on, please. Not tonight.

I turn the key once more, twisting with all my might.

It's no use. I'm stranded.

Nerves absolutely shot, I fall back against the headrest, close my eyes, and take several deep breaths.

It's okay. You're okay. Don't panic, I tell myself. *Call Daniel. With any luck, he's still in the area.*

It's then, as I'm reaching into my purse for my phone, that I realize I'm no longer alone. A figure stands in the middle of the barren street, watching my every move.

My heart thuds and my stomach drops.

With fumbling fingers, I swipe my phone awake, torn between calling Daniel and dialing 911.

Don't be ridiculous. I shake my head. Whoever is out there is probably a straggling member of the search party looking for his car. There's no need to call the police.

But then, as though he senses the shift in my reserve, the silhouette in street begins to move steadily and purposefully in my direction. I still can't make out who he is, but something in his stride leaves me feeling exceptionally vulnerable sitting here all alone in a car that won't start.

Anxious, I make the hasty decision to jump out of the car and face him. I keep a firm grip on my keys, however, just in case. My mother taught me at a young age that in a worst-case scenario, I could use them to defend myself. I pray tonight that I won't need to.

"Hello there, Eloise," the shadowed man greets me with a voice that sends a shiver of dread down my spine.

Cortland Hill.

"What are you doing here?"

He doesn't answer. Not directly, anyway.

"Having car trouble?" His question is casual enough, but there's something off about his tone. It's almost as though he isn't surprised to find me out here. "Maybe I can help."

"Actually, I was just about to call Daniel."

Stupid! I scold myself immediately. I shouldn't have admitted that I hadn't called him yet. I should have told him Daniel was already on his way. That unless he's looking for a fight, he should probably clear on out of here.

"You don't really want to bother him with this, do you? It's so late, after all. He should be getting home to Addie. Like you said."

My entire body goes cold as the meaning of his words sinks in.

"You.... you..."

Oh, *God.*

He'd been listening. How close had he been? *Where* had he been?

And how long has this been going on?

He takes another step closer to me.

"It's all right, Eloise. Come on, you know I'm not going to hurt you."

But I don't. I don't know that. And as he reaches out to take my hand, every instinct in me screams at me to flee.

And so I do.

I take off like a bullet through the dark, the icy wind biting at my face and making my eyes sting with tears. I don't think Cortland is running after me, but I can't say for sure that he isn't, either. So I keep running.

I bolt between buildings and into the poorly-lit back alley. I can barely make out anything through the darkness, but I know that if I keep going, I'll reach the bookstore's back door. That's my destination.

Cortland probably expects me to seek sanctuary there, but he can't possibly hope to follow me. Even if he does, I doubt he'll be able to find his way to the back door by the time I've locked it again. From the alley, all the backsides of the buildings look pretty much the same, especially in the dark.

Finally, I reach my bookshop. My hands shake with icy adrenaline as I unlock the door. Then, with a quick glimpse over my shoulder, I duck inside the pitch-black storage room and slam the door behind me. Once I've locked and deadbolted it, I take a few moments to catch my breath.

I need to call Daniel. I need to call Mom. I need to call anyone.

It's only then that I realize that I don't have my phone. It's back in my car, along with everything else.

That's okay. That's fine. I have a landline here.

Unwilling to alert anyone to my presence, I keep the lights off and stay low to the ground as I maneuver my way out of the storage room and into the store itself.

It's a different world in here at night. During the day, Blue Ridge Books is warm and inviting, almost magical in my mind. When the sun is shining, I feel peace and hope surrounded by so many books, so many thoughts and dreams and words. But in the dark, those pages of passion seem more like ghosts, forgotten and discarded. And I can't help but feel like those ghosts are watching me.

My senses are on high alert as I move carefully through the aisles. I'm aware of every creak of every floorboard, every particle of dust drifting through the air.

Then I hear him breathing.

Stricken with sheer terror, I whirl around just in time to see Cortland Hill hurtling towards me, his amber eyes flashing with wild determination.

I don't even have time to scream as his hands close around my throat.

Chapter Thirty-Three

The smell of musty wood and moldering paper stirs me to consciousness. The hazy glow of wintry pink sunlight shining in through a pair of dirty windows tells me it's early morning. I blink, willing my eyes to adjust to the light. My head is pounding and I can't seem to make sense of my surroundings. Stacks of cardboard boxes sit collecting dust and cobwebs in every corner. Broken bookshelves full of antiques and assorted knick-knacks line the wall on the far side of the room. Off to my right, a makeshift bed of faded blankets and frayed comforters lies wrinkled on the floor. I also see discarded food wrappers, a pile of new books, an old camera, and an open suitcase.

Where *am* I? And what am I doing here?

"... El...?"

The raspy voice startles me and my gaze flies to the far corner of the room, a shadowed area I completely overlooked.

For a moment, I think my eyes are deceiving me. It *can't* be him. I can't even be sure that it *is* him. But the longer I stare, the clearer he becomes.

"Jason!" I gasp.

Like me, he's sitting upright, propped up against a wooden column. He's bruised and bloodied and his head is drooping off to the side like he's having trouble supporting it. But he's here, and as far as I'm concerned, that's a miracle.

Acting on impulse I move to get up and rush over to him, but I very nearly topple over myself. It's only then that I realize my hands are tied behind my back and my ankles are bound together with zip-ties.

Eyes wide with panic, I look to Jason for answers.

"What... what's going on?" My voice is rough, hoarse, and it hurts to speak.

"... It's him... Hill..." Jason winces, breathing heavily. His face is as white as a sheet. "... I saw he was here... so I... confronted him..."

"He was here?" I croak. I don't know what he means by that.

"He's... living here..."

"Where?" I press him for clarity. "Where is here?"

"Book... store..."

As soon as he speaks the words, the blood drains from my face.

Of course. The shelves. The boxes. How could I not recognize it? We're in the long-forgotten loft of my bookshop. The same space Logan wanted to convert into his Bogman Research Center. In hindsight, perhaps I should have let him.

Unfortunately, this upsetting revelation raises more questions than it answers.

"How?" I whisper, horrified.

"My... keys..." Jason answers. "He... took them."

That's right. Jason lost his keys. The set with his spare key to the bookstore. When even was that? It feels like a lifetime ago.

Hill's been up here all this time? Oh, God...

"Why?"

But Jason only closes his eyes and shakes his head.

Just then, a door opens from somewhere below us and someone begins moving up the stairs. I don't have to wonder who it is.

"Oh, Eloise! You're awake!" Cortland Hill greets me with a wide smile that doesn't quite reach his eyes. "How are you feeling?"

"What do you want?" I whimper. "Why are you doing this?"

"Shh... shh... There's plenty of time for questions later," he says, crossing the room and kneeling down next to me. He's carrying a white paper coffee cup, which he presents to me as a sickening sort of peace offering. "Here. I got you a vanilla late. Your favorite."

"How do you know that?"

"Oh, I know everything about you, Eloise," Hill replies. "I know you prefer simplicity, that you would rather be content than take any unnecessary risks. I know that you like to curl up with a blue fleece blanket when you read. And I know your life revolves around your son. Or at least, it did. Before you had the misfortune of falling in love with Daniel Brunsworth."

It isn't until he mentions Isaac that my stomach begins to twist itself into an icy knot. I'd been so preoccupied trying to figure out where I was and how I'd gotten here that I failed to consider what my mother and son might be going through. They must

323

be worried sick. My mother, at least. Maybe she hasn't told Isaac. Not yet. I don't think she'd want to worry him. Not until she knows for sure that I'm not coming home.

Oh, God. I might not be going home.

What would that do to my mother? What would that do to my boy? My sweet, gentle, innocent baby boy?

No. I can't think that way.

My mother knows it isn't like me to stay out all night. And it especially isn't like me to disappear without a phone call. As soon as she started to suspect something may be amiss, I'm all but certain she called Daniel to see if I was with him. Then he would know that I might be in trouble as well. Surely, someone has reached out to Emma Jean by now.

"You're not going to get away with this," I scowl, fighting back tears.

"I know. That's why we can't stay here," Hill says, holding the latte back up to my lips. "Are you sure you don't want a sip? It's going to get cold."

"I *want* to go home."

"Your home is with me now."

I expect him to elaborate, but he simply rises up to his full height and walks past me toward the back of the room. I turn, straining my neck to watch as he retrieves an old brown suitcase and begins to assemble his few belongings; two pairs of pants, three shirts, about a dozen copies of his books, and a framed photograph. He stops for a long moment to gaze at the picture before dropping it into the suitcase.

Observing his strange, almost sentimental behavior, I can't help but wonder if I might be able to break through to him. Maybe if I'm able to establish some sort of rapport, he'll let his guard down and cut me loose.

"You travel light," I observe, my voice quivering.

He looks up at me and smiles, almost as though he thinks I'm being cute.

"Are you afraid I won't be able to provide for you?"

"No! No, I... I think it's very efficient."

Hill accepts my praise with satisfaction.

"I promise, it's only temporary. Once we've found a place of our own, you and the kids will never want for anything."

"The kids?"

"We'll pick them up this afternoon on our way out of town."

"Where... Where are we going?" I ask, not altogether sure I want to know the answer.

"Wherever we want," he replies. "California, Montana, maybe New York? Isaac would like that, wouldn't he? To live close to Broadway?"

"No!" I gasp.

Hill flinches, clearly startled.

"You don't think he'd enjoy living in New York?"

"No, I... it isn't that," I reply, struggling to contain my emotions. I should have known Hill was planning to abduct Isaac, too. He wants to make me happy and he knows I can't be happy without my son. But I *cannot* let this man anywhere near him. Even if it means I disappear and Isaac never knows what happened to me. I would rather him be here, safe with my mom and Lenny and the people who know and love him than an unstable man who resorts to stalking and kidnapping to get what he wants. "I don't want him to come."

"What are you talking about?" Hill asks.

"He wouldn't be happy. He loves it here. He loves his school, his grandparents... I couldn't take him away from his life here."

"But you'll never see him again."

"I know," I whisper, choking back tears. "But I want what's best for him."

Moved by the sentiment, Hill walks back over to me, kneels down, and strokes my cheek with cold, clammy fingers.

"You're a remarkable woman, Eloise," he breathes. "Losing you is going to be devastating."

"What do you mean?"

"For *him*," he answers, a sort of dark delight dancing in his amber eyes. "He really cares about you, you know. I might even go so far as to say he loves you."

I can feel my brow furrowing as understanding dawns on me.

"What does Daniel have to do with any of this?"

Hill clenches his jaw, stands up, and storms back to his suitcase.

"Daniel Brunsworth does not deserve you," he spits. "He doesn't deserve a *stroke* of his good fortune. And we're going to remind him of that."

By now, my heart and my mind are racing.

"I don't understand."

"He isn't who you think he is, Eloise. He's a liar, a traitor. And he takes everything for granted."

"I - I really don't think - "

"You don't *know* him!" Hill snaps, slamming his suitcase shut. I flinch, stunned and shaken by his outburst. "Do you know what he did, Eloise? He walked out on his wife and his daughter. He abandoned his family. A family that he should have loved and cherished. But he didn't appreciate them. He *never* appreciated them."

Terrified of setting him off again, I consider my next words carefully.

"Maybe... you don't know the whole story."

"No, Eloise. *You* don't know the whole story. But you will," he assures me.

Then, he grabs Jason's stolen keys off of one of the old bookshelves, picks up his suitcase, and disappears back downstairs.

As soon as he's gone, Jason looks up at me and grimaces.

"You've... got to get out of here," he rasps urgently.

"We've *both* got to get out of here," I correct him.

He responds by shaking his head.

"No. He's... not safe. For you."

"What do you mean?"

"He's... obsessed. He's been following you. Ever since... you and Daniel..."

It isn't anything that, deep down, I didn't already know. Still, it's jarring to hear it confirmed, and even more so to look back and wonder. How often was he there in these last few weeks? How much did he see? I think of that night in my kitchen; the night I tried to read Daniel's book. Something was off. I felt it. And then the following morning...

Oh, God.

That was the morning Isaac woke up and announced he'd seen a monster in our front yard. But it wasn't the Bogman. It had never been the Bogman.

It was Cortland Hill.

"But why?" I ask. "What did I do? What did Daniel do?"

To that, Jason doesn't have an answer.

The minutes tick by, the sun rises higher into the sky, and all the while, I wriggle and writhe against my plastic shackles. I jerk my shoulder forward, kick my feet apart, but my bonds hold fast.

There has to be a way, I tell myself. Maybe if I can find a loose nail in the floorboards, I can maneuver my way around it to cut the zip-ties. Or if I can get my hands on a discarded key. Or even a piece of broken glass.

I scan the contents of the room for what must be the hundredth time since Hill vanished, but there's nothing useful within my reach. Discouraged and exhausted, I close my eyes and rest my head back against the wooden column behind me.

That's when the downstairs door opens.

He's back.

"Okay, Eloise. I think we're just about ready," he announces once he reaches the top of the stairs. "I have food, water, blankets... I even took the liberty of buying you and Adelaide a few new outfits."

"Addie?" I ask. "What... why...?"

"You know, you are well-loved in this community," he comments, disregarding my question completely. "Everyone is out searching for you. Including your beloved *Daniel*."

"You saw him?" I breathe.

"He looked defeated. Like a man who'd lost all hope." Hill's face breaks into a twisted, satisfied grin. "And he's about to lose so much more."

Addie.

That's why he bought clothes for her. That's what he meant earlier when he mentioned picking up the kids. He's going to abduct Addie.

He's trying to steal Daniel's entire world.

But *why?* Is it because of his success? Is he trying to claim that sort of renown for himself? Or is he simply a crazed fan who's lost touch with reality?

"You don't have to do this," I tell him. "You still have time to make things right. If you just let us go, we promise we won't tell a soul. Isn't that right, Jason?"

But Jason is unresponsive.

And he's pale. So, so pale.

My heart stutters with fear.

"Jason?" I call out. "Jason!"

I hold my breath, waiting for my best friend to move. To blink. *Anything* to let me know that he's okay.

Meanwhile, Hill simply stares down at him, looking bored and utterly unconcerned. Perhaps to appease me, however, he kneels down to examine him.

Tears stream freely down my face as Hill presses two fingers to Jason's neck.

"I think he's slipped away."

My mind rejects his words immediately.

This isn't real. It can't be real. It's just so, so *wrong*.

Jason is fine. He's downstairs right now, smiling and laughing and organizing the shelves. He's dreaming about the documentary that's going to catapult him into supernatural superstardom. He's going to travel the world, discovering new mysterious cryptids, and regaling the rest of us back home with his wild tales.

His life is just beginning. It isn't possible that he's slipped away...

"No..." I moan. "No! Jason! Jason, wake up! Please, wake up! Please..."

That's when violent sobs begin to wrack my body. I'm crying so hard I can barely breathe.

"I'm sorry, Eloise," Hill tells me. "I know how much he meant to you."

"You killed him," I weep.

"He brought this upon himself. It really is a shame. But now, it's time for us to go."

He kneels down, and I realize he intends to lift me up in his arms... without cutting my bonds. Instinctively, I begin to thrash in a futile attempt to ward him off.

"No!" I spit. "I'm not going *anywhere* with you!"

Frustrated, Hill grabs my arm. His grip is so firm, I'm certain it will leave a bruise. Still, I fight back.

"Eloise, we don't have *time* for this," he scolds me through gritted teeth. "Now, if you'll just hold still - "

But before he gets the chance to finish, Cortland Hill is flailing backward and stumbling into a heap of old, decrepit packing boxes. Startled and confused, I turn my eyes to the man who towers over Hill. His broad shoulders are tight. His fists, ready to fly. And when he speaks, his voice is a menacing, guttural growl.

"You go near her again, and I'll rip your goddamn throat out."

Chapter Thirty-Four

"Daniel!" I cry out.

"Eloise," he breathes. He's by my side in a heartbeat, taking me in with tired and tortured blue eyes. Hill was right. He looks like he's been through hell. "God, Eloise. Are you hurt?"

"No. But Daniel, it was him. It was him the whole time. Jason..."

"I know," he says, cutting my ankles and wrists loose with his pocket knife. "Come on, let's get you out of here."

"I don't think so," Hill snarls, appearing over Daniel's shoulder.

In that moment, I can only watch, frozen in horror, as Hill kicks the knife out of Daniel's hand and snatches it up off the ground. Then, he pulls back and thrusts the blade into Daniel's back.

"No!" I scream.

Grimacing with shock and pain, Daniel attempts to throw his assailant off his back. But Hill has the advantage now. He pulls the knife out of Daniel only to plunge it back in again.

"Stop!" I beg. "Stop! Please, Cortland..."

The sound of his name seems to elicit something akin to mercy because Hill momentarily ceases his assault and looks up at me.

"You want me to stop, Eloise? Okay. I'll stop. In fact, I will get in my car, drive out of this town, and Daniel Brunsworth will never see hide nor hair of me again," Hill promises. "But only if you say you'll come with me."

My breath catches in my throat. This is what he's wanted all along.

And I'm playing right into his hands.

"She'll never go with you, you son of a bitch," Daniel snaps through gritted teeth.

"Tell him, Eloise," Hill urges, his eyes suddenly wild with a strange, unnamed fervor. "Look him in the eye and tell him that you choose me over him."

Trembling, I turn to Daniel.

"Don't do this," he whispers. His plea is desperate, almost pitiful.

His eyes, however, are as cold and hard as ice.

He's playing Hill's game, too.

This is how we save each other.

Finally, I find my voice.

"I'm sorry, Daniel," I speak slowly and clearly. "I'm going with Cortland. I *want* to go with Cortland."

Grinning with absolute delight, Hill releases Daniel and walks over to me. Without a word, he takes my hands and lifts me to my feet. Then, he wraps his arms around me and aggressively presses his mouth to mine. Somehow, I resist every instinct to recoil.

"I'm going to make you happy, Eloise," Hill tells me. "I'm going to provide for you and take care of you. And once we have Adelaide, we're going to be a family." Then he sneers down at Daniel, who winces at the sound of his daughter's name. "So much for the great D.H. Whittaker. Do you see now, Daniel? Do you see what happens when you take people for granted?"

Daniel glowers up at him.

"I don't know what you want me to say."

Hill scoffs, as though amused by some twisted inner joke.

"You really don't remember me, do you?" he asks. "I guess that comes as no surprise. After all, it's been what? Almost eighteen years now?"

Shaken by this new information, I look down at Daniel.

"You *know* him?"

"I don't... I don't know..." Daniel admits. He's broken out into a sweat and he's wrapped his arm around himself in an attempt to reach his wounds. "I'm trying..."

"Let me give you a hint," Hill offers. "*The Nebula Effect.*"

The shift in Daniel's demeanor is immediate as his eyes widen with recognition.

Encouraged, Hill continues.

"*Although they remain unseen, our ever-expanding galaxies are electrified by the great forces of time and nature and fate. These universal forces are constantly at work, shaping our destinies, uplifting the weakened, and punishing those who allow evil to dictate their lives...*"

"Cal," Daniel finally murmurs. "Cal Sheridan. Shit, Cal, of course I remember you. Gary Lund's creative writing class at Columbia." Turning to me, he says, "Cal was the best writer in the class."

Hill, chuckles mirthlessly.

"Yeah, well, that's what I thought, too. But Gary sure seemed to prefer you. You had no experience, no ambition, yet he was constantly singing your praises and submitting your work to literary contests and journals. I wasn't bitter about it, though. I even offered to take you under my wing, be a mentor of sorts."

"I remember," Daniel says. "You thought... that we would make a pretty good team."

"That's right. I did. I figured with my years of experience perfecting my craft and your raw, untapped talent, we'd be rising through the ranks of the best sellers lists by the time we were twenty-five. But you didn't have any interest in that. You said, 'Thanks, but I don't think writing is really my thing.'"

"I never thought..." Daniel sighs. "I really had no intention of pursuing it as a career..."

"I didn't hold it against you. If your heart wasn't in your work, we were better off going our separates ways. And to be honest, I really didn't think about you too much after that. Until one day, maybe three or four years after graduation, I was flipping through a copy of *Publishers Weekly*. There was an article I wanted to read about horror's hottest rising star; a young man who, at my age, was already being lauded as 'The Next Stephen King.' You can imagine my surprise when that young man... turned out to be you." Hill keeps his voice calm, his tone steady. "Do you remember what happened next?"

"You... reached out to me. Email."

"That's right. I wanted to extend my congratulations. You said you appreciated it and you seemed sincere. You asked how I was doing, probably more out of politeness than genuine interest, but I answered you anyway. I told you I'd taken a day job as a substitute teacher. I told you I was engaged to the woman I adored. And I told you that I was writing a book."

Daniel closes his eyes, as though he knows what's coming.

"I wrote back... that I was happy for you."

"But that wasn't all you wrote, was it?" Hill asks. "You also offered me your full support and said that if there was anything you could do to help, all I had to do was ask. And so I did."

"Shit," Daniel mutters under his breath.

"Granted, I took my time getting back to you. It wasn't until a few years later, after I'd been rejected by every agent and publishing house I queried, that I reached out to you again. Of course, if I had known your offer had an expiration date, I would have been in touch sooner."

"Cal, listen to me," Daniel pleads. "I am so sorry I let you down. But you've got to believe me when I tell you that your email never reached me. I don't know if it went to the wrong address or if my assistant at the time deleted it by mistake, but I never saw your email. This is all just a huge misunderstanding."

"No, Daniel. It isn't. Because that wasn't the last time I tried to track you down. I saw you a few years later at one of your book signings. By that point, Mia and I had married. We even had a daughter, if you can believe it. A beautiful little girl named Maggie. And I had made them a promise. You see, Mia was working full time to support us while I wrote, but I assured her it was only a matter of time before I could provide for all of us with my books. Which is why I sought you out."

"I don't remember that."

"That's because you barely looked me in the eye. To you, I was just another faceless fan, worth little more than ten seconds of your time. But I was determined to track you down. That evening, I followed you to your hotel. I tried to stop you in the lobby, but you brushed right past me as though I didn't even exist."

"I'm sorry..." Daniel breathes. He's losing strength. I can see he's beginning to fade.

"We need to get him to the hospital," I say. "Cortland, please..."

But Hill... Cal... ignores my plea.

"Do you have any idea what you cost me?" he asks, his voice harsh, sinister. "After you failed me at the book signing, Mia and I began to fight. She lost her faith in me, and in my ability to give her the life she wanted. The life I had promised her. Eventually, I signed a multi-book deal with an up and coming publishing house, but in Mia's eyes, it was too little, too late. So she left me. And she took Maggie with her. Of course, as fate would have it, that was right around the time that you married Lisa and welcomed little Adelaide into your lives. That was when I realized... you had everything in the world that I wanted. But you know what? I could live with it." Hill glares down at Daniel with disgust. "Then, you left them."

"Cal..."

"I would have given anything, *anything*, to have my wife and daughter back in my life. To have what you had. But you? You just walked away. When I heard, I'll admit that I couldn't wrap my head

337

around it. How could the universe see fit to bestow everything that I yearned for... upon a man who couldn't have cared less about any of it? Who parades around as though his publishing contracts and adoring fans meant nothing to him? Who would turn his back on his beautiful wife and baby girl without so much as a second thought? You never deserved them. You never deserved *any of it*," Hill sneers. "And that's why I'm not going to kill you. Because I want you to know what it's like to lose everything. And I want you to have to live with it."

As soon as he says the words, something inside of me reacts.

He isn't going to kill Daniel. He was never going to kill him.

That means that I don't have to bargain for his life.

I'm not strong enough to fight Hill, but I might just be quick enough to escape him.

If you're going to do it, do it. Don't think. Don't look back. Just run.

And so I do.

Breaking away from Hill's hold on me, I make a mad dash across the room.

"Eloise!" Hill bellows. I can hear him barreling after me as I fly down the stairs.

Good. I'd rather have him chasing after me than upstairs with access to an incapacitated Daniel.

Running on pure adrenaline, I sprint through the store that was once my sanctuary. Hill's heavy footsteps fall closely behind.

Don't think about it. I tell myself. If I can just reach the front door, if I can just make *someone* see me, then it will all be over.

I'll be safe. Daniel will be safe.

We're going to make it. Just. Keep. Go -

I'm nearly there, the front door mere yards away, when, out of nowhere, a swift blow knocks my legs right out from under me. I hit the floor so hard my kneecaps crack, and in my left ear, I hear a sharp, high-pitched ringing. Nearly blinded by pain and struggling to regain my equilibrium, I glance over my shoulder in time to see Hill tossing my fire iron aside.

"I never wanted it to come to this, Eloise," he sighs. "I wanted us to be happy. Don't we deserve that? After everything he's put us through?"

"You're wrong about him," I wince. "Daniel's a good man."

"How can you say that? Look at what he's done to you. You're in the situation you're in now because of him."

"No. It's because of *you*," I spit.

Hill sighs.

"We can talk about it in the car. It's parked just outside the back door. Come along, now."

Again, he kneels down to scoop me up in his arms. This time, however, Daniel doesn't swoop in to save me and I'm in too much pain to fight him off.

Carefully, Hill carries me across the store, through the storage room, and into the alley where, sure enough, an old navy-blue Chevrolet is waiting for us. I recognize the car immediately. It's the same one I saw outside my house on Saturday morning. The one I mistook for a reporter's car.

He really has been there the entire time, in the background of every moment since Daniel first moved to town.

"No..." I moan, my heart thudding with dread as we draw nearer and nearer to the car. "No... please..."

"Cal Sheridan!"

Hill freezes in his tracks as Emma Jean Wilde and one of her officers appear in the alley behind the car. Three more gather, guns drawn, around the hood of the car.

Daniel must have managed to alert them.

Overwhelmed by relief and gratitude, it's all I can do to choke back a sob.

"Let her go, Cal" Emma Jean orders.

But Hill doesn't give up so easily.

"What?" he laughs. "No. No, no, no. This... this is all a misunderstanding. Eloise is injured, you see. I was just about to drive her to the hospital."

"Well, good news. We've got an ambulance on the way. So, why don't you just set her down and let the paramedics take care of her?"

"No. She wants to go with me. She chose *me*," Hill argues.

"And I'm sure she still will. If you let us get her the help she needs. Right, Eloise?" Emma Jean asks me.

"R-right." My voice is barely a whisper.

"Tell him."

Slowly, I turn my gaze back toward Hill.

"I'll still choose you," I say with as much sincerity as I can muster.

Hill must know on some level that it's over; that once he lets me go, I'm not coming back. Instead of acknowledging this, however, I think he chooses to let himself believe me for as long as he's able.

Closing his eyes, he presses his lips to mine one last time. Then, he sets me down on the ground and surrenders.

Excerpt from *Renfield*
By D.H. Whittaker

Brimming with pride and fit to burst with anticipation, Robert straightened his tie and knocked on the door to his master's study. It was done. The business was secure. His oath was fulfilled.

Now it was his master's turn to uphold his end of the bargain.

"Yes, come in."

As usual, the vampire sat at his desk, his striking features illuminated by the soft glow of his computer screen. At a glance, one could almost certainly mistake him for a human, but Renfield had long since familiarized himself with the subtle distinctions that set his master apart from mortal men. His power, his perfection... his divinity.

And soon, Robert would share in his divine nature.

"It's official, Sir," he announced. "Carfax Incorporated is yours."

The vampire smiled.

"Excellent," he declared, rising to his feet. "You've done well, Renfield. I am truly in your debt."

"A debt that can easily be paid," Robert replied in earnest.

His master's smile faltered just ever so slightly. "Indeed."

Then, without meeting Robert's eye, the vampire crossed the room and gazed into the fire crackling on the hearth.

Robert watched, confused by his master's elusive demeanor. What was he waiting for?

Emboldened by the vampire's words and driven by a near-maddening desire for that which he had been promised, Robert stepped forward.

"You know what I want," he reminded him.

"Yes," the vampire confirmed. Yet he remained motionless.

Robert felt his hopes begin to wither.

"You gave me your word."

It was then that his master shut his eyes.

"You don't know what you're asking,"

"I know exactly what I'm asking," Robert argued. "I want to be as you are; exceptional, powerful, immune to the passage of time. You live the life that every man craves."

"It is not a life!" his master bellowed, whirling around to face him. "It is a curse! I am a condemned man, Renfield. Not even a man. A creature. One that should not be permitted to walk the Earth."

"You are more than a man could ever hope to be! Second only to God Himself!" Robert hollered back. "You have the power to defy death, to create life!"

"I do not create life! I destroy it! Have you not seen enough of my daily existence to know this?"

"I have seen you perform wonders! You travel as swiftly and silently as the shadows of the night. You speak to the beasts and they obey you. You summon fire and diamonds with a mere thought and the winds bow to your will."

"I also slaughter the innocent and commit unspeakable acts in order to survive. Is that really what you want?"

"I want what you promised me," Robert growled.

The vampire scoffed.

"You are a fool."

"And you are a coward!" Robert countered. "Tell me something. The day the deal was struck, did you ever intend to follow through? Or were you just playing me? Deceiving me as you do everyone else?"

His master didn't answer him. Instead, he turned and walked back to his desk. Robert watched as he opened a drawer and produced what looked to be an antique jewelry box. Unlocking the box, he reached inside and pulled out a stack of fresh currency bills. Then, with an icy sneer, he shoved the money into Robert's hands.

"Do not seek me out again, Renfield," the vampire spat. "And for God's sake, do not envy me."

Epilogue

It's a beautiful summer's eve in Cedar Ridge.

The setting sun paints the sky a brilliant orange and illuminates the forest with golden light as a warm breeze dances through the fields. Isaac's laughter echoes through the twilight as he chases Addie around in silly circles. In the seven months since the bookstore incident, they've become thick as thieves. Isaac adores and looks up to Addie. And Addie? She's an absolute angel with him. Every time I see them together, a little piece of my heart melts.

"What do you think?" Daniel asks over my shoulder, slipping his arms around my waist. "Maybe give them ten more minutes?"

"I think ten sounds fair," I agree. We've been out here almost four hours hiking, exploring, taking pictures, and simply enjoying the day. At this point, I think it's pretty safe to say we're all going to be ready for dinner by the time we get back to Daniel's house.

"Are you and Isaac staying over tonight?"

"We might," I reply with a coy smile. "I'll ask him how he's feeling."

Knowing Isaac, he'll be all too eager to stay in the "cool" room that Daniel set up for him. In fact, if it were up to him, we'd probably be living at Daniel's ice castle all the time. And I'm sure someday soon, we will be. I'm just not quite ready to give up our house. I love it too much.

Besides, I've done about as much moving this year as I can handle.

After Jason's funeral, I couldn't bear to even set foot in my bookstore without him. And that absolutely broke my heart. I wanted to honor his memory by keeping the store going. I wanted to prove to everyone, especially to myself, that I was strong enough to stay there, despite everything that had happened. But I wasn't. I let the demons drive me away. And to tell you the truth, that's something I still struggle with.

I am very happy with my store's new location, however. It's a charming free-standing building with much better lighting and a lot more space than my previous site. With so much extra room, I've seen to it that each section is a celebration of its genre with quotes, posters, and artwork on display. The horror section is particularly festive with a whole table dedicated to Harberger's Favorite Frights, featuring D.H. Whittaker and an array of other books and authors that Jason loved. I like to think that wherever he is, he's geeking out over his spooky shrine. And basking in the knowledge that Daniel's latest book is going to be dedicated to his memory.

God, I wish he were here. We all do.

His death hit everyone in town pretty hard, but I don't think it affected anyone the way it did Logan. After everything that happened, Logan Taylor is not the person he used to be. His spirit is completely shattered. And as strange as it is for me to say it, seeing him like that is absolutely devastating.

As it turned out, Emma Jean did end up charging him and Santiago with influencing and interfering with law enforcement, to which they both pleaded guilty. They were convicted, fined, and sentenced to carry out one hundred hours of community service each.

It probably goes without saying that Santiago didn't stick around Cedar Ridge after his hours were up.

"Hey, kids! Ten minutes!" Daniel calls out to Addie and Isaac.

"Nooo!" Isaac cries and flops dramatically down onto the soft ground.

"Yes! It's almost time for dinner!" I inform my sweet, silly boy.

"Can we have pizza?" Addie asks.

"We had pizza two nights ago!" Daniel reminds her. "You two are going to turn into a couple of giant pepperonis."

Isaac and Addie both burst into fits of giggles. I find myself laughing right along with them. It feels good to laugh. It's a wonderful reminder that I'm healing. We all are.

The kids still have questions, of course, and Daniel and I try to be as open and honest as we can. Granted, we make sure to spare them the more traumatizing details, but for the most part, they know and understand what we went through.

Most recently, Addie asked Daniel, "How did you know where to find Eloise?"

"I followed the man who took her," he answered. "As soon as I saw him, I remembered everything she'd said about him. That day, all it took was one look and I knew she'd been right."

"Is he going to jail?" Isaac wanted to know.

"Yes," I assured him.

Once in custody, Cal Sheridan, known to his readers as Cortland Hill, pleaded guilty to four counts of first-degree stalking and two counts of involuntary manslaughter. As it so happened, before he followed Daniel to Cedar Ridge, he'd set his sights on Lisa Bell. The night she died, he was waiting for her in her bedroom. She tried to run, but he caught her at the top of the stairs. She fought back. He let her go. She fell.

The news made Daniel sick. He hasn't told Addie yet. Perhaps one day he will. For now, he's just glad that Lisa and her family will have justice.

"Okay, time to pack it up! Let's go!" Daniel announces.

Isaac protests, but Addie reluctantly begins gathering their scattered water bottles, cameras, and butterfly nets.

"Come on, Isaac. You too!" I tell him. "Don't let Addie do all the work."

Isaac heaves an exaggerated sigh, but he obeys. Meanwhile, Daniel and I work on folding the blanket we've been camped out on for the past hour.

Overall, I think we're doing pretty okay. Of course, we still have our off-days, but both of our therapists say that's to be expected. When everything is said and done, all that really matters is that we're still here with our children... and with each other. And for that, I will always be grateful.

"Mom, I can't find my binoculars," Isaac declares.

"Where did you see them last?"

"Somewhere..."

Typical seven-year-old response.

Shaking my head, I traipse down to where Isaac and Addie had been playing and begin combing through the wild mountain grass. I locate them in less than a minute.

"Found them!" I call to my son's retreating back. He, Addie, and Daniel are already slowly making their way back to the car.

"Thank you!" he hollers.

Smiling to myself, I turn and take one last look at the rich, glorious world around me. The fields are still dancing with the wind, the trees, still illuminated by the warmth of evening's glow. Everything is as it should be.

Then a sudden movement catches my eye.

Curious, I raise Isaac's binoculars up and gaze into the grove.

There, just beyond the edge of where the meadow meets the woods, a massive figure rustles through the foliage. It moves swiftly, surprisingly so for a being so large. But when it senses me watching, it stops just long enough for me to catch a glimpse of its warm russet fur and its white fangs glistening in the sunlight.

Then, with a flash of golden yellow eyes, the creature turns and disappears into the deep shadows of the forest.

Acknowledgements

Thank you, as always, to my God, my Lord and my Savior for this life, for your guidance, and for walking with me throughout these past crazy months.

Thank you to my parents, David and Susan, for your constant love and support.

Thank you to my sister, KJ, my best friend, my manager, my quarantine buddy... You are the Niles to my Frasier.

Thank you so much to Amy Mire for your encouragement, your support, and your proof-reading skills!

Thank you to my friends, Hannah, Julia, Jessica, Jalitza, Kara Maria, Kat, and Stephen for helping to keep me sane.

Thank you to all the healthcare workers for your dedication, your sacrifice, and your bravery. You are our true heroes.

Thank you to my colleagues, my fellow writers, including but not limited to Miracle Austin (*Boundless*), Cody Wagner (*The Gay Teen's Guide to Defeating a Siren*), Margie Longoria (*Living Beyond Borders*), Katelynn Rentería (*The Other Side of the Law*), Terri Farley (*Seven Tears into the Sea*), James William Peercy (*The Wall Outside*) and his amanuensis, Claudette, Manuel Ruiz (*The Dead Club*), B. Ellen Gardner (*Shae's Song*), D.C. Gomez (*Death's Intern*), April L. Wood (*Winter's Curse*), Kendra L. Saunders (*Dating an Alien Popstar*), Jessica Wayne (*Blood Hunt*), Sandy Lo (*Dream Catchers*), and countless others! Thank you for your stories, your inspiration, and your love!

And as always, thank you, thank you, thank you to my dear friends and readers around the world. Honor, Morgan, Natalie, Kayla, Cassandra, Marine, Danika, Kaylin, Sandra, Lindsey, Marialena, Tamar, Christina, Candice, Camile, Prar, John, … I love you all so very, very much!

Image Courtesy of Fervent Images.
https://www.timmalek.com

Jacqueline E. Smith is the award-winning author of the *Cemetery Tours* series, the *Boy Band* series, and *Trashy Romance Novel*. She was born and raised in Dallas, Texas. She attended the University of Texas at Dallas, where she earned her Bachelor's Degree in Art and Performance in 2010. Two years later, she earned her Master's Degree in Humanities. Along with writing and publishing, Jacqueline loves photography, traveling, and nature.

Made in the USA
Coppell, TX
14 January 2021

48193182R00215